Chasing Romeo
The Jungle War

Kregg P.J. Jorgenson

BookLocker

Saint Petersburg, Florida

Copyright © 2020 Kregg P.J. Jorgenson

ISBN: 978-1-64718-051-5

Published by BookLocker.com, Inc., St. Petersburg, Florida.

Printed on acid-free paper.

This is a work of fiction. All characters, names, persons, military units, incidents, locations, and events described in this book are solely products of the imagination or are fictional in this representation. Any resemblance to actual persons living or dead is unintentional and purely coincidental.

BookLocker.com, Inc.
2020

First Edition

Library of Congress Cataloging in Publication Data
Kregg P.J. Jorgenson
Chasing Romeo: The Jungle War by Kregg P.J. Jorgenson
Library of Congress Control Number: 2019917922

Cover art by Glen Carey, Artist for Hire

This book is for Kappie, Jon Frantzen, and all of those good friends and loyal readers who have patiently stuck with me over the years. You are all much appreciated.

Chasing Romeo

"It's not the critic who counts, not the man who points out how the strong man stumbles or where the doer of deeds could have done them better. The credit belongs to the man who is actually in the arena whose face is marred by dust and sweat and blood..."

- Excerpt from the speech, "Citizenship in a Republic," given by T.R. Roosevelt at the Sorbonne in Paris, April 23, 1910

Welcome to the arena...

Chapter 1

It was a sweltering 101 degrees and weeping humidity. The staggering steam bath that was the remote stretch of Vietnamese jungle along the Cambodian border, in this far reach of Tay Ninh Province, had U.S. Army Specialist-4 Darrell Thomas feeling like a worn and wrung-out, dirty sponge.

The dark blotches of salt-stained sweat that had spread out from under his armpits and lower back had the sun faded and damp camouflage jungle fatigue blouse sticking to him like badly peeling adhesive tape. When he wasn't lazily slapping at mosquitoes or wiping away the small, annoying beads of perspiration that had pooled and were slowly dribbling down his forehead, ears, and upper lip, he was flicking away predatory blood-sucking leeches that were looking to latch onto any exposed flesh they could find. The heat, bugs and leeches only added to the fraying strain of the daylong wait in a jungle that Thomas figured time had either forgotten or had seriously overlooked.

High up above the jungle floor a once promising breeze that had pushed in from the South China Sea one hundred miles to the east, had withered in the heat and distance. What little remained barely stirred even the thinnest leaves in the canopied treetops where the jungle met the sky, 140 or so feet above him.

Thomas, like his four teammates on Ranger Team Nine-One, passed the time he wasn't on watch in the their makeshift 360-degree perimeter, stretched out and leaning back against his rucksack trying to find a modicum of comfort.

The mind wearies and wanders during the slow and quiet moments in the heat on these long-range reconnaissance patrols, so the 21-year-old's thoughts went from the *'Greeting: You are hereby ordered for induction into the Armed Forces'* Draft notice to thinking of better times and much better places.

His thoughts drifted from the war to the wonderful redhead he'd met on his R&R in Australia the week before, and he was smiling to himself, oh so happy in the remembering.

When he and his two Army buddies had spotted the three swimsuit clad young women sunbathing on the crowded beach at Nielsen Park in Sydney they made their way around the beachgoers, and casually laid out their towels beside them.

While the other two GIs got busy with introductions to the young women in the bikinis they'd eagerly targeted, Thomas nodded and smiled at the attractive red haired, emerald eyed twenty-something that had turned and looked up questioningly at him. He was also thinking that she had filled out the one-piece bathing suit quite nicely.

"My, oh my, oh my," he said, by way of hello in a pronounced East Texas drawl, "ain't this the prettiest part of the beach?"

"A Yank, is it?" she said, holding up one hand to shield her eyes from the sun.

Thomas leaned back, held a contemplative pause, and then grinned.

"Well, I must admit that's a pretty straight forward and tempting offer, Missy, and while I'm not necessarily opposed to it, I think we should begin by introducing ourselves to one another first and then see how it goes from there. I'm Darrell, Darrell Thomas," he said, maintaining his grin as he held out his hand.

There was a brief hesitation and a slow chuckle as she sized him up with a sidelong glance and exaggerated sigh. The American GIs on their seven-day leaves from the war in Vietnam seemed to be all over Sydney these days, but this was her first personal encounter with one. That he was sandy haired, fit, and smiling with a likeable lopsided grin, helped with his brash banter.

"Trying for clever and naughty at the same time, are we, Darrell Thomas?" she said.

"Could just be a simple misunderstanding due to both of our wonderful accents," he said, with pleasing ease and charm.

The young woman chuckled again as she reached out to shake the proffered hand.

"Mattie, Mattie Lindsey," she said.

"Mattie? Wait! As in Waltzing Matil..."

"...As in, I *prefer* Mattie," she said, cutting him off. "Are you always this simple and bold?"

"I am simply a man who believes that fortune favors the bold, Mattie Lindsey."

"Oh, and why do I think you don't have a fortune?"

"Well, I've heard beaches are the best places to find treasure, and low and behold missy, here you are."

Lindsey rolled her eyes and laughed.

"Has that line ever worked for you before?"

Thomas shrugged. "Never tried it before. Is it working now?"

"No, not really," she said. "Anyone ever tell you you're an idiot?"

Thomas' grin widened.

"Frequently," he said, "but I'd be a bigger idiot if I didn't at least try to chat you up. You're so pretty you make my eyes blur, Miss Mattie Lindsey!"

There was more laughter, more small talk, of course, and a lot more flirting in the days that followed. Fueled by youthful surging hormones, lustful loins, and shared yearnings, it was the best and happiest week he could ever remember.

She was, she said, *'just a sales clerk at a downtown store, refolding clothes, arranging small displays, nothing all that exciting or amazing, actually,'* but the night before he was to leave to go back to Vietnam and the war, Darrell Thomas was excited and amazed with what she had on display for him in his hotel room.

"*Oh, Army boy,*" she cooed playfully standing in the bathroom doorway wearing only a sly smile and a white cotton hotel room towel that served as a sexy sarong.

Her left arm was up along the doorframe with her head seductively leaning in and resting against the crook of her elbow while her right hand was pinching the towel closed at the top.

"Oops!" Mattie said, giggling as she let the towel drop. The giggles gave way to a startled flight of birds high up in the trees that instantly brought a startled Thomas out of his musing and immediately on alert.

His eyes went wide, darting towards what little he could see of the trail in front of him, as he realized where he actually was, and what had caused the disturbance.

Mattie, the joyfully smiling redhead, the hotel room, and the lusty thoughts of his R&R were gone in an anxious blink, along with the familiar noises of the rain forest, all replaced by an unnatural and unnerving silence.

His adrenaline was pumping and he had to force himself to take in slow and steady breaths to remain calm, or as calm as he could be considering the circumstance. Carefully and very deliberately he rolled over, leaned forward on his elbows, and took up the hand-held triggering device to the three daisy-chained Claymore Anti-personnel Mines set up in ambush ten yards out, facing the small trail.

During his eight months in-country on other recon missions and patrols he'd taken part in, he'd gotten familiar and even somewhat comfortable with the natural sounds of the jungle. Somewhat. But it was those telling moments of abrupt and awkward quiet, like now that had set his nerves on edge and the veteran Lurp team members in motion. For these long-range patrols it was just a series of staggering hikes and bad camping until the war, once again, reached out to find you.

The East Texan Assistant Team Leader, the A-T-L on the patrol, watched and waited with three of the other experienced members of the five-man team who had recognized the warning for what it was. Like him, they quietly went on alert and began readying themselves.

The four were keyed in on the path in front of them; their designated kill zone. Their hide site was well hidden behind a living screen of broad elephant ear-like leaves, tangled branches, and plush, tropical underbrush. There were just enough small openings in the natural screen to target that section of the trail while remaining unseen by any casual observer.

It was the jungle's alarm system that told the Lurps of Team Nine-One that, someone, or maybe even a few someones, were moving on the trail to the east and working their way towards their kill zone.

With no friendly units operating within the Lurp Team's patrol area, and the team deep in enemy territory just this side of the border, Thomas had little doubt just who that *someone,* or those *someones,* could be.

This isolated part of the Province along the Cambodian border served as one of the primary off-ramps for the Sihanouk Trail, a Khmer stretch of the better-known Ho Chi Minh Trail. Every day thousands and thousands of enemy soldiers that had made the long journey down from North Vietnam, through Laos and Cambodia, had used the cover of the massive swath of jungle to slip across the border to attack South Vietnam, and the sudden flutter from the disturbed birds told the GIs some of those NVA units were using it again.

Four of the five members of the team were down, in position, and ready; the exception was the team's FNG, Private First Class John Blake Bowman.

Bowman, 18, who looked like somebody's kid brother playing army, had graduated from William Wyatt Bibb high school in Alabama seven months before, and from Romeo Company's intense and compacted three week, in-country, LRRP/Ranger training course a day prior to the start of this mission. He had a plastic spoon upside down on his tongue and was busy digging through his rucksack. Blissfully unaware of what was going on around him, his determined focus was on finding a better tasting, freeze-dried, dehydrated Lurp ration that he'd packed for his very first combat patrol four days before.

Spaghetti, maybe, he was thinking? Yeah, it wasn't bad, or better still, nom, nom, nom, Beef and Rice.

"Oh yeah, baby, definitely Beef and Rice," he said to himself as he sifted through the contents of the rucksack, pushing aside the other O-D colored freeze-dried ration packages, extra radio batteries, Claymore Mines, other assorted mission related items he was required to carry on the five-day mission. He knew he'd packed two of the Beef and Rice ration pouches and had one yesterday, so he was sure he had one left. Finding it in the heavy and crowded rucksack, though, was another matter.

Ah, but when he did, he'd mix his lukewarm canteen water into that sucker, and stir it like whirlwind to bring it back to edible life. It wasn't fine cuisine, but it was fine for the jungle. Never mind the occasional leg or wing of some dead insect, or the one or three mixed in mosquitos, let alone trying to spoon them out. That was just part of the mission menu, too. Protein on the fly, *a la Carte*. No extra charge. Enjoy! Well, enjoy or go hungry.

The rations would be eaten cold. There would be no campfires or heat tabs or pieces of C-4 to light and heat the Army rations on Lurp missions. Sergeant Ben Carey, the Team Leader, made that abundantly clear during the team's Op Order mission briefing back at Camp Mackie. He wouldn't allow it. Nor would he allow smoking.

"Wafting food odors, tobacco smoke, or other man-made smells carry," he said, "and there is no mistaking their origins. Everyone copy?"

Heads nodded, and the word, *copy*, echoed from the team members during the pre-insertion mission briefing. There was more.

"Did he just say, wafting?" Thomas said to Warren, the team's Radioman, who nodded and grinned.

"He did. And I don't believe he was referring to those little rubber boats, either."

"He wasn't. As he is our talented and articulate team leader, his wisdom wonderfully wafts for our benefit."

"We are indeed amongst greatness."

"Indeed."

Carey frowned as he stared them down. "As Lurps you're supposed to remain unseen and quiet. It says so in the job description. So, if you two are done blowing smoke up my ass and will let me finish the Op order, later, I'll introduce you to a few other big words for your edification as well."

"Damn! I hope he brings a dictionary."

"He will. He's our Team Leader. He's thorough."

"You done?" asked Carey.

The two nodded with smartass smiles and the mission briefing continued.

Carey was correct. The primary goal of a Lurp mission was to remain unseen and unheard in the jungle on patrol, which was why he was adamant about the team members eating their freeze-dried or canned C-rations cold, or what passed for it in the jungle heat.

Even if Bowman couldn't find the ration pouch of Beef and Rice, the best he could hope for was something that had a little better flavor when he poured in the tepid canteen water, stirred the contents until they became less crunchy, and took the first bite.

Yeah, it would taste like oddly flavored lumpy oatmeal, complete with a Rice Krispies snap and crackle. Adding more water, he knew, eliminated the pop.

It wasn't a cheeseburger and fries, but after three days into the patrol, it would do. Now, if he could just find the damn thing.

On this, his very first 'cherry' mission, and with his focus on finding his lunch, Bowman hadn't recognized the startled birds that had suddenly taken flight, or the odd silence that followed for the danger they foretold.

Sergeant Carey angrily snapped his fingers twice in his direction to get the new guy's attention. Sound carried in the jungle, but the finger snaps would barely be audible more than a few feet away.

When the teenage soldier looked up from the opened rucksack, he found the stern-faced team leader pointing to his right ear before pointing back out at the trail. The Sergeant had his short-barreled CAR-15 submachine gun leveled on the path even as he looked to Bowman. Over Carey's shoulder the team's Radioman was sneering at Bowman and quietly mouthing, '*FNG.*'

Being new was never easy, but the now surprised Bowman had gotten the unspoken message. He immediately stopped what he was doing, gave a slow nod, and picked up his M-16.

Thumbing the selector switch from SAFE to FIRE, he spit out the plastic spoon as he eased himself down to the ground, and used his rucksack as a tripod.

When it came to FNGs-those '*Fucking New Guys,*' in the jargon of combat, and their cherry missions, the more experienced veteran team members were never sure how a new guy would act and react under fire, or in the stressful calm that preceded it, so Carey watched for a critical moment to see how Bowman was managing the threat.

With, quite literally, a handful of Rangers making up the team and operating deep within enemy-held territory, the Team Leader needed to be sure that Bowman wouldn't panic, and that he'd do what needed to be done when trouble came.

It would be a critical moment, and for Carey and the others, a necessary one. Two weeks earlier, another FNG, two days into his first mission, had panicked when the team was pulling surveillance on another similar jungle trail along the Song Be River when 20 to 30 unsuspecting NVA soldiers began passing in front of the Ranger team's hide site.

Just as the line of heavily armed enemy soldiers were filing by that other FNG violently began to tremble. Overwhelming fear overtook him, and when he started to cry out and get up to run both Carey and Warren, the Radioman, quickly and forcefully held him down. The muffled cry in angry hands kept the team from being compromised and thrust into a deadly firefight they likely couldn't win. The NVA soldiers never saw or heard the scuffle.

They walked on.

Once Carey was certain the last of the North Vietnamese Army soldiers were well passed the team's position, and seeing that the FNG was still terrified and whimpering, the Team Leader got on the radio and called for an immediate extraction.

With a five to six-man team, a panicking soldier was a deadly liability, and with three more days to go to complete the long-range patrol, they couldn't trust him from doing something else just as dangerously foolish. You didn't have to be John Fucking Wayne on these patrols, but you had to be cowboy enough to rein in your fear, and do what was necessary.

After making their way to a pre-designated pickup zone and being flown back to Camp Mackie, Carey was met by a less than pleased Ranger Company Commanding Officer on the helicopter flight line wanting to know just what in the hell had happened, why the immediate extraction was called in, and why the mission had been cut short.

As the frustrated Carey explained what had taken place, Thomas and the other team members nodded along. The hang dog look of the new guy's embarrassed face confirmed it.

"I...I can't do this, sir," the FNG quietly admitted. "I can't go back out there."

The Ranger Company Commander nodded. "And we can't allow you to," agreed the CO. "Pack your bags."

The next morning the FNG was transferred out of the unit.

Fear was a given on long range patrols but managing it was a desperate necessity for these small teams operating in enemy occupied areas. It wasn't always courage under fire that sustained them, either. More often it was fright and fight and making that fear work for you and not against you. A healthy amount of caution and worry kept one on alert and focused on task.

With that ill-fated patrol still fresh in his mind, Carey kept a cautionary eye on Bowman. But other than looking a little nervous by squeezing and re-squeezing the stock and grip of his M-16 and taking in slow and steady breaths to calm himself as best he could, Bowman seemed to be handling it as well as could be expected. If he was scared shitless, then he was hiding it well. Good.

It was one thing to train for a fight, but something else entirely to step into the proverbial arena, and face off against an equally determined enemy whose sole purpose was to kill you as quickly, brutally, and efficiently as possible.

When Bowman caught his team leader staring at him, he gave Carey a nervous chin-up nod. The Team Leader nodded back then turned his attention back to the jungle trail.

For the last eight hours and change, the team from MAC-V's Company R, 75th Infantry-Ranger, had been set up in the hide site to observe the trail with little to show for the daylong wait. Patience may have been a virtue in long-range reconnaissance, but it was also a physical pain in the ass at times.

The team had been inserted by helicopter into their area of operations three days earlier, two and a half clicks from their insertion site. Their mission was to reconnoiter a remote four-grid map section of the vast jungle adjacent to the border. They would check out if there were recent enemy activity in the area, and if so, they'd plot the enemy's numbers, direction of movement, equipment, and other pertinent information to pass along those findings to the Intel people upon completion of the mission.

Over the course of five days of humping heavy rucksacks through the jungle searching for the elusive enemy, they would note any Viet Cong or North Vietnamese Army hidden jungle bases and bunker complexes and record them on their operational map, without being seen or compromised. If possible, they were to ambush small patrols as *targets of opportunity*, capture any POWs they could, and then *di-di-mau* to a pre-planned exfiltration point.

POWs were a highly sought after prize for the teams. The Romeo Company Commander made it so by offering an in-country, three day R&R at Vung Tau for any team member who captured an enemy soldier, brought him back alive, and in a better mood to talk.

For Team Nine-One, though, the first forty-six hours into this five-day mission were a bust. Prior to finding the well-used trail near sunset the day before, they hadn't found squat. They had spent the time much the way they had on other long-range reconnaissance patrols, slowly and carefully pushing away large fronds and vines as they quietly moved through the vast stretches of primordial jungle searching for the fresh or recent signs of enemy activity.

Some parts of these vast and ancient swaths of rain forests were so far removed and remote from what passed for civilization that they even held arrays of flora and species of fauna yet to be scientifically discovered or named. But the opposing armies weren't there for scientific or geographical exploration. They weren't botanists or explorers. They were there to remain hidden and unobserved, and when the time came, ready to capture or kill their enemies in an ugly and deadly combined game of military styled *Hide n' Seek* and terminal *Tag*.

When the five Lurps took a much-needed break and rested in place, or remained in overnight positions on patrol, the team would set up in a wagon wheel formation with weapons facing out in a tight circle. At night they kept watch using a rotating guard system between the members of the team in two-hour shifts until sunrise.

Then the team would repeat the process. Focused vigilance, in the morning gave way to bored yawns and the stretching out of kinks after the previous long, shivering night of woeful sleep on the jungle's cold and often wet ground.

The month of September in this part of the world meant steaming heat followed by heavy rains in the late afternoon. The Monsoon Season's on-again/off-again downpours fell on the treetop canopy above them, and indirectly worked their way down to the fetid ground below. There were open spaces in the jungle canopy, but not many. An army could hide unobserved in the vast swaths of jungle and often did.

The tropical rain was moving in but the sunlight that had filtered down through the foliage had the various shades of green vegetation momentarily glistening like precious emeralds. The hothouse light that added flickers of radiance to the colorful and sweet smelling wild orchids and other blossoms peaked through the brush and trees and dazzled the senses.

But this abundant and naturally verdant beauty would be muted in the next downpour; when the wind-whipped rains out of the South China Sea pelted the jungle, its overhead tangle of broad leaves, twisted vines, and scribbled branches would then only make a poor awning.

Like the previous evening the five Rangers would once more be soaked and sitting in wet, soggy soil, struggling through the night and in the early morning hours trying to stay warm until the inevitable heat of day could take over, evaporate the layers of mist, and turn the jungle once again into a living greenhouse.

This was the seasonal Monsoon cycle and directional change in the winds that repeated daily. Sweat, rinse, and soak. Shiver, dry out, and repeat. The dry season wasn't far off and then there would only be the miserable heat.

For these Lurp Rangers there were no tents, shelter halves, or sleeping bags in the field; there were no air mattresses, or even ponchos to keep them dry, warm, or even moderately comfortable on the five-day surveillance and ambush patrols.

What poor and little material comfort there was came in the way of small sections of O-D olive drab colored towels or the short pieces of camouflage poncho liner they used to cover their faces when it was their turn to sleep.

Although the small, wash-cloth sized pieces of camouflaged cloth helped keep the swarms of mosquitoes at bay, they didn't do much to stop the bites or stings from red ants, centipedes, and other painfully annoying insects on the back of exposed necks, ears, or hands.

During the near pitch-black night, when the two-hour guard shift was done, the team member would wake the next man in line and pass over the handset to the team's backpacked radio before settling in to find some something that was a poor substitute for sleep. Sleep, on combat patrols in the jungle, always came in fits and starts, when the jungle wasn't yet a battle zone and something unseen slithered, groaned, or grunted nearby through the thick brush.

The croaks from *Fuck You Lizards* kept some new team members, like Bowman, nervously awake at times while veteran team members and those who'd been, in-country, in the jungle, for any length of time, recognized the offensive sounding calls as little more than a peculiarity.

"Sarge! Sarge!" whispered Bowman to his sleeping Team Leader the first time he'd heard the sound the night before. "I think I hear..."

"It's a lizard," said Carey, without opening his eyes. The lizard was still grunting away.

"A lizard? But..."

"It's a lizard," he said, again. "Don't wake me up again unless it's my turn for guard, you actually see an NVA out on the trail, or something chuffs or growls. You got that, new guy?"

"Yes, sergeant," said the embarrassed FNG.

The uneventful night wore on.

Low or even loud chuffs and growls from the occasional tiger, weren't out of the scope of probability in the Southeast Asian jungle. On other patrols, when the unmistakable sound of one was heard, everyone on a team came awake wide-eyed, on guard, and anxious. Those nights were infrequent, but when they happened, or when a poisonous snake bit someone, or a crocodile stared at you as you crossed a muddied stream, soldiers on both sides of the conflict were reminded that the jungle war was being fought in a zoo without cages.

The miserable nights became the routine until dawn, or what passed for it in the rainy season, as the Lurps rose for the day to continue their patrol.

They were young men, and at times their thoughts wandered to an always better elsewhere before their focus returned to the task at hand, and taking care of the basic necessities.

They knelt when they had to take a piss and ventured out a few meters to take a dump and then bury it while another Ranger kept guard over the activity. Weapons were always kept within reach, regardless of what they were doing.

And now because of the frightened birds that took wing they were hugging the ground, facing the trail from their hide-site, and waiting for the enemy to show. The much too calm jungle, the oppressive heat, and the wait only exacerbated the tension.

Team Nine-One was in position and ready as the war, at least the war they knew was coming towards them.

Chapter 2

The weather was turning, again. The once sunlit afternoon sky, or the little that could be seen through the heavily canopied trees towering above them, was turning grey and foreboding. The jungle was on the verge of being pounded by another seasonal downpour.

Like clockwork, the Monsoon's rain would begin shortly before sunset with a trickle and later there would be another long, miserable night of heavy rain before it pushed on. But that would be later. The *now* was the pending ambush behind enemy lines. The trickling rain was not the problem. There was another storm coming closer.

While there were some who naively believed there were no actual enemy lines in the war in South Vietnam, there were those that knew that the ownership lines in the jungle areas outside of the cities and villages, were clearly defined. The jungle belonged to their enemy. Everyone else was just visiting. While chemical spraying of Agents Orange, Blue and White killed large sections of the Tropical forest and its trees, broadleaf plants, brush, and grasses, the Viet Cong and North Vietnamese Army adapted by moving through these areas under the cover of darkness.

In these remote and troubled regions throughout the four tactical Corps regions of South Vietnam, the Viet Cong and North Vietnamese Army Battalions and Regiments relied on the protection of the seemingly endless stretches of canopied tropical rain forest, swamps, mountains, and caves to hide their bases and covert staging areas. It was their concealed sanctuary, their masked refuge where they planned, prepared, and positioned their forces for coordinated attacks on the villages, cities, and people of the Republic of South Vietnam.

The five Lurps from Team Nine-One were indeed operating behind enemy lines and the well-used, heavily trodden trail they'd found said as much. There was no mistaking the many imprints from the soles of the NVA's soldiers canvas issued boots, nor the deep bicycle tire tracks in the wet or damp orange soil. The NVA were strategically shifting their fighters again and Nine-One had found one of their operational routes. The NVA were on the move.

They were set and ready to ambush a small patrol, and hopefully snatch up an enemy POW or two.

Hot and grubby as he was, Thomas was thinking that a little in-country R&R in Vung Tau was a nice little incentive right about now.

Yep, we bring a stunned or wounded NVA soldier back with us and pack our bags, swimsuit, and sunscreen! Oh Hell, I'll even chase one of the little suckers down and tackle his ass, if I have to!

These five-day long-range reconnaissance patrols in enemy held territory took their toll of these soldiers; physically and psychologically, so the R&R incentive loomed large to these young LRRP/Rangers.

Officially, they were designated as 75th Infantry, U.S. Army Rangers, but were better known as *Lurps,* for the job they did. The initials, L-R-R-P proved too long and awkward for most people to say or spell out, so it became *Lurp,* much in the same way *As Soon As Possible* became abbreviated to *A-SAP,* and the acronym, *REMF* stood for *Rear Area Mother Fucker.* GIs had their own, distinctive lexicon and applied it liberally, especially when it came to REMFs.

Those doing the actual fighting, humping the boonies, slogging through the mud one wet and sucking boot step at a time, and staring into the pitch black jungle at night, swallowing panic at the sound of something or someone, slithering or creeping through the brush, didn't just despise those military personnel working and living in the safer rear area support centers, they envied them. They envied the clean barracks, the access to snack bars and readily available hot pizza, Enlisted, NCO, and Officers' clubs with rock bands and Go-Go girls, and other support services and comforts the likes of which the combat soldiers seldom, if ever, enjoyed.

More so when an inch-long green slime-colored leech attached itself with its teeth to an exposed piece of flesh and gorged and plumped up on a victim's blood, or when a swarm of mosquitoes flew in like determined Kamikazes at night in the jungle and attacked a GI on his eye lid one too many times so that even opening the eyes the next morning became a struggle. The jungle sucked in ways most people could only imagine and not fully comprehend.

But there was pride too in the combat jobs and some distorted braggadocio in the shared misery. In their forward operating basecamp the LRRP/Rangers proudly sported black berets with *Sua Sponte* crests, and the red, black and white 75th Infantry scrolls sewn high on the sleeves of their left shoulders over their parent unit patches to show that they were U.S. Army combat Rangers. The bulk of those serving in combat Ranger units in Vietnam received their training in-country, with any fine tuning coming from MAC-V's Recondo School up north in Nha Trang.

But the clean and decorated jungle fatigues and highly polished boots they wore in the rear areas were for award ceremonies and base camp formations only. On patrol in the jungle, they wore sterile camouflaged fatigues with no patches or symbols of rank to identify them. They camouflaged their faces with green, black, and sand-colored grease paint, camo paint, to better blend into their jungle surroundings on their surveillance or ambush patrols.

Bowman, the new guy, was worried about more than just remaining unseen and unheard by the enemy. What bothered or maybe even worried him more than a little were the Claymore anti-personnel mines that his team leader- the T-L, and his assistant team leader, his A-T-L, Specialist Thomas, had placed and hidden just a few yards off of the trail.

During stateside infantry training he was taught that the minimum safe distance for the back blast for a Claymore was sixteen meters, which was what, forty to fifty feet?

Romeo Company, though, had another take on it.

"Out in the jungle on patrol you'll be lucky if you can maybe see fifteen to twenty yards in any direction. The jungle's thick, which means you don't have the luxury of distance when you're setting up your Claymores," explained Sergeant Rob Shintaku demonstrating the working placement technique during the ambush phase of their training. "So, you set them up twenty feet or so away."

"Twenty feet?" questioned one of the remaining would-be Rangers in Bowman's class with upraised eyebrows and a pretend *I'm not really worried, but damn it, I'm actually worried* tone.

The Ranger trainee doing the asking was a Sergeant E-5 on his second tour of duty. During his first tour of duty he'd served as a combat Engineer and was very familiar with explosives.

Of the forty-seven volunteers that had begun the Company's LRRP/Ranger training and selection process, only seven had remained.

"That's right," said Shintaku.

"Isn't that, like, you know, danger close?"

"You need to be able to keep them close enough to keep an eye on them so Charlie doesn't turn them around on you," said Shintaku. "That's the real danger."

"Okay, but what about the back blast?"

The southern Californian shrugged off the concern. "You angle the mines away from the hide-site, and yeah, you'll feel the heat and force of the blast before you'll hear the BOOM, and it'll be a massive amount of bell ringing in your ears, but, here's the thing; you'll survive, the bad guys don't. Now, let's get started."

To Bowman, the twenty feet, and never mind the fucking *'or so'* distance from the trail was much too close for comfort to safely serve as an effective ambush hide site.

While Bowman still had his concerns about the proximity and placement technique of the anti-personnel mines none of this seemed to bother Carey, Thomas, Doc Ryan Moore, or Jonas Warren, the team's Radio Telephone Operator, the RTO.

"Good Lord!" thought the new guy. Warren is smiling. He's either way too Gung fucking ho or crazy, but then it occurred to Bowman that maybe they all had to be a little gung ho and crazy to be out on patrol behind the lines in the first place. Bravery, or what passed for it, always seemed like a good idea before it was confronted and called into play.

Still, he doubted he'd ever smile at times like these and instead, took in another slow, deep breath, and stared out towards the trail, hoping he wouldn't freeze up when it came to the fight. No, not that. Never that.

The trail the team was monitoring was little over three feet in width at most and, with the exception of an open area beneath the trees across from the kill zone, it was walled in by heavy vegetation and brush.

Both the trail and the open area below were protected from any aerial observation Scout helicopters or any other low flying aircraft by the heavily foliaged canopy, so the NVA Companies and Battalions believed they could move and operate with impunity.

The trail that snaked its way through the jungle wasn't *the* main off-ramp for the infamous Ho Chi Minh Trail, but the many boot imprints and deep bicycle tracks showed it to be at least a lesser exit and something Carey knew would be well-worth noting and monitoring when Thomas, who was walking point, found it.

Unable to move large, motorized vehicles through these trails, the Viet Cong and NVA used specially modified bicycles to transport heavy weapons, equipment, and war materials through the jungle maze. The bicycles could cart and carry hundreds of pounds of war materials stacked high through the jungle via the labyrinth of a trail system.

After finding the well-used trail and calling in the find to Romeo Company's Tactical Operations Center, the TOC, Carey set the team up in a small but tight, three hundred-and-sixty-degree perimeter to keep anyone from sneaking up on them. Attacks could come from any direction, so they planned for it accordingly.

Once the hide site was selected, both he and Thomas had crept out closer to the trail to set up the Claymores. They selected two ideal target locations that covered both avenues of approach, and another that split the difference in the center. While one man covered the other they took turns planting the Claymores in the ground. Using the folding scissor-like metal adjustable prongs that were attached to the mines, they tilted the anti-personnel mines up to better aim them to take out anyone caught in their destructive path.

Before returning to the team's perimeter they blanketed the Claymores with clumps of brush and leaves, and covered any disturbed ground or sign they'd left behind. Pulled vines, bent or broken branches, and turned leaves left markers or natural flags for an observant enemy point man, so Carey took his time to carefully cover any traces of their actions.

When it came time to trigger the anti-personnel mines, Thomas would be the one to do it once Carey gave him the nod. A fourth Claymore was set up behind them to protect the way they had come, and if need be, Carey would trigger it, if they, themselves, had been tracked or followed.

Nobody spoke, so communication was kept to an operational minimum with barely audible hushed tone whispers and the use of hand signals. It was rumored that the North Vietnamese Army leaders had placed a bounty on Lurps who they called the 'men with their painted faces.' Whether the rumor of a bounty was true or not, the Lurps weren't taking any unnecessary chances.

A clear and distinct crack of a branch snapping in the near distance, followed by another a few moments later, told the five Americans someone was moving on the trail just east of their position so they remained motionless, breathing slow and steady breaths, much like hunters in a hide, waiting for their prey, and waiting to see who, and how many, would show.

What they could make out of the small section of trail in front of them through the interlaced leaves and branches was empty, and then suddenly it wasn't, as the first enemy soldier came into view and stopped.

Thomas was thinking that the soldier was surprisingly tall for a North Vietnamese soldier and that either he was Chinese, or his Grandfather was.

He was maybe five-eight or nine, and weighed, what the A-T-L estimated was a good one hundred and twenty pounds. He looked like a ranked bantamweight complete with a veteran fighter's confident scowl. His sun-faded, lime green uniform was weathered and worn, and his issued pith helmet was branch scratched, sun mottled, and aged from both the jungle and the war.

A khaki-colored backpack hung from his shoulders and he was gripping a well-maintained Chinese-made Ak-47, which he held at the ready. He had a light brown carrying vest strapped to the front of his chest that held three additional thirty round magazines for his assault rifle. He was ready to fight as he carefully turned and studied the small, natural opening beneath the trees to his right before slowly sweeping his gaze and assault rifle to the much thicker wall of jungle to his left.

"Spot us, you little peckerhead! Recognize the ambush for what it is and you're history!" thought the Texan, ready to blow him away.

He and the others watched as the lone NVA soldier continued his cautious look around, and then when the enemy soldier seemed satisfied that all was good, he shouldered his weapon, and turned around, and stood facing back down the trail with a heavy, frustrated sigh.

The short wait brought two more North Vietnamese soldiers into view. They, too, had stopped in place on the trail, directly in line with the three hidden anti-personnel mines, and turned and faced back the way they came.

All three of the enemy soldiers were unaware that they were in the Lurp team's ambush kill zone, and only seconds away from dying.

Bowman glanced over to Warren and, for a stunned moment, gaped at him.

The RTO's smile had grown wider.

Chapter 3

With a quite literal death grip on the *clacker*, the Claymore's hand-held triggering device, Thomas was ready to squeeze it three times as fast and as hard as he could to detonate the mines. Although, he was holding the fate of the enemy soldiers in his hands, that wasn't his only pressing concern.

The young soldier from Athens, Texas was fighting the panicky urge to slap at his left trouser leg where something, a large spider, centipede, or scorpion perhaps, had crawled inside his pant leg and was slowly moving up his left calf. He knew it wasn't a leech because it was moving too fast. However, knowing that didn't provide much in the way of consolation.

He squirmed as he felt the tiny needle-like legs tapping against his skin as, whatever it was, was working its way up towards the inside of left knee and thigh.

Tap, tap-tap, scurry, tap, pause, and then once again, tap, tap-tap, scurry, tap, and pause.

Thomas was doing everything he could to keep from jumping up, dropping his trousers, and yelling, '*Fuck, fuckity, motherfucking jungle!*' as he slapped away whatever it was, only he remained motionless. He kept his eyes glued to the jungle trail, where they needed, and had to be. One wrong move would give the team's position away and the gates of hell would burst open in an instant.

He was thinking; *maybe if I was careful enough I could slide one hand down, find the head of whatever it was and pinch it inside the pant leg between my thumb and index finger until it popped like an ugly zit, then maybe I wouldn't get bitten or stung or whatever the hell a large spider, centipede or scorpion did that might not necessary kill me, but would certainly fuck up my day, thank you very much.*

Yeah, thought Thomas, and maybe all would be well, too, if the Viet Cong or NVA patrol didn't spot us before we spring the ambush.

I squeeze the clacker, three times real fast, and KA-BOOM! We eliminate the three little yeller fellers; gather up their weapons, maps, equipment, or any stunned survivors, and then *di-di the fucking mau* to the designated pick up zone.

Job done. Mission completed. Adios, and hopefully not hasta fucking manana!

But Ranger Thomas couldn't kill the spider, centipede, or scorpion because he had to remain calm, and had to keep both hands holding the clacker so he could blow the enemy soldiers away once Carey gave him the nod.

With his eyes on his Team Leader and his peripheral vision on the NVA soldiers out on the trail, the spider, centipede or scorpion that was crawling up his pant leg wouldn't get crushed, pinched, swatted, or flicked away just yet. The pattern continued.

Tap, tap-tap, scurry, tap, and pause. Tap, tap-tap, scurry, tap, and pause.

Whatever it was was now almost up his thigh and his family jewels, and it was scaring the piss out of him. And that's when it occurred to him that there was one thing that might work and he wouldn't have to move all that much to do it.

Putting his weight on is knees and easing his hips up just a bit to find the right angle, he began to urinate. The warm urine spilled down his thigh and pant leg and the steady flow and stream drove the unseen pest back the way it had come in a flooded frenzy.

As good as he momentarily felt there was little in the way of any actual comfort or relief. The three enemy soldiers were still out on the trail in front of them. The bug was the least of his problems.

Come on, Ben! What in the hell are they waiting for? Thomas wondered but the question was soon answered. They were waiting for a pudgy, disheveled looking, moon-faced young soldier, who was caught up in several low-hanging 'wait-a-minute' vines, and struggling to free himself.

The fourth and final NVA soldier's uniform was soaked in sweat in dark blotches and displayed small torn flaps from sharp thorns or broken branches showing that the jungle was just as hard on the NVA and Viet Cong as it had been on the Lurps. His newer looking pith helmet had been knocked askew by low hanging vines and tangle of branches, and had dropped down over his eyes, blocking his vision and a goofy-ass apologetic smile. FNG's apparently were universal.

The bantamweight in the lead was glaring at the sad looking straggler and then muttered something to the soldier that had the two other fighters in the enemy patrol chuckling and slowly shaking their heads.

It made for a good show, and his critics in the small enemy patrol didn't know that they too had an audience.

Three quick squeezes of the Claymore's *clacker* in rapid succession would send the hand-generated electrical charge to the three anti-personnel mines and set them off. Shintaku had taught them that one good squeeze might do it, but three guaranteed it.

"You keep squeezing it until you hear the boom. Got it?"

Thomas did and all of the trainees that went through their Lurp training did as well. This was deadly business.

The coordinated blasts from the three anti-personnel mines would send a combined wall of 2,100-buckshot size ball bearings and a hellish concussive wave of heat from the C-4 explosive that would rip and shred the enemy patrol and bug-infested section of jungle in its path.

Damp and wet as the day had been, the palms of Thomas's hands were unusually clammy. His heart was racing, and the spider, centipede, scorpion, or whatever the hell it was crawling up his leg hadn't helped calm things down.

'Come on! Come on! Come on, Ben! They're right in front of us!' Thomas said to himself, eying the kill zone and then his team leader waiting for the signal, but for some reason Carey hesitated.

What the fuck, Ben?

Instead, Carey, who was up on his elbows, looking to his right where the still smiling Jonas Warren had one hand holding his rifle and the other holding the radio's handset ready to call in 'Contact!' once the Claymores were detonated.

Carey turned to Doc Moore, the team's stoic medic, who was next to Warren and was covering their rear, then to Bowman, the new guy, who was covering their nine, and then back to Thomas on his left who was completing the protective circle like critical spokes on a wheel.

They were set, their weapons were ready, and the enemy soldiers were in the kill zone, dead center. Thomas was beside himself and his was mind was screaming.

For crying out loud! What are you waiting for, Ben? We can take three of them out with the claymores and maybe even capture the Buddha-looking butterball, if he doesn't catch up to the others in the next few moments. Come on! Come on! Gimme the nod so we can blow them away, you can call for our extraction bird, and we can get the hell out of here. Nod, Ben! Do it! Damn it! Do it! Give me the fucking nod!

But the nod still didn't come. Instead, Carey motioned for Thomas and the others to lower themselves back down as the straggler finally bumbled his way out of the vines and branches that were holding him back, and caught up with the others.

After admonishing him a second time, the frustrated NVA Patrol Leader pivoted back around and led the other three out of the kill zone until, out of view, and further up the trail.

Seriously? What the fuck, Ben? Why did you let that happen? Thomas was frowning at his team leader when, out of the corner of his right eye, he caught new movement on the trail.

He froze as the first in a long and steady line of NVA soldiers quietly began to file by the five prone Lurps following the route of their comrades in the lead had taken.

The file and flow of NVA soldiers moving past their hide site didn't stop. There were no breaks in the seemingly endless enemy line. This was a Company size element or more. These weren't stragglers moving from a lost battle, just disciplined men moving with purpose.

Thomas took in a much slower and steadier breath concentrating on his new task of counting every tenth man to get an approximate average count of how many enemy soldiers there were trooping by, knowing that Carey was doing the same.

Later, if they lived to see a later, they'd compare numbers, if the 70-enemy soldiers he had counted so far, and the others that followed, kept walking. Any sense of bravado had disappeared. All that mattered now was for the long, continuous line to keep moving.

For a moment, as one enemy soldier turned and spit in the team's direction, the Texan held his breath, lost his count, and almost set off the Claymores. When the soldier turned back and kept walking with his shouldered AK-47, the A-T-L breathed a sigh of relief.

The long line of enemy soldiers continued with enemy soldiers toting the heavier RPD machine guns, RPGs, or struggling to push the dozen or more modified and overburden bicycles that were packed with mortar base plates and tubes, wooden boxes of mortar rounds, Chi-com grenades, ammunition, large fifty-pound bags of rice, and other boxed or bagged military supplies, along the muddied trail.

Thomas went back to the count. Taking in a calming breath, he let it out slowly, trying to regulate his breathing and heartbeat that his adrenaline was manipulating. He continued to quietly mouth the NVA's growing numbers. It was now looking to be at least two or three NVA companies, possibly a Battalion. The first four enemy soldiers were only the point element.

The A-T-L still had his hands on the claymore's firing device, but now prayed that Carey wouldn't give him the nod. He felt a slight tremble in is hands, and he fought to steady them as the enemy line trooped on by the hide site in a long, seemingly endless procession.

Keep walking! Don't stop, he said to himself. Jesus, keep fucking walking.

Chapter 4

Camp Mackie was a low-rent, hastily erected, compact Forward Operating Base. It was strategically placed northwest of Saigon between the larger 25th Infantry Division headquarters basecamp in Cu Chi and south of the Division's Forward Operating Base in Tay Ninh. Squalid to a civilian's eye, it was acceptable to the military's.

Mackie was put in place to supplement on-going tactical operations after the cross border incursion into Cambodia in May of 1970, and to hinder the flood of North Vietnamese Army soldiers infiltrating into the Republic of South Vietnam through the neighboring nation.

In truth, the new Camp, which was still accommodating itself to the war, was a pebble in the boot of a North Vietnamese Army who were bent on running through the province on its push to take down the Saigon regime.

The boomtown outpost, ringed with trip flares, concertina wire, and guard towers frustrated the enemy's advance by standing directly in the path of one of their major infiltration routes into the province. Mackie was a functioning outpost with two artillery batteries, an airstrip with a troop of scout, lift, and gunship helicopters and other fixed wing aircraft, a tank battalion, a platoon of MPs, one company of Engineers, a beefed up Aid Station, and the rear area to house an infantry battalion and the battalion's line units as they rotated in and out of the field to man the base, the small camp had some military muscle.

The Camp also had a mobile-home sized PX operated and managed by a civilian contract employee who must have believed that he'd been exiled with this latest assignment and that someone higher up in his civilian chain-of-command must have hated him. The small PX provided some small niceties that were well received by those in the Camp.

With all of the man and firepower, necessary support services, and supplied military equipment contained within its well protected perimeter, Camp Mackie was formidable for its size.

Mackie was also the home for R Company, 75th Infantry-Ranger. R Company was better known by the military's phonetic designation, as Romeo Company. In reality, though, the Ranger Company was only a Detachment.

The 51-man Ranger unit that came into being six months earlier, was brought in to play at the request of MAC-V Command, when someone, somewhere higher up, decided they needed more and better snooping eyes and ears on the ground.

By 1971 U.S. Troop strength in South Vietnam had been cut in half to slightly over 150,000 even as the fighting was heating up in Vietnam and in Cambodia. With anti-war rallies and protests flooding the streets, parks, and campuses back home and around the world, and with the anti-war sentiment growing in Congress no politician looking to be re-elected, including President Nixon wanted to have to explain higher casualty rates this late in the war on the campaign trail.

As a result large scale operations were being curtailed with whole Divisions and Battalions being pulled back from their once operational forward patrol areas, leaving the job of finding the enemy to Scout helicopter teams, Recon platoons, and LRRP/Ranger teams.

For the forces remaining, better intelligence was needed from the field, the kind that Lurp patrols could provide, which was why the fourteenth semi-consecutive lettered Ranger Company in the U.S. Army, Company R was officially added to the 75th Infantry roster.

In reality, the better military minds behind *we who grant you lettering naming* Ranger units bypassed the letter Q in favor of the next alphabetical letter in line, as they felt it had more cache, or because the decision maker with the final say, overlooked or possibly hated the letter Q. Stranger things had been known to happen in the Army.

Regardless, R Company came into being, At present, though, the new Ranger unit could only field four to five functioning teams until the latest batch of trainees in the unit's abbreviated, but intensive in-country LRRP/Ranger training cycle, were ready to graduate.

Team Leaders and Assistant Team Leaders came to the new unit from previously disbanded Ranger companies, or from Grunt, or Aerial Rifle Recon Platoons. The bulk of the team members, though, came from newly arrived FNGs who'd volunteered for the LRRP/Ranger training and had successfully completed the difficult and exhausting selection process.

Whether they'd joined the army or had been drafted, all of the volunteers were welcomed into the Romeo Company fold upon completion of the training.

The only exceptions to the training requirement were Romeo Company's Commanding Officer and First Sergeant who came from the 5th Special Forces Group and had served multiple combat tours of duty. It was they who had designed the training curriculum and set it in place.

Not all of those who served in the Airborne designated unit were parachute qualified, or were graduates of the eight-week Ranger school at Fort Benning, Georgia. Some weren't even Infantry qualified, but they all were eager volunteers, who, after the in-country LRRP/Ranger training, took on the second, working Military Occupational Specialty of 11-B, Infantry with the LRRP diploma added to their 201-personnel records file.

Petty critics would say they weren't *real* Rangers while the Viet Cong and NVA regulars they targeted might argue otherwise. Those who served on these five to six man teams behind the lines in enemy held territory did indeed range and carried on the 75th Infantry Ranger legacy in combat patrols.

They were a proud, at times loud, and an unlikely mix of young adventurers. Like the population of the U.S. most were white, but there was a hefty percentage of Blacks, Hispanics, Pacific Islanders, Americans of Asian extraction, and even one Native American. While they'd all had received their red, black and white Ranger scrolls and identifying black berets upon successfully completing the difficult in-country training, respect or at least, begrudging admiration, came one harrowing mission and firefight after another.

In the process they would forge true bonds and become part of a brotherhood that more than a few University Sociologists with furrowed brows would scratch their heads at, struggling with to fully comprehend.

The team members would become brothers, or at least, much appreciated cousins when it came to a fight. For some, there were still dislikes and ingrained prejudices to overcome or tolerate, but for the many, the layers of learned or perceived biases were slowly being peeled away with admirable respect, one mission, and one individual, at a time. Those who couldn't fit in, or who'd caused problems, were sent packing.

The Romeo Company home, their Ranger compound, such as it was, wasn't much to the discerning eye. There were two platoon-size, sandbagged ringed Quonset hut-like hootches, a large, semi-underground, heavily sandbagged TOC-Tactical Operations Center bunker, a third well-protected similar hootch pulling duty as the Arms Rooms and Supply Room, a fourth hootch, divided into living quarters for the company's First Sergeant and Senior NCOs, and a GP-medium tent that served a temporary home for the LRRP/Ranger trainees. A fifth and final Quonset hut served as the unit's Orderly Room with separate sleeping quarters for the Commanding Officer and XO, the Executive Officer. In this case the XO was a newly arrived West Point graduate named Marquardt, who had completed the Lurp in-country training the month before and who was immediately put to work overseeing the TOC and making the compound more livable for its inhabitants. There was much to do.

The packed-dirt compound featured a four-seat Outhouse, several piss tubes, and a shower point with two nozzles, and four fifty-gallon drums for the non-potable water to service it. There was a small motor pool area really for the company's one jeep, two flatbed 'Mules,' to ferry the five and six man teams to their awaiting helicopters, one deuce and a half truck, and the occasional stolen jeep or three-quarter ton truck that turned up in the company area from time to time, and then disappear during an announced Inspector General inventory inspection.

At the company's eastern perimeter two chest-high wooden tables with covered awnings served as weapons cleaning stations, accompanying sand-filled fifty-gallon drums dug into the ground and placed at an angle were provided to clear weapons. Scattered around the company area were strategically placed fortified, sandbagged, bunkers used primarily for better protection against incoming enemy rockets and mortars; all of which needed to be maintained for the unit to function.

To an onlooker the Ranger compound had the appearance of a poor looking cul-de-sac. Its horseshoe shaped perimeter was a four-foot high barbed wire fence that opened to a driveway and one of Mackie's many interconnected dirt roads. At the driveway's entrance facing out, a large sign in red, black and white paint proudly announced in bold, block print: R Company- Ranger 75th Infantry, *Audentis Fortuna Iuvat.*

The new Ranger unit with its Latin claim that *fortune favors the brave* was one more reason why the Viet Cong and NVA wanted to knock the American Camp out of their way, and why Mackie was the frequent target of rocket and mortar attacks, targeted sniper fire, and an occasional ground probe to Camp Mackie's perimeter.

The latest round of incoming mortars and rockets began falling in rapid succession over the remote base shortly after 2 p.m. with a flurry of hastily fired .122mm rockets and .82mm mortar rounds aimed in on the American Forward Operating Base.

After launching the rockets and mortars the NVA gunners quickly began breaking down their weapon platforms and high tailing it away before the Camp's Fire Direction Center could key in on their positions for return fire.

While it was just another harassing attack on the Camp, with only a small number incoming rockets and mortar rounds, it was the frequency of the attacks that demonstrated that the Viet Cong and NVA were upping their game. It was the fourth one this week.

Today, the first of the three .122 mm rockets that hit the camp, scored a direct hit on a UH-1H 'Huey' helicopter parked in its revetment on the flight line. When the rocket found its target the explosion ignited the helicopter's fuel tank and sent a fiery thermal column of flames, choking black smoke, and debris from the aircraft mushrooming into the sky.

The incoming rockets and mortars sent waves of whistling splinters of shrapnel radiating out from their impact areas. The blistering hot shrapnel blew through the surroundings like a drunken fireworks display.

Just as the first enemy round hit, the camp's incoming siren came alive, its wailing punctuated the methodical series of explosions and sent Mackie's occupants into their sandbagged covered bunkers or running for immediate cover.

The enemy combatants targeting the Camp, hurriedly sent their deadly barrage from one end of the jungle base to the other, trying to inflict as much damage as they could before they packed up and scurried off to plan their next attack.

To say they were *under the gun* wasn't an exaggeration. The artillery unit's Fire Direction Center was already yelling out commands to return fire on the calculated launch sites.

However, as quickly as the attack began it was over within minutes, with the incoming siren's blaring wail already diminishing to a dying whine.

An *'ALL CLEAR!'* command was given and soon echoed in shouts throughout the camp as GIs slowly began coming out of their bunkers, drainage ditches, and hiding places to once again secure the camp's perimeter, or to inspect the damage.

In this latest aftermath it was learned that other than the helicopter that had been hit, a second .122mm rocket, which was in theory targeting a 155-Howitzer cannon position, had missed its intended target and scored a direct hit on the artillery unit's plank-board, tin-roofed Outhouse. The rolls of toilet paper in the heavily damaged Outhouse would be sorely missed.

Considering that the replacement cost of the helicopter would run to a few million dollars, the NVA had taken out a valuable piece of equipment. Toss in the cost of the destroyed planked board, mesh screened, four-seat shitter, which some GIs estimated to be no more than $27, then the Viet Cong or NVA gunners had had a reasonably good, if not profitable afternoon.

Although the attack was over, the base camp would remain on high alert while some units began to clear away debris, working to get things could get back to what passed for normal.

One obstacle to normality was a third incoming .122mm Katyusha rocket that had landed inside the Romeo LRRP/Ranger Company's compound.

The rocket, filled with a warhead of 41-pounds of high explosives, had not only missed its the Command hootch and TOC, and the Company's Tactical Operations Center, but also had failed to detonate. The five-foot-long, ninety-three-pound missile, had instead bored a few feet into the damp, orange soil leaving the tubed engine and fins hissing, smoking, and leaning at an awkward angle within a few yards of the TOC's entrance.

The unexploded enemy rocket was proving to be a problem for Romeo Company's training NCO, Sergeant Rob Shintaku, too.

The veteran LRRP/Ranger was annoyed because the rocket and mortar attack had delayed the five-mile rucksack run, which was the final testing requirement for this latest class of selection candidates. The unexploded Soviet rocket delay it further.

Of the forty-seven volunteers in this training cycle who'd hoped to make the cut to become R Company Rangers, only nine remained. The dropout rate was typical of the selection process. The Lurp training was demanding and rigorous, but then it had to be. The rucksack endurance run, during the heat of the day would be their final challenge. That is, once they were allowed to begin. Shintaku and the nine would-be Lurps waited out on the perimeter road. *Hurry up and wait* seemed to be an Army maxim. The unexploded enemy rocket was a curious delay as it still had the potential to explode.

The war, that Shintaku knew, and the war the others would soon come to learn, had its own unique challenges, this interruption to the training being a minor, although a frustrating one.

The trainees weren't alone, other frustrated Lurps in the Company were standing out on the road with the soon-to-be Rangers watching, waiting, and wanting to get on with their day, too. The veteran Lurps on the road were on stand-down, meaning they had a one or two-day break in-between missions, so the downtime was theirs.

For the daily routine to continue, the missile's warhead would first need to be made safe before it could be dismantled and removed. The problem was the EOD- the Explosives Ordnance Disposal people who'd arrived on site said it would, perhaps, be a '*good hour or so*' before the LRRP/Rangers would be permitted to return to the company area.

Because of the unstable World War II Soviet-made rocket, those within the potential blast radius were evacuated from the potential danger area.

Well, except for the LRRP/Ranger Company Commander, Captain Johnston Bennett Robison, and his acting First Sergeant, Walter '*The Brick, as in Wall, but don't ever fucking call me, Walter,*' Poplawski. The two, who had just finished stacking a protective three-foot high wall of sandbags in front of the TOC's entrance, were now standing just in front of the small wall, only a few yards away from the unexploded rocket.

Rangers lead the way was the Ranger's motto earned on the D-Day beaches of Normandy. It was partially a show of balls and swagger, sure, but, in fact, it meant a great deal more, it was the creed of the Rangers who followed.

The Romeo Company Commander and First Sergeant were there, leading the way, because the TOC was the radio lifeline to their teams in the field. They wouldn't abandon their people.

The TOC's Operations NCO, Sergeant Tomas 'Tommy' Cantu, had volunteered to stay behind to monitor the bank of radios, which was why Robison and Poplawski had built the temporary wall. A portable, back-packed radio, an AN/PRC (prick)-25, rested just behind the protective sandbags. Its volume was turned up high and tuned to the teams' primary operating frequency keeping both men within hearing distance. A two-man radio team from Romeo Company, stationed atop the Nui Ba Den Black Virgin Mountain, relayed transmissions to the Company TOC at Mackie.

The trouble was the PRC-25 radio had limited range, and a host of other communications issues that '*hindered*' its overall effectiveness and reliability. *Hindered* was a polite way of saying that at times the radio didn't work worth a shit. The more powerful radios in the TOC were the true lifelines.

Normally, the Company's X-O, Lieutenant Ryan Marquardt, manned the TOC with Cantu and one other Lurp who had worked in scheduled twelve-hour shifts, but Marquardt had asked permission to insert a team in the field, so Captain Robison gave the Lieutenant the go-ahead knowing that he needed the experience, and had volunteered in the TOC in his stead.

Poplawski had joined him after seeing where the rocket had dug itself into the ground, and had quickly gone to work with the Captain to build the small protective sandbagged wall.

Once done the dark-haired and dark-eyed thirty-two-year-old Ranger Captain, who was of medium weight and height, and who, some said, could easily double for an albeit shorter version of the Boxer, Mohammed Ali, calmly began sipping on the cup of coffee he'd retrieved from the TOC and watched with mild curiosity as the EOD team arrived and set up to do their work.

At five-nine and two hundred and thirty pounds, Poplawski, who was all muscle and neck was standing beside Robison with crossed forearms was visibly annoyed at the morning's inconvenience, and specifically at the young EOD Second Lieutenant who'd asked them to leave the immediate area even as they were constructing the small sandbagged wall needed to help protect the TOC.

"Gentlemen, you'll need to remove yourselves from the immediate area," said the young EOD Second Lieutenant to the two veteran soldiers. "Those sandbags won't do much if this thing explodes. I can't guarantee your safety, if it detonates."

Robison nodded, shrugged off the concern, and took another sip of his coffee. The EOD officer, who looked to be the same age as many of the young Rangers in the company, also looked painfully new to Vietnam. His not yet scraped boots and still dark green jungle fatigues told the Ranger Captain that much, which probably explained why the EOD Lieutenant didn't understand why the two veteran soldiers remained where they were, even after he'd given them the warning.

Captain Robison would enlighten him.

"As of this moment, Lieutenant, I have two teams in the jungle on patrol, with another getting ready to deploy. This TOC is their only lifeline."

To Cantu inside the TOC he yelled, "Any SITREP update on Niner-One?"

SITREPs were situational reports, the called in reports from teams in the field.

"Negative, sir," came the shouted response from deep inside the bunker.

"Then, there it is," said the Captain.

"Yes, sir…but…"

"No buts, Lieutenant. Someone needs to be here to monitor the radio traffic and order up a Quick Reaction Force, if one or both of my teams hit the shit, which is more likely to happen than that WW-II surplus Soviet rocket going off. Besides, it's my Company area, and I haven't given the rocket permission to explode Have I, First Sergeant? Have I given the rocket permission to explode?"

The Ranger Captain turned to his First Sergeant for the answer.

"No, sir, you haven't," said Poplawski, dutifully matter of fact.

"See? Then, there you go," said Robison, holding out his arms in a *There's nothing I can I do* gesture. Back to First Sergeant, he said, "You can leave, First Sergeant. I'll mind the store."

"That's a negative, sir. I'm not going anywhere. Someone needs to be here to look after my fine Italian Alfonso Bialetti coffee maker in the TOC, and that someone is me. You know how much I do love my coffee, Captain."

"I do, indeed. I just don't understand why," Robison said, staring into his coffee cup and frowning at the coffee the First Sergeant had made. "I do hope you put a sandbag or two in front of the coffee creamer and sugar that makes it considerably more tolerable."

"Done and done, Captain."

"Outstanding! Then your job here is done, too, First Sergeant. I'll watch over your precious coffee maker, too. You may leave now."

"No, sir, no can do."

"Excuse me?"

"Did I mention it's my fine Italian Alfonso Bialetti coffee maker, sir?"

"You have, and I believe I have as well."

"It's crucial to my sense of personal well being. To those who don't know beans, coffee is life, Captain."

"Granted. However, what if I order you to leave, First Sergeant?"

"Can't, sir."

"You can't?"

"No, sir, I'm afraid that at this very moment I'm too fucking petrified to move."

"Can't or won't?"

"Tomato, tah-mato, sir. I'll stand my grounds."

"Ah! Another coffee reference."

"It is indeed."

Like a terrible toddler who didn't want to take a time-out, the First Sergeant crossed his heavily muscled forearms over his broad chest showing some of the size and bulk, along with several pale and troubling looking shrapnel scars in a defiant gesture to the young EOD officer.

"So I take it then you would ignore this young Lieutenant's request and my direct order to remove yourself from the immediate area, if I gave such an order?" Captain Robison said to Poplawski.

The First Sergeant nodded.

"That's affirmative, Captain," said Poplawski. "Paralyzing fear makes me incapable of comprehending or carrying out such an order, sir. I suspect, too, that when, or if, say someone tries to remove me I might panic and there's no telling how uncontrollably angry or violent I might become. And later, if I'm court-martialed for disobeying your direct order, and any mayhem that followed sir, I suspect the presiding judge, who sympathizes with career soldiers, would see the violation as combat stress and would probably recommend that I be placed in a nice warm Veterans Hospital stateside and be given a coloring book and a dull set of fucking crayons, so I won't hurt myself. Hot cocoa too, I imagine."

All the while he was speaking he was staring at the young EOD officer with a direct and defiant challenge. Senior NCOs, and especially those with considerable more life and combat experience were not to be trifled with.

"Are you talking hot Swiss cocoa with those tasty, little marsh mellows?" Robison asked, mimicking stirring a spoon in his coffee cup.

"I am, indeed, sir. Little bit of heaven, Captain. Little bit of heaven."

Captain Robison turned back to the young EOD Officer and shrugged.

"You see my dilemma, Lieutenant, do you?" he said.

"Yes, sir, but..."

"No buts, Lieutenant. So, I'd say the best course of action would be for you to just carry on and get that dud-fucking rocket out of my company compound so we can get back to the business of trying to win the war. Roger that, First Sergeant?"

"Loud and clear, Captain. Loud and clear!"

The First Sergeant smiled the smile of a junkyard dog with a far too loose choke chain, unsettling the young officer.

To his Training NCO and the nine remaining volunteers, who were standing back at a safe distance on the nearby road, the Ranger Captain bellowed, "Are you going to let a little thing like a war get in the way of the trainees final training exercise, Staff Sergeant Shintaku?"

"No, sir!" said Shintaku from the hard-packed dirt road.

"Out-fucking-standing, Staff Sergeant. Carry on!"

To his First Sergeant he said, "Perhaps a good cigar will help calm your nerves, First Sergeant." Robison pulled out two good-size cigars from his jungle fatigues breast pocket and handed one to his senior Non-commissioned officer.

"*Romeo y Julietta*," said Poplawski, studying the cigar with obvious admiration and approval. "Gotta hand it to those beard growing island commies. Those sonsofbitches really know how to make a fine cigar."

The senior NCO bit off the end of the cigar and spat it away it while removing a small piece of dried tobacco leaf from his teeth. Pulling out an engraved Zippo lighter from his right jungle fatigue trouser pocket, he flipped the metal lid open with his thumb and offered the flame to his Commanding Officer before lighting his own cigar.

The end of the cigar grew to a dull orange glow with a slowly growing ash grey edge as Poplawski drew in a deep lungful of smoke and then blew a small grey plume skyward.

"Nothing like a good cigar to keep me from pissing all over myself at a moment like this," he said to the Ranger Captain.

"Look, Top..." said the Second Lieutenant trying one more time to reason with the Ranger Company's stubborn First Sergeant.

"What did you just call me?" growled Poplawski, taking the cigar from his mouth, as he stepped forward and loomed over the now startled officer like a menacing human tornado.

"Top?"

"TOP! TOP? Do I look like a fucking Dreidel to you, Lieutenant, some kind of goddam toy for you to grin and spin?"

"No, I just..."

"You just what? Disrespected me by referring to me as some cheap ass children's toy? Is that it, Lieutenant, you insulting me instead of showing me the proper respect that my hard-earned rank, time in service, and multiple combat tours warrant and deserve? You implying I don't deserve that respect, sir?"

"No, First Sergeant, I, eh ..."

"You, eh, what? Forget that Non-Commissioned Officers carry the disproportion of the burden in any and every conflict and war?"

"They do, indeed!" agreed Captain Robison. "It's no secret that the NCOs are doing the bulk of the heavy lifting, just like your NCOs are doing with that rocket, Lieutenant."

The Ranger Company Commander tilted his head towards where the two-man team of EOD enlisted men; a veteran looking Staff Sergeant and a short-timer E-4, had paused in their disassembly of the unexploded missile, and with tools in hand, were now enjoying the show. Second Lieutenants always made for cheap entertainment.

A bead of sweat that was trickling down behind the EOD Lieutenant's right ear likely had something to do with the 100-plus degree temperature, but not all. Clearly intimidated and disrupted, he looked around nervously hoping to find support, but found none. It was Captain Robison that offered him a way out.

"Dial it back, First Sergeant," he said, intervening in the verbal dispute.

"Sir?"

"I'm sure that this fine young officer in no way meant to demean or disrespect you or NCOs in general, let alone your years of dedication and service. Did you, Lieutenant?"

"No...no, sir. I did not."

"There you go, First Sergeant, so how about we leave him be so he, and his outstanding people, can do the important job they came here to do? They deserve some respect as well."

Still scowling, Poplawski was momentarily unresponsive.

"First Sergeant, did you hear me?"

"Sir, Yes, sir," came the reluctant reply. Properly chastised Poplawski took a step back.

"Thank you, First Sergeant," said Robison, as his First Sergeant appeared to regain a modicum of self-control.

Back to the young EOD officer Robison added, "Everyone's a little on edge here, Lieutenant. Best to look to the task at hand. Please, carry on with your mission."

The junior officer officer took the hint. The two weren't going anywhere. More than a little irritated, he'd bring this up to his own Commanding Officer once he got back to his own Detachment. For the moment, the now, he was not only outranked by the Ranger Company Commander, but was more than a little intimidated by the Ranger First Sergeant as well.

A .155mm howitzer cannon boomed from the Artillery Battery in the near distance and the young Lieutenant flinched, as the two Rangers casually smoked their cigars.

The Lieutenant turned back to his people muttering something under his breath that brought smiles to both Robison and Poplawski.

When the EDO Lieutenant was out of hearing range, Robison said, "A little harsh on him, wouldn't you say, Top?"

Poplawski turned to his Commanding Officer and smiled a wide grin as he checked the ash at the end of his cigar. "It's just how you spin things, Captain."

"Quite the performance, I must admit. Well played."

"Not too audacious or over the top, sir?"

"No, I'd say fine and quite fitting for the role. You loom menacingly and quite convincingly. However, I suspect he probably thinks you're one of those pain in ass, knuckle draggers he has to contend with from time to time."

"Huh? Well then, I guess he's more perceptive than I gave him credit for."

"Have we received any SITREPS from the teams in the field, yet?"

"One. A negative SITREP from Team Niner-three. We should be hearing from Niner-One any time now," the First Sergeant said, checking his watch.

"All quiet on the western front, then?"

"Hopefully," said the First Sergeant.

"I haven't seen Lieutenant Marquardt about the Company area. I take it he's not back yet."

"No, sir, I believe our new Upper Hudson is still somewhere near Cu Chi inserting team Nine-Two for a mission."

"*Upper Hudson?*"

"Yes, sir, it's one of those playful and endearing nicknames we enlisted folk call all fine West Point graduates behind their backs until they've proven themselves useful."

"That, and other things, I suppose? You know, of course, that I, too, am a graduate of West Point?"

Poplawski nodded.

"Yes, sir. I gathered that from the heavenly choir and blinding glow emanating from your class ring. However, because you're also Special Forces qualified and have proven yourself nicely as a man amongst men, it gives me hope for our young Ranger officer. That, and because I'm pretty certain he's capable of tying his own boots and not spilling his juice from the sippy cup that's attached to his canteen."

Robison chuckled. "You are a cynical man, First Sergeant?"

"Yes, sir, and observant too."

"Once the EOD people get the rocket out of here and the TOC people are back in place, we'll head over to the Mackie TOC to find out what air support they have laid on in case one of team's get hit."

"Sergeant Cantu nicknamed it BIG-TOC."

"Given who all resides there, I'd say that's pretty accurate," chuckled the Ranger Officer. "Did I mention they have better coffee there, too? No offense, but your coffee tastes like horse piss."

"No offense taken, sir. And may I say it's always good to have firsthand account and confirmation from someone who actually knows what horse-piss tastes like, Captain. You truly are an inspiration."

"Glad to see I'm appreciated."

"That you are, sir. That you are."

Chapter 5

It was a tense, white-knuckled wait even after that last NVA soldier had walked out of the kill zone and presumably had kept moving further down the trail. Out of sight didn't necessarily mean out of danger. Out of sight in the jungle could just as well mean that an unseen someone was still only a few yards away. Still ready to fight, the Rangers waited, watched, and listened. All was quiet for a few tense and drawn-out moments.

Carey needed to be certain that the enemy soldiers were well past the team before he oh-so-cautiously, lifted his head up to get a better view of the trail. When that was enough to see all that he needed to see, he rose to one knee.

The trail, or at least what he could see of it through the lattice of leaves, branches, and brush, looked to be clear. Even so, he lowered himself back down and kept the others down for a few anxious minutes longer. They waited, watched, and listened on.

They would remain at the ready in case any of the enemy soldiers had doubled back or that there were no more stragglers or rear scouts trailing the main column. When you only had a five-man team operating behind the lines, you didn't push your already pushed luck.

Carey motioned to his RTO for the team's backpacked radio's handset and Warren passed it over to him. Depressing the talk button, Carey whispered, "Valhalla, Valhalla. Longboat Niner-One. Over."

Valhalla was the call sign for the Romeo Company TOC, the Ranger Company's communication bunker and Tactical Operations Center back at Camp Mackie.

He waited for the response and when it didn't come, he tried again.

"Valhalla, Valhalla. Longboat Niner-One. Over."

No response, again. Nothing. Just white noise static.

The Sergeant frowned and changed the radio to a secondary frequency.

"Valhalla relay, Valhalla relay. Longboat Niner-One. Over."

Nothing.

To Warren he said, "You replace the battery, Jonas?"

The radioman nodded. "New battery before the parade started."

"Toss up the long-whip," said the team leader.

The RTO nodded again and then removed the folding, ten-foot 'long whip' antenna from its canvas, carrying bag, and pulled it together like a tall, thin folding, fishing pole. Once done, he quickly attached it to the team's radio.

"Good to go," Warren said, once it was operational.

The long whip antenna would give the team a better reach when it came to commo, up to eighteen miles, in a better world. But the jungle war wasn't a better world. The dense rain forest, rolling topography, and the terrible weather could and would play havoc with normal radio communications. Even with the better antenna, it was a crapshoot. Combat was always a game of luck, where few who took enormous chances knew that there was no such thing as luck, but rolled the proverbial dice anyway.

"Valhalla, Valhalla. Longboat Niner-One. Over," said the Team Leader again, his voice taking on a new urgency.

Still there was no response. The on-going white noise static crackled in his ear.

Carey tried several more times but with the same frustrating response. He wasn't happy about it, but outwardly he kept his cool.

"Keep trying," he said handing the handset back to Warren.

"Roger that, Sarge."

Carey's mind was busy. There was much to weigh and consider. How far had the NVA soldiers moved? Did they keep going or stop? Were they just out of sight? Were they moving on the nearby Fire Support Base? If so, then there had to be more on the way.

The very real danger was still there and perhaps more so, now that the enemy soldiers could no longer be seen. Without commo there was no way to let the TOC know what they'd witnessed. No way to pass this important Intel along.

The teams were required to radio in their locations and situational reports status, their SITREPS, once an hour for the duration of the mission. Significant findings, like the one they'd just had, direction of enemy movement, numbers, found enemy weapons caches, occupied bunker complexes, tunnels, or whatever else the teams came across on the patrols were radioed in as they were discovered. This was significant, and there was no way at this moment to report it.

Standard Operating Procedure was that when the TOC hadn't received one of the hourly SITREPS, the TOC would then initiate radio contact with the teams. However, they too knew that the weather, dense jungle foliage, a bad battery or handset could affect radio transmissions, so some leeway was allowed before they'd send up a helicopter to try to re-establish radio contact.

At night, if a team was set up in their RON, their rest-over-night position, and a team member manning the radio fell asleep on guard duty, another procedure was applied. If the company TOC hadn't heard from the team in the field after two to three required check in times then the TOC would request an illumination round from a nearby Fire Support Base be fired in the team's general direction.

The loud cannon fire and falling flare would startle those sleeping, radio contact would be re-established, and the Team Leader and the rest of the team members would be pissed off at the man who'd fallen asleep on guard duty. A five-man team in enemy territory couldn't afford stupid or critical mistakes.

But Warren had just called in the latest SITREP shortly before the initial enemy sighting so the TOC wouldn't even begin to contact the team for another forty minutes or so. That left a big window of opportunity for things to go to fuck all in a hurry.

"Let me know when you have commo," Carey said, back to Warren and then waved over his Assistant Team Leader.

"What's up, Ben?" asked Thomas, scooting over to Carey's side.

"No radio contact."

"Lovely, just fucking lovely, so what do we do? The URC-10?"

In GI speak URC was pronounced *erk* much the way the PRC-25 was referred to as the Prick-25. Unlike the backpacked radio the URC-10 was a small, hand-held FM emergency radio, a pocket-sized backup radio.

Carey kept the small radio in is trouser cargo pocket. He pulled it out and set it on the top of his rucksack, ready to use in case Warren couldn't get any commo with the PRC-25.

The trouble was both radios had problems in valleys, thick jungle, tunnels, or other physical obstacles that interfered with frequency modulated transmissions. The PRC-25 was still the team's best option.

Carey was thinking he'd have Warren move over to the cover of a nearby tree and then stand with the radio over his head to try to make radio contact, but decided against it. Something more was nagging at him and he couldn't quite place it, yet.

"We wait," he said eyeing the still jungle around him.

The wait didn't last long as one more long line of enemy soldiers soon followed the first line down the jungle trail. Only this time, a few minutes into the procession, the line of NVA soldiers stopped on the trail. Seven to ten of them were visible through the leaves and brush screen while more could be heard further up and down the trail.

The NVA soldiers began dropping their packs, pulling out their canteens, and cooking pots while the small American patrol began making themselves even smaller.

This battle, if it started, would begin from thirty feet away.

Chapter 6

Captain Tony Adler looked at his military watch, yet one more time, shook his head, and then slowly blew air out through his teeth in exasperation. The Senator and his entourage were running late, again.

Of course, they were.

The VIP visit was turning into a cluster fuck.

Still, it was good to be out of his khakis and back into his jungle fatigues with a holstered .45 strapped to the pistol belt. The familiarity was comforting.

"Any update, sir? Any word, yet?" asked the mustachioed helicopter pilot from the opened door of the Huey's cockpit.

Adler shook his head.

"Naw, apparently we're still standing-by," he said, and the pilot nodded.

The pilot, or more formally, the aircraft commander, twenty-two-year old Chief Warrant Officer-2 Michael Corsi was on a six-month extension to his one-year tour of duty. Corsi's dark, drooping mustache made him look like a short and grinning Wyatt Earp. His co-pilot, Scott Kehr, was a tall, lanky Californian with only five months in-country. His job was to learn from the more experienced combat pilot. With the war as an on-going classroom, Kehr had much to learn and Corsi was a patient instructor. The two obviously got along, which Adler knew, wasn't always the case.

Both the pilots and crew were on loan from the 229th Aviation Battalion to serve as a taxi service to the VIPs, and, given that their actual job was hauling grunts in and out of combat landing zones and hot pickup zones, where they'd taken hits from enemy fire, this TDY task was a picnic. They, along with their crew chief and door gunner, didn't mind the wait and took it in stride.

The Senator was the Honorable Henry Howard Russell, a four-term career politician from the mid-west who wasn't worried about being unseated anytime soon.

As a ranking and well-respected member of the House Armed Services Committee, he spearheaded budgets for the Department of Defense, and was a mover and shaker in Congressional circles. At least that's how he had been described in the briefing when the Captain was handed the job of coordinating the air and ground transportation for the VIP visit.

"He's a *somebody* in the VIP world of somebodies," said Lieutenant Colonel Albert Bainbridge, explaining the tasking to the two MAC-V Public Affairs Office staff officers under his command.

The air conditioner that cooled the Saigon office was doing its job, but it couldn't do much for the stuffiness conveyed by the Colonel's personality.

"It's important that we make the Senator, and those traveling with him, feel welcome for the time he and his people are with us."

"How long is the visit, sir?" said Adler.

"Three days," said the Colonel. "After that he's making stops in the Philippines, Japan, and Taiwan."

"How many people in his party, Colonel?"

"Two, besides the Senator, I'm told," said Bainbridge. "His Chief of Staff, one S. Orlov, and the Senator's teenage son, Zackary."

"I'll be accompanying the VIP party while they're here in Saigon, on Days One and Three, but I'm relying on the two of you to get the Senator to and from his scheduled stops in-country for the Day Two visits."

Adler started to ask another question but was cut off by the Colonel. "And before you ask to and from where, Tony, tentatively three stops are lined up for day two; Cu Chi, Tay Ninh, and Phuoc Vinh."

To the Major standing beside Adler the Colonel said, "Bob, let's make sure we have jungle fatigues, ball caps, and boots for each member in their party. Get with the Senator's Chief of Staff to coordinate sizes, etcetera upon arrival. Oh, and make sure they have MAC-V patches and nametags as well."

"No problem."

"Good, and I'll need you to coordinate with the PIO office to lay on a photographer and Information Specialist, preferably one and the same. Someone from Stars and Stripes will cover the Saigon visit. As for the other stops along the way, coordinate with the PIOs at those locations. We'll want some good press and photos out of this, so you'll be handling the press release as well. You'll be shepherding the party once they leave Saigon. You'll be the official glad-handler on the other in-country visits."

Of course, he will be, thought Captain Adler. Haverly was tall, ruggedly handsome in an Army recruiting poster kind of way, and had all of the practiced and calculated charm needed to feign gravitas and sincerity- characteristic traits that Adler figured the Major had fine honed to his benefit on the job and his career.

Adler was everything Haverly wasn't. He was older, shorter, deceptively average looking, and was someone who tended to speak his mind when asked a question, which weren't necessarily attributes when it came to the Public Relations glad-handing business.

Also, Tony Adler was an actual soldier and decorated combat veteran, who wasn't much on Dog and Pony Shows, which was this VIP visit was all about, which was also why he figured the Colonel left him out of the initial meet-and-greet.

Turning to the Captain, the Colonel said, "Tony, you'll coordinate the air and ground transportation on Day Two. Check with the motor pool for the appropriate vehicles and then get with Flight Operations about the necessary aircraft needed for the visits we have laid on. Make it a Huey."

"Not a Chinook?" questioned Haverly, registering some concern.

"No, let's give them the whole Vietnam experience."

As he was speaking, Bainbridge began passing over typed copies of the schedule to the two junior officers. The agendas were stamped in red ink block print with a SECRET classification as it contained the times and locations for visits to the U.S. Embassy, MAC-V headquarters, with flights to the basecamps in Cu Chi, Phuoc Vinh, and Tay Ninh, with a brief visit to the Cao Dai Temple in Tay Ninh City.

"Any questions?"

"Security teams, Colonel?" said Adler as Colonel Bainbridge dismissed the Captain's question.

"Not our concern. I've been told by MAC-V command that the MPs will be handling the security aspects of the visit at each of the locations. Heavy Gun jeeps and the whole nine yards."

"Perhaps even the whole ten yards," laughed the Major, "considering who the Senator is."

Bainbridge chuckled as well while Adler forced a smile.

"We have 72-hours before the Senator's plane touches down and I want every wrinkle and possible wrinkle ironed out before it does, so let's get on this, A-SAP. Any more questions?"

The Major shook his head while the Captain, once again, spoke up.

"Yes, sir," he said. "I take it these aren't precise times, Colonel?"

"Excuse me?"

"I know that these, eh, visits tend to fall off schedule pretty quickly, so what's the wiggle room on these movement times, sir?"

Bainbridge frowned.

"The wiggle room, Captain," said the somewhat annoyed Colonel, "is whatever it is. You need to be flexible in that regard, from the time we pick them up at the airport to the time to the time we put them back on the plane out of country. Is that understood?"

"Yes, sir."

"Good. Now get it done. I want to see your game plans on my desk by close of business today."

The plans were delivered on time and, with the exception of one or two minor changes, they were approved to the Colonel's satisfaction.

Wiggle room was shown to be needed on Day One when the Senator's visit ran long at each of the Saigon locations, from the greeting at the airport, to a brief stop off at their temporary quarters, to MAC-V Headquarters for status briefings with General Abrams and his staff, and finally to the U.S. Embassy for a visit with the Ambassador, where the Ambassador invited them to stay overnight at the Ambassador's residence.

On Day Two Tony Adler had ground transportation back to Tan Son Nhut arranged and available for 0700, with what was to have been the actual movement time being 0900 after breakfast at the Ambassador's residence.

The helicopter flight to Cu Chi was laid on for 0930, after yet one more Show and Tell from Colonel Bainbridge.

By Adler's watch, it was almost a quarter past ten and the VIPs and accompanying entourage were still nowhere in sight. A half hour more and one of the stops and visits in the preplanned agenda would have to be scrubbed.

Of course, they're late. Adler thought to himself as he slowly shook his head, again. *A Dog and Pony Show* best summed up what it was, with staff briefings, long lunches, and grip and grin photo opportunities. Just as the schedule had been skewed on the previous day, Day Two wasn't starting off any better.

More than likely the Senator was still sipping coffee and looking thoughtful, or at least photographically concerned as Bainbridge and Major Haverly went about their informal briefing as the PIO photographer took photos of Russell, his Chief of Staff, the Senator's fifteen-year-old son, and a beaming Public Affairs Colonel and Major.

Photo Ops made for good campaign images back home and the Senator was up for reelection in his district, not that there was anything for him to worry about; the polls had him in a substantial lead over his nearest opponent.

The visit to the war zone was probably his way of drumming up support from both the pro-war and anti-war voters, audiences that the Senator would work to his political advantage.

Incumbents knew the political score and capitalized on such overseas troop visits; they made for good PR, especially when it came to fund raising for the next election campaign drive. Good PR was also good for the careers of those in Public Affairs Office positions; something Colonel Bainbridge and Major Haverly were fully aware of and using to their best advantage.

Although the Senator wasn't a big name in politics; not a Kennedy, Humphrey, or Goldwater, he was big enough to have sway and influence over all of them when it came to key Senate votes or placement on important committees.

Russell was part of the inner circle of Congress, so the Army higher ups gave him more than a little leeway with the visit, offered much glad-handing, and produced enough custom-made unit caps, plaques and giveaways for the Senator to pass along to his Chief of Staff, who in turn, passed them along to Lieutenant Colonel

Bainbridge, then to Major Haverly, who passed them along to Captain Adler, along with a mailing address for what they didn't want to carry.

Meanwhile, Tony Adler and the aircrew on the tarmac would continue to stand-by as long as it took for the VIP's social wiggling. The helicopter would wait and so would Adler.

"Mister Kehr wants to know if there's time to grab a quick soft drink, sir?" the helicopter's crew chief asked Adler, tilting his head towards the helicopter co-pilot.

Standing beside the 20-year-old veteran crew chief was his door gunner who'd be making the snack bar run. The door gunner, who looked hopeful, also looked to be eighteen, tops. Both had attempted to grow mustaches. The attempts were on going.

"Is that okay, Captain?" asked the crew chief.

Tan Son Nhut air base was a modern, sprawling military facility with amenities that could rival most stateside bases, including clubs and snack bars that sold burgers, fries, and cold soft drinks. The one the door gunner was referring to was just across the flight line, at best five minutes away.

"Apparently, there's time," replied Adler. "Sure, go ahead. Just be back in a few. You copy?"

"Yes, sir," said the crew chief who turned to the door gunner and said, "Hey Petey, make it quick."

Petey, the young looking door gunner said he would. When he started to go the crew chief grabbed him by the elbow.

"Can we pick up something for you, Captain?" asked the crew chief.

"Naw, I'm good. Wait, hold on a minute..."

Adler reached for his wallet and retrieved a $10 MPC note. He said, handing it to the door gunner. "Let's make it my treat."

The crew chief grinned as he turned and yelled to the pilots, "He's buying!"

The two pilots for the UH-1H 'Huey' that looked all too painfully young to Tony Adler as well grinned and gave him a thumbs-up as the door gunner took off at a quick pace.

"God, I'm old," he thought as the two pilots and crew chief were still nodding their thanks.

"Appreciate it, Captain," said Mister Corsi as Adler acknowledged him with a quick nod before turning his attention back to the road adjacent to the airfield.

Still no VIPs.

Adler smiled to himself; a resigned smile that he was all too familiar with and had come from his nearly three decades of similar situations in uniform.

With the Army it was always '*hurry up and wait.*' He even harbored a suspicion that Leonidas' Spartans probably felt the same way when they got to the pass at Thermopylae and had to wait a day or so before the Persians showed up. With the King's permission a few of his Spartans probably even went looking to find a halfway decent gyro and a grape soda at a nearby snack bar as well.

It had been that way in England twenty-nine years earlier, too, when, the then seventeen-year-old pimply-faced Private Anthony *'Call me, Tony'* Adler, sat in a parachute harness, cradling an M-1, and waited on another tarmac with the other equally young paratroopers to board the C-47s for the jump into Normandy.

He'd parachuted into combat on D-Day with the 101st Airborne then, and again in Holland on Operation Market Garden. By the war's end, the Army Private with a combat star on his jump wings had risen to the rank of a seasoned Staff Sergeant, complete a Bronze Star for Valor and Purple Heart for a number of shrapnel welts and divots to his chest, back, and legs from a German grenade.

"No sweat, kid," said the medic who treated him outside of a small village in Holland when the grenade peppered him with the splintered metal fragments. There were seven small wounds in total and they'd left a blood dripping display of nasty-looking gouges. "Nothing serious," added the medic. "They only nicked you. If you're lucky, a good woman will play connect the dots and eventually discover your dick."

By the Korean War, the still hard charging Tony Adler had been promoted to the rank of E-7, Sergeant First Class, with another Bronze Star for Valor while serving with the 187th Regimental Combat Team.

By the early 1960s, he had been promoted again, this time into the Officer Corps as a Second Lieutenant. As such, he was a '*Mustang Officer*,' as those enlisted men who had been selected for the promotion, were better known.

It was a badge of honor to the enlisted men he'd led, who knew how he came up through the ranks, as well as to some of the OCS and West Point officers who, at times, viewed the Mustang Officers as the proverbial red-headed bastard step children.

Adler begrudgingly earned their respect of those he commanded by leading from the front, whether it was in Marksmanship, PT, or the back-burdening, full rucksack carrying, grueling twelve-mile forced marches.

The Infantry School's motto of '*FOLLOW ME*' was something he took to heart. It was more than just a slogan to him. He believed you never asked a soldier to do something you yourself, couldn't, or wouldn't do.

By the mid 1960s, and at an age for what some considered to being '*a little long in the tooth*,' the newly promoted First Lieutenant Adler had applied for the Special Forces and made the selection process. He had earned his tab and coveted Green Beret, along with more than a few tired and strained muscles during the grueling training at Camp McCall and the final *Robin Sage* phase of the course at Fort Bragg, North Carolina.

At graduation, over a beer with another graduate he admitted, "If you told me I was going to wear a beret when I joined the Army, I probably would've told you to go fuck yourself. But now, I can't think of any headgear I'd be more honored or proud to wear."

After a year in Bad Tolz, Germany, followed by a six-month stint in North Africa working with the French, he volunteered for combat duty in Vietnam. There he eventually led a Special Forces A-Team on missions in the Central Highlands.

One more Bronze Star and a South Vietnamese Cross of Gallantry with Gold Palm later, Adler's career was on the rise. That is, until his second tour of duty in the Central Highlands, where he was wounded again.

This time, though, it was more than minor shrapnel wounds. When the CIDG camp they were on was hit and almost overrun, he led a small team of Montagnards to take on an eight-man squad of Viet Cong sappers who had breached a hole in the wire of the camp's eastern perimeter.

Adler and two of his *Yards* took out the sappers but not before he took a three round burst from an Ak-47 to his chest. Two of the rounds shredded his left lung while the third broke some ribs, somehow missed the vital organs, and exited out his back.

Although he was violently knocked down when he was hit, and was struggling to breathe he shot and killed the enemy soldier who'd shot him. When he tried standing he couldn't find the strength. Worse still, he found himself drowning in his own blood.

He was rescued by his A-Team medic who raced in, pulled him back to cover, and immediately began treating the miserable wounds. A shot of morphine helped but it blurred what followed as he was Medevac'd out by helicopter to the Third Field Hospital in Saigon and rushed into the Operating Room. The gunshot wounds proved severe and he lost a lung. Lieutenant Tony Adler's once promising career came to a sudden, bleeding halt.

When his wounds stabilized, he was evacuated to Camp Zama, Japan, and finally to Walter Reed in Bethesda, Maryland. Along the way, though, pneumonia set in. With one lung and with each breath feeling like it came with broken glass, Adler struggled.

Three weeks later, and with a severe drop in body weight, he finally was well on his way to a reasonable recovery. For his defense of the Montagnard camp he received a Silver Star for Gallantry. The medal was pinned to his hospital pajamas by a Full Bird Colonel who was surprised to find a First Lieutenant who was only slightly younger than he was.

With the medal also came a promotion to the rank of Captain, the last being a 'gift' for the medical retirement everyone was expecting him to take. The promotion and accompanying disability benefits from the Veterans Administration would've made for a halfway decent retirement check, if he chose to put in his papers.

Only he didn't take the retirement. Instead, he talked the medical board into letting him remain in uniform on active duty.

While he may have convinced one or two well-meaning military physicians that he was still fit to serve, those in Command at the Pentagon, no longer saw it that way. Because he couldn't meet the rigorous physical standards required for the Special Forces, let alone for any combat status, he was transferred out of the Special Forces and away from any combat duty.

Upon his discharge from the hospital and after a two-week leave, he found himself at his next duty assignment running a Basic Training Company at Fort Dix, New Jersey.

Two months into the job where he and his cadre had been teaching enlistees and draftees the basic concepts of soldiering, he was bored out of his mind. He was in a dead end position and he knew it, which was why decided to call his former World War Two Platoon Leader from the 101st who was finishing his time in the Army at the Personnel Center in Alexandria, Virginia.

The former Platoon Leader, Colonel Sam Mayhew, had visited Adler during his recovery at Bethesda, saying that while he was getting ready to retire, if there was anything he could do for him or his career before then, all he needed to do was ask.

"They're easing me out," Mayhew said. "I'm little more than a paper pusher these days, so maybe it's time."

"When do you retire?"

"This coming April."

"I should be out of here by then and in my new assignment but I have enough lave time so I'll be there to help you celebrate."

Mayhew nodded. "Honored to have you, Tony," he said "And, by the way, I meant what I just said. If there's something I can help you job wise before I go, let me know."

Tony Adler said he would. Just prior to Mayhew's retirement in late February, he took him up on the offer. When he called the Personnel Center, he was put on hold, and waited a few moments before Mayhew's familiar deep bass voice boomed over the telephone line.

"Tony! Great to hear from you," said Mayhew. "How in the hell are you doing? You still coming to my retirement party, I hope?"

"I am, indeed, sir," laughed Adler. "I just need the when and where for the celebration?"

"April 12th, at noon at the O-Club at Fort Meade, and its Sam, not sir. You've earned that."

"Sam," said Adler, reluctantly.

"So how's the Basic Training Company treating you, and have you heard yet where you are on the promotion list?"

"The job is mind numbing and there's no news on the promotion list."

"Well, you'll make a fine Major and those trainees and even the young cadre at the Basic Training Company can use your experience. I doubt too many soldiers have ever seen someone with two stars on their Combat Infantryman's Badge. That's as rare as spotting a unicorn!"

"More like a dinosaur to some," laughed Adler and after a brief pause got to the primary purpose of the call. "I was hoping to take you up on your offer, and maybe bug you for another assignment? Anything you can do to help me out?"

Mayhew didn't hesitate. He said, "Let me see what I can do. Give me a good number and I'll get back to you with something in a few days."

"Good enough, sir," said Adler, passing along his contact number and feeling chipper about his prospects.

"Sam."

"Sam," echoed Adler.

There was a reason why Sam Mayhew wanted to help Adler out. Mayhew had been his Platoon Leader on the predawn jump into Normandy on D-Day, and when he came down in a farmer's pond the weight of his British leg bag had pulled him underwater. Worse still, he was wrapped up in his parachute risers. The pond was maybe ten feet deep and the surface was just beyond the reach of his outstretched and wildly flaying arms.

Mayhew was choking on the putrid water and desperately struggling to free himself from the parachute harness and leg bag in a seemingly losing battle. He was about to drown when he was dragged out of the pond by a cherub faced Private. On his butt and digging his boot heels in to anchor and hold him in place, the Private had wrapped the bulk of Mayhew's parachute canopy in his arms and then using every bit of strength a skinny 18-year-old could muster, he reeled Mayhew in. That Private was Anthony Adler.

Mayhew never forgot what the young soldier did for him that day or in the difficult days that followed, fighting from hedge row to hedge row, village to village. Of course, he would return the favor. He was happy to. The two had stayed in touch over the years and when he'd heard that the former enlisted man had become an officer the then Major Mayhew believed the Officer Corps was made better for the likes of Tony Adler.

The conversation that began with pleasantries two days later when he got the return call gave him a sinking feeling that the news wasn't good. After some brief banter, a more subdued Mayhew passed along some more news.

"Tony, I don't know how to tell you this, but you've been passed over for promotion. I got a sneak peek at the Major's list and I'm sorry to say, you're not on it. I don't know what in the hell they were thinking. I'm so sorry."

The phone went silent for an uncomfortable moment. Being passed over meant that he would eventually be forced into retirement once the promotion list was posted. He remembered a dark joke with a punch line about a newspaper reporter who'd interviewed Mrs. Lincoln, and asking, *'Sure, but other than that, what did you think of the play?'*

Without the promotion his career was dead. The news was its death knell.

"When does the list come out?" Adler asked. "When will it be posted?"

"Thirty days out. Forty, at best."

Not much time. The solution, well, one anyway, he quickly figured, was to volunteer for a third tour of duty in Vietnam before the promotion list was announced. There was always a shortage of volunteers for the war zone, so with that in mind, he called in a favor.

"Okay then, can you get me back to Vietnam? Anything, Colonel, anything at all, I'll take it."

"You sure this is what you want, Tony?" said his friend, warily.

"I do. I'll need one last tour of duty for a better retirement."

"Given your medical records it won't be a combat assignment."

"I'll take whatever you got, if it buys me a little more time."

"Then I'm on it," Mayhew said. "Let me see what I can do."

Sam Mayhew came through for him three days later when orders came down for Adler to report to MAC-V Headquarters in Saigon in two weeks time, he was elated. At Mayhew's retirement party he thanked his friend who said he wasn't sure he was doing him a favor.

"It's an office job with MAC-V and the best I could do," Mayhew said.

"It's appreciated," said Adler. "Thank you."

MAC-V headquarters, the Military Assistance Command-Vietnam, operated out of a sprawling office compound adjacent to Saigon's Tan Son Nhut airport. What began in the early 60s as a temporary advisory and assistance command soon grew to encompass all combat and pacification operations in the four tactical corps regions of Republic of South Vietnam.

Besides its unofficial and more acceptable nickname of the *Pentagon East* it also was referred to as *The Puzzle Palace.*

Unlike the bulk of GIs on the World Airlines flight to South Vietnam, Tony Adler knew that whatever his job at MAC-V Headquarters would be when he arrived, it would be relatively a lot cleaner and more comfortable than what they'd find. Some of these rear area bases and camps had all of the comforts of stateside bases and more.

The 18-hour government contract flight out of McChord Air Force Base south of Tacoma, Washington, touched down in Bien Hoa, Vietnam, after a brief refueling stopover in Japan. After gathering up his duffle bag, he made his way down to Saigon and Tan Son Nhut where he reported to the security desk at MAC-V Headquarters.

"Looks like I'll be assigned here," he said, presenting his orders and photo ID to the MP manning the desk.

"PAO-Liaison Office?"

"Apparently, although I'm not quite sure what that is, exactly."

The MP chuckled. "I'm not sure, either, sir," he said. "I'm new here as well."

"Well then, I think we're both in for a few surprises," laughed Adler. "Would it be alright if I leave my duffle bag here while I report in?"

"No problem, sir," said the MP who directed him to the PAO-Liaison office halfway down a long and highly polished corridor on the first floor.

While Adler was familiar with Public Affairs, the *Liaison* aspect added a new and confusing twist. Entering the office, he announced himself to the smiling civilian secretary inside and was told to take a seat while she relayed his arrival to the Colonel in the next office.

The Colonel was Lieutenant Colonel Albert Bainbridge, the Public Affairs-Liaison officer in charge.

"Sir, a Captain Adler to see you," she said pressing a button on a small intercom.

"Fantastic! Send him in," came the squeaky speaker reply.

"Right this way, Captain," said the secretary rising from her desk, opening the inner office door, and ushering him in.

"Thank you," said Adler, smiling, and earning a smile in return.

Inside, he found a stout-looking senior officer, dressed in a starched and tailored Class-B Khaki uniform with two and a half rows of colorful '*I was there, but nowhere near combat or anything that ever goes boom*' ribbons, seated behind an ornate and impressive teak desk.

A highly polished brass nameplate, front and centered on the desk read, LTC Albert Bainbridge. The large desktop held a leather blotter, a telephone, and a small intercom. An IN basket that held a small stack of papers and files was positioned on the right side of the desk while an empty OUT basket hugged the left side, indicating there was much to be done.

The Lieutenant Colonel, who was on the phone, held one hand up to have him wait, but didn't motion for him to take a seat. A thin file was opened on the desk in front of him. Even upside down from his point of view Adler recognized his name and attached photo in the file.

"Can you join us? Good," Bainbridge said into the phone before he hung it up on the cradle.

"Captain," said the senior officer, but younger and less weathered man.

"Colonel."

In Army speak Lieutenant Colonels were always referred to as 'Colonels' unless it came to a pissing match with a full bird Colonel, the next rank up. Tony Adler knew Army speak and the courtesies that went with it.

"We're waiting for Major Haverly, who'll join us shortly," Bainbridge said. "So, eh, where you from?"

"Chicago, sir. South side."

"Wrigley Field!" said the Colonel uncertain exactly where the *South side* was.

"No, sir, that's the North side. Lakeview."

"Ah," replied the Colonel, not pursuing it further.

"You married?"

Adler shrugged and smiled. "Was," he said and earned another '*Ah*' from Bainbridge after that, but nothing more. It made for an awkward beginning.

Lieutenant Colonel Bainbridge was a good ten years younger than the Captain standing in front of him, although near nowhere in the same physical condition. His career behind a desk gave the senior officer a portly look, and for that the senior officer was somewhat envious of the former Special Forces Officer.

Also, he couldn't quite hide being both a little intimidated and perturbed by the career soldier in front of him dressed in starched and tailored jungle fatigues, complete with the Special Forces combat patch, a Combat Infantryman's Badge with two stars over the wreath showing that he had served in combat in three wars. In addition, there was the cloth paratrooper wings patch above the CIB, a Recondo V pocket patch, and French Parachutist wings over his top right pocket that only added to Bainbridge's social discomfort.

When he'd been told a week before that an older, former Special Forces Captain would be assigned to his command, the Light Bird Colonel wasn't quite sure what to do with him. Truth be told, Bainbridge wasn't even certain if he wanted him under his command.

More experienced soldiers, and especially combat soldiers, tended to second-guess decisions of those younger in command and with less experience, or at least with registered disdain, something Tony Adler suspected the Colonel was thinking.

But Adler's time in camouflage face paint, and on recon patrols in the jungle had taught him how to better mask his face and place. If his facial expression were a color, then it would've been bland.

"We're waiting for my Public Affairs Officer Liaison Officer," said Colonel Bainbridge, sipping on a cup of coffee as he leafed through the file on his desk.

Tony Adler wasn't offered a cup of coffee. A pecking order was being firmly established early on.

While waiting he took in the Colonel's *I LOVE ME* wall behind him. There were a number of framed 8 X 10 photos of a smiling Bainbridge with various celebrities; Bob Hope, Sammy Davis, Jr., Martha Raye, Joey Heatherton, and Anne Margaret, all obviously, from USO Tours or troop visits. Another showed the Colonel with a grip and grin with General Creighton Abrams. The Colonel was good at posing with people.

Next to that particular photo was a framed Army Commendation medal certificate. The stylized bold print was big enough for Adler to make out the Colonel's name, but not the smaller block print that revealed why he'd received it. Although, given everything else on the wall Adler made a reasonable guess. The LOVE ME wall gave it away.

"Impressive wall," Adler said, giving a nod to the framed photos. Martha Raye was a favorite of the Special Forces community. He'd never met her, but had heard good things about her from other Green Berets he respected.

Colonel Bainbridge smiled. "Yes, we've had the pleasure of playing host to some fantastic people."

Several awkward minutes passed before they were joined by a tall, sandy-haired Major who, at best, looked to be in his late twenties or early thirties. Adler stood when the Major came through the doorway. The Major gave Adler a cursory glance, instantly dismissed his importance, and turned to the Colonel. The visitor, after all, was only a Captain. Tony Adler was becoming increasingly well aware of his place in the office pecking order.

"You wanted to see me, sir?" the Major said to the Colonel.

"Bob, this is Tony Adler. He'll be joining us. Well, you, specifically."

The black plastic nametag on his crisp khaki- uniform read: *Haverly* in block print, white lettering. Adler pegged him at six-two or three and felt that the Major's Patrician's nose suited him for the habit he had of looking down at those with lesser status like he was doing now. In the time that followed he'd come to understand that the Major's height had nothing to do with his persona, but the first meeting set the belief in motion.

Haverly shook his hand with mild enthusiasm. Adler couldn't decide if the expression on the Major's face was guile or indifference and decided it was perhaps a little of both.

"Captain," said the Major.

"Major," said the Captain.

"Tony's assigned to our liaison office, which means he'll be working directly for you, Bob, in the VIP Liaison capacity."

"PAO, sir?" said Adler, surprised and more than a little uncomfortable by the position he was being placed into. PAO was the Public Affairs Office.

"Yes, Captain. You'll work directly under Major Haverly. He'll get you settled in and show you the ropes. We have quite a number of VIPs lined up for in-country visits, so we can always use another competent hand to insure that what we do here at MAC-V is on message, timely delivered, and that the guests are carefully shepherded..."

"Shepherded?"

"Well, yes, arrange schedules, coordinate transportation, and then properly and safely escorted to and from wherever they need to go while they're in-country. Put succinctly, your new job will be to put our best foot and face forward for our office and MAC-V. Bob here will show you how best to accomplish that. He's very good at what he does."

"Thank you, sir," said Haverly beaming while Tony Adler, no poker player, gave a hesitant half-smile that gave away what he was thinking.

"Something bothering you, Captain?" asked the Colonel, noticing the Captain's hesitation.

"Yes, sir."

"Spit it out."

"Don't take this the wrong way, Colonel, but I don't suppose there's anything else available for me? Some other real job I can do?"

Adler realized his mistake with the *real job* remark right after it came out of his mouth, as did Colonel Bainbridge and Major Haverly.

"Excuse me?" said the Colonel.

"To be frank, sir, I'm not exactly cut out for PR work, let alone shepherding VIPs. I tend to say 'fuck' a lot," Adler said with a small laugh, hoping they'd see the humor.

They didn't. His laugh died painfully in an awkward silence when neither the Colonel nor the Major had found it funny. Bainbridge, in fact, was bristling at the verbal affront, and his casual attitude took a decisive authoritarian turn.

"No, there isn't another job available to you, Captain," he said, slowly and deliberately and emphasizing each word of the comeback. What came next wasn't welcoming or pleasant.

"I understand how you former combat types feel about these type of assignments that you refer to as REMF work, but this too is another very real part the army that some of *you* don't seem to recognize for the importance it serves."

"No, sir, it's..."

"At ease!"

There was no *ease* involved with the sharp command and argue ending rebuke, nor was there any missing the way that Bainbridge used the word '*you*' like a slur.

"In case you don't know it, this war is being fought on two fronts, the kind in the jungle that you're used to and the kind in the streets back home. Those of us in both battles are trying to win them as best we can, including the hearts and minds of all of the VIPs that come over here. So your job is the job I need you to do, and that you will do, and do to the best of your ability. End of story."

No stranger to command structure, Tony Adler ate the scolding and remained quiet.

"I also understand that you requested this tour of duty," the Colonel said, breaking the awkward silence by thumping the file on his desk.

"Yes, sir."

"And what, you have twenty-seven, twenty-eight years in service?"

"Twenty-eight, sir."

"Which makes you..."

"Forty-seven, Colonel. I was seventeen when I enlisted in 1943."

"1943? My God, I was still in Junior High back then!"

The Lieutenant Colonel leaned back in his swivel chair, chuckling at the revelation. The Major Haverly joined in the snide revelry, both enjoying the humor at Adler's expense. He took them for generational frat boys while he was the reluctant pledge.

They were worlds and wars apart. Both the Colonel's and the Major's branch was Admin while the bulk of Adler's career had been Airborne Infantry. He was a combat soldier and his time as a Green Beret only better honed his fighting skills. He was thinking a throat punch might not help him reach his thirty-year goal, so he smiled at their sarcasm.

He figured they probably viewed him as a Neanderthal, necessary perhaps outside the proverbial cave, but not so much inside the air-conditioned offices and polished corridors of MAC-V headquarters. Here it was political finesse that dictated career advancements, and, Tony Adler was keenly aware that the Army he loved was indeed political and that he wasn't. He lacked the required guile. He'd always been a soldier first.

"I suppose with this tour you were hoping to make it thirty years before retirement?"

Adler nodded. "Yes, sir," he said, "or at least get in a few more years in. Well, that was my original plan before I lost a lung."

"A lung?"

"Yes, sir, took a few AK rounds to my chest on my last tour."

"My God, man!" exclaimed the Colonel. "You'd think they would've given you a medical retirement after that!"

Adler shrugged. "They offered," he said, "but I turned it down."

"Turned it down?" echoed a stunned Major.

"Yes, sir," Adler said to the Major. "Like I said, I'm hoping to make it to thirty years."

The Colonel said, "Word has it that you've been passed over for promotion, Adler?"

Adler pretended to be surprised by the news.

"I wasn't aware the list was out."

The promotion list wasn't out. It hadn't been officially posted, and he knew it, which meant the Colonel also had friends in the Army's Personnel Office.

"Soon to be announced," said Bainbridge. "And what, no prior talk of a RIF?"

Adler shook his head. "No, sir. No one has mentioned a RIF."

RIF stood for *Reduction in Force*, a weeding out of the Officers Corps where some Officers were allowed to remain in uniform after having been reduced back to an enlisted rank.

But, there hadn't been a mention of a RIF, which meant that he'd be out of the Army at the end of this final tour of duty.

"Well then, let me assure you that this job you're being assigned can be a fantastic way to prepare you for your civilian career once you retire. There are a lot of powerful and influential VIPs who come through this office, so you'll have an opportunity to make some new and important civilian contacts; something I suspect you'll need in the near future. Do a good job for us and all things are possible. Is that understood, Tony?"

"Yes, sir," Adler said, dutifully, noticing that the Colonel was addressing him as *Tony* again, the rebuke short-lived, and the proverbial stick put aside with the proffered carrot in its place.

"Good," replied the Colonel. "Morning briefings at 0900, but I want you in your office by no later than 08:30. Major Haverly will show you to your living quarters and the Liaison office. He'll brief you as to your duties and responsibilities. I'll expect to you to be up to speed soon. There's much to be done. Any questions?"

Of course, he had questions, but Tony Adler had been in the Army long enough to know that was a rhetorical question.

"No, sir," said the veteran soldier.

"Very well. You're dismissed. And oh, the uniform of the day here is Class-B khakis."

"Yes, sir."

"Good," said the Colonel pushing aside Adler's unofficial file and going back to his cup of coffee.

The meet and semi-greet was over.

Like it or not, Adler was now a full-fledged REMF, but not what he considered the good kind, either. He wasn't a doctor, nurse, medic, and a hospital tech working in the rear area evacuation hospitals, not an MP, Intel analyst, or a pay clerk, or any of the other important and critical support jobs, but in this position as a VIP greeter and glad hander he'd be more like a used car salesman eager to sell you that undercoating you weren't certain you needed, let alone ever knew about.

"Fantastic," he said to himself already hating the word and the hyperbole the Colonel had given it.

Judging from the cool to cold reception he'd just received, and from how he was treated over the following three and a half months working in the PAO- Liaison office, Tony Adler figured he'd be happy to leave the army with twenty-nine years and change.

He'd have a decent retirement check and some disability check from the Veterans Administration for the lost lung, that is, if he could manage to smile and keep making nice to Bainbridge and Haverly, which was proving more difficult to do on a daily basis. Over the years he'd worked with many decent and even stellar Officers, but Bainbridge and Haverly weren't anywhere near the top of his list.

Early on the Major had relegated him to what he thought were the *shit jobs*; picking up the Colonel's dry cleaning, making sure the sedans assigned to the office were washed and vacuumed, and overseeing having award or other special plaques made and ready for out-going senior officers and visiting VIPs.

He also took on the job as an occasional chauffer, or when Haverly preferred to drive, literally riding shotgun for the Colonel and Major on their drives into town to hobnob with a few prominent visiting journalists. The get-togethers were usually at the rooftop bar on the tenth floor of the Caravelle Hotel or at what some reporters referred to as the *Continental Shelf* at the Continental Palace Hotel in downtown Saigon.

"You think that weapon's are really necessary?" asked the Major when the Captain showed up with a shotgun slung over his shoulder and a .45 strapped to his hip on the first time driving his bosses.

"Better to have one and not need it, than..."

"Yeah, yeah, than need it and not have it," said the Major, dryly. "This isn't the Wild West, Captain. It's Saigon, and between the Military Police and the National Police, things are pretty much under control in the city. And I have it on good authority that various foreign military attaches employ their own expert security at the hotel. There's talk the Australians are looking to move their embassy personnel to the Caravelle, so we're good."

Adler nodded. "Yes, sir, I'm just watching out for you and the Colonel to make sure the bartender doesn't overcharge you for drinks."

At that Colonel Bainbridge chuckled. "Good one, Tony! Come to think of it, last time I believe the bartender charged me for three Martinis when I only had two. However, Bob's correct about the security and besides, we have an image we want to portray. Much of what we do is about perception. Can't have the press people thinking we're not winning this war if you're going around armed in the bar looking like Have Gun, Will Travel, so next time, just bring that Special Forces scowl of yours. That'll be enough."

"Yes, sir," said Adler, thinking next time out he'd leave the long gun, ditch the pistol belt, and holster, keep the .45 under the driver's seat of the sedan, and tuck a .38 pistol in an ankle carry.

Tony Adler soon came to realize that perhaps some things associated with the job were, in fact, about perception, especially when he came to realize that some of these '*Special correspondents*' seemed to be spending more time filing their reports from the hotel bar over Scotch and sodas, Gin and Tonics, or Whiskies-neat than they did from the field.

When one such noted TV news figure of that ilk they frequently met with informed them that he'd sent his cameraman out to get footage of the city in case anything like Tet ever kicked off again, Adler pointed out that TET this year would be in early February, but that if any attacks happened, then the bar would make for comfortable viewing.

Cool as the Caravelle's rooftop bar felt, the social temperature around the table chilled considerably. Later, on the ride back to Tan Son Nhut Major Haverly suggested to the Colonel that the Captain's services might be better suited keeping an eye on the Army sedan parked on the street.

"Given the occasional attacks in the city by the Viet Cong, then if anyone can keep the vehicle or us safe and provide our security, then our very own Green beret is the right man for the job," said the Major. "I suspect he's getting a little bored by these meetings, anyway. That right, Captain?"

The Major gave Adler his patented bullshit smile. Adler, who being a quick study, returned it with an accompanying nod.

"Might not be a bad idea to keep an eye on the car, and make sure the local Viet Cong won't leave us a nasty little surprise," he said into the rearview mirror.

"Good, then it's settled," said the Colonel.

The decision didn't bother Adler. He preferred the livelier Saigon streets, especially Dong Khoi where the Vietnamese went about their day-to-day less deceptively and with a frenzied appreciation for life or purpose.

As the decision wasn't his to make, Tony Adler accepted it, and in the days that followed he remained outside whichever hotel entrance he had driven them to, and in sight of the car while the Major and Colonel met with some of these so-called. 'War Correspondents.' Adler suspected that when a few reported that 'war is hell,' it was likely because the bar ran out of lemon slices or cocktail olives stabbed with toothpicks. There were good ones, sure, but not all, and certainly not the ones secretly looking to gain celebrity status rather than being recognized for their journalistic achievements.

So no, Tony Adler didn't mind not having to meet with some of those types, nor did he really mind the personal slight his bosses had given him. He'd stay with the car. Besides, the street was where he could find the best Pho, share a cigarette and small talk or banter with the locals, or have some meaningful talk with a handful of actual working reporters who'd recognized his experience from his combat ribbons and awards on his uniform, and his time in-country and wanted to bend his ear. It was these journalists that would grill him for the best ways to hop helicopter rides to the combat areas, where to go, who to talk to and interview, and why, once they got to those destinations.

The budding acquaintances that he had with a handful of working journalists from the AP, UPI, and Reuters, and the attention he drew as a result, however, introduced one more snub.

When the Major and the Colonel noticed that Adler was greeted with '*Hey, Tony! How are you doing?*' and '*Got a minute?*' by several of these reporters who immediately began picking his brain when as they pulled up to the Caravelle or the Continental Palace on one of the outings, his chauffeuring responsibilities into the city were no longer required.

Following one such outing and after one morning staff meeting in the Colonel's office the following day, Adler was informed of the latest change.

"We need you here back at the office to handle other important tasks while we're out," said Bainbridge. "Bob will fill you in."

Adler nodded and took the change in stride. He was the square peg in the round of schmooze.

His first *important* task the Major had assigned involved procuring a mimeograph machine for the Public Information Office. That was followed by a six-week stint working with an Information Specialist and photographer in putting together a MAC-V yearbook. In that time frame he spent hours going through dozens and dozens of photos, interviewing various department heads and personnel, finding, and then coordinating with a printer in Japan to work out the pricing, printing requirements, and a delivery timeline for the project, only to have the assignment scrubbed by the Major.

"Budgeting issue," Haverly said with an indifferent shrug before he moved the Captain on to another *important* task.

This time out Adler was tasked with designing and ordering five-dozen embroidered give-away ball caps from a local Vietnamese vendor in Saigon for the Liaison office. This one, apparently, was the Colonel's idea and delegated to Haverly, who in turn, immediately passed it along to Adler.

"Do a bang up job for us, Adler," said Haverly, when he was presented the task at a morning Liaison office briefing.

"Yes, sir, will do. Turn around time?"

Bainbridge looked to Haverly.

"What do you think, Bob?"

"Custom hats, local vendor? Three weeks, maybe. Four, tops."

"Good enough, get it done," said Bainbridge. "Stay on top of this, Bob."

"Roger that, sir," said the Major.

Back at their office Haverly told the Captain to get right on it.

"Rough out a working design and show me something that'll wow me by close of business today."

"Yes, sir," said Adler, finding it odd that there was a '*business day*' in Vietnam. His previous wars had never been nine to five jobs, but then he hadn't served in a rear area capacity prior to this tour of duty.

There were times when he felt that fighting a war was always easier than managing one, and his biggest fight would be adjusting to the bureaucratic difference.

He got to work on the cap design and near the end of the business day the design he came up with was a simple, yet stylistic MAC-V logo that wasn't anything outlandish or over-the-top butt ugly. It featured the letters MAC-V in gold superimposed over a khaki-colored outline of South Vietnam on a black ball cap.

Haverly, of course, immediately dismissed the design and ball cap color.

"No, no, no," he said, pushing the proposed artwork aside. "This won't do! I want it to pop. It needs to zing. Give me a flashy red and gold dragon around the MAC-V. Maybe some fire coming out of its throat and sharp claws on a khaki-colored cap."

"Talons."

"What?"

"The front feet on dragons are talons. The back feet are claws."

The now annoyed Major stared at the Captain for a reproving moment.

"I don't actually give a rat's ass what they're called, Captain," said the Major. "Just make it happen. Do it."

Adler made it happen, going with Haverly's design. Five-dozen ball caps were ordered, procured, and to his surprise, the caps were well received. A second order was soon placed for four-dozen more, with an additional dozen of black ball caps that Adler had procured, on his own, for proposed variation on a theme.

"I didn't okay this," Haverly said, when the caps were delivered.

"No sir, I thought maybe you'd like to have a few more options to make your design zing. The black makes the dragon stand out better. Don't you think?"

Haverly reluctantly agreed. The color scheme worked, so much so that the black caps soon became the most highly prized and sought after. While the Major wasn't initially impressed with the black caps, it didn't stop him from taking credit for the change.

"You two did some quality work here," said a beaming Bainbridge. "Got some nice compliments and feedback from a few Generals and Full birds, especially with the black caps."

"Glad you liked my design, Colonel," said Haverly. "Had to stay on Adler here until he finally got it right."

"Fantastic!"

Adler nodded and held his tongue. In the nearly five months he'd been assigned to the Liaison office, he was never *'Tony'* to the Major. He was always *Captain* or *Adler*, and Adler was convinced that the assigned tasks were kept mundane to humble him or keep him in his place, possibly both.

While the Colonel kept a professional distance, the Major seemed to enjoy lording over the Captain. Adler knew that there were those in life who relished making other people's lives miserable, simply because they could. Haverly was one of those people.

While the Major was doing his best to remind the Captain of his place at seemingly every opportunity, Tony Adler was doing his best not to slap the piss out of the arrogant and condescending prick, which he didn't necessarily rule out as a possibility. Yeah, there was always that.

Now, on the tarmac waiting for the VIP party to show, Tony Adler checked his watch, again. It was 10:37 and still no VIPs.

The wait continued.

Chapter 7

Petey, the door gunner with the fledgling mustache, returned with a box full of soft drinks and snacks just a few minutes before a highly polished Army sedan, and trailing open jeep, drove onto the far end of the flight line and slowly towards the awaiting helicopter.

The O-D green, four-door, air-conditioned, Ford Fairlane sedan looked sorely out of place while the Jeep had a more authentic appeal and the gravitas for a war zone, at least this side of a rear area military flight line. Gravitas, though, didn't translate to comfort. Major Haverly and, the Jeep's driver, along with a third soldier in the token back seat of the Jeep were considerably less comfortable. Army jeeps are basic utility vehicles. They weren't designed for luxury or fitted for creature comforts.

As both vehicles came to a braking halt, Haverly frowned at Adler who had arranged the transportation that had the open jeep following the official army sedan and eating road dust. The Army photographer assigned to the Public Information Office, however, seemed to be enjoying the assignment as he leapt out of the back of the jeep, and quickly went to work.

His camera caught Colonel Bainbridge as he stepped out of the front passenger side of the sedan dressed in ribbon-adorned Khakis before turning back to the Major who was outfitted in heavily starched, nicely ironed, and slightly dust covered jungle fatigues for the day-long visit to the semi-field. The sharp creases on the Major's uniform belied field duty and could've easily sliced paper.

The two pilots and crew members hurriedly finished their snacks and sodas, stuffing their mouths, or putting the leftovers aside to eat later, as they went to work. Donning their flight helmets, they settled into their start-up routine as the photographer turned his 35mm Nikon camera in their direction. The photographer's shot caught Mister Corsi smiling and the young crew chief scratching his balls.

The sedan's driver, an E-4 enlisted man borrowed for the occasion, opened the front side passenger door for the Senator while Major Haverly, with his Aviator sunglasses and smarmy disposition in place, was quickly up and out of the jeep and hurrying over to open the far side door for the rest of the VIP party. Of course he was, smiled Adler watching and knowing why. S. Orlov, the Senator's Chief of Staff, was a woman. The S stood for Stephanie.

Haverly was holding the car door for an attractive, early forty-something-year-old brunette, offering her a hand, which she politely declined. Stephanie Orlov was dressed in standard issue jungle fatigues, without a name patch or any other markings.

Unlike the Senator and his son who were sporting the new red and gold dragon MAC-V black ball caps, the dark haired, pale skinned Orlov was wearing a floppy hat- a boonie cap, to shield her neck and face from the burning sun. The sleeves of her jungle fatigues were buttoned at the wrist.

Before slinging a shoulder bag over her left shoulder, she pulled a clipboard and ballpoint pen out off the bag, clicked it alive, and made a notation on the day's itinerary. Adler suspected the itinerary also contained the names and ranks of important personages they were to meet that day on the outing, or perhaps, a list of items and things to ask for or check off. After a quick read she lowered the clipboard at her side and turned her attention to the helicopter, giving the Army Captain standing beside it a curt nod.

Adler returned it with a pursed lipped, chin up nod.

Orlov, was tall, lithe, and carried herself with unapologetic self-confidence, her bearing showed that she could hold her own in a man's world and frequently had to.

Ever the official face of Public Affairs Liaisons, Haverly was doing his best to charm her, and, Adler suspected, trying to hit on her as well.

Tony Adler smiled to himself when he saw that it appeared that Haverly's advances weren't getting him anywhere, or at least not to the *where* that the Major was hoping to go.

Watching the Major's latest swing and miss, and from the little interaction he had had with her the day before when the VIP party arrived at the airport, Adler realized something important that the Major had apparently missed, Stephanie Orlov was more than just a good looking woman.

From what he'd witnessed, albeit brief, and at a distance, she came off as a quiet, competent professional who understood the significance of her job as well as the purpose of the visit. Unlike Haverly, she wasn't a kiss-ass. That she hadn't fallen for the Major's play made Adler like and appreciate her all the more.

Following Orlov out of the vehicle was Zackery Russell, the Senator's fifteen-year-old son. The boy who preferred to be called, Zack, was a freshman cadet at a Military School in upstate New York, and Tony Adler suspected the Senator had brought his son along on the trip to show him the reality of the profession beyond the elite school's parade field.

While the Colonel, Orlov, and the Major were momentarily in a huddled conversation with the Senator, the Senator's son was looking more than a little uncomfortable amongst actual soldiers. The boy, who recognized, and seemed awed by Adler's impressive uniform patches, started to come to the position of attention only to have Adler wave him off. The boy gave him a nervous smile and awkward nod.

Adler nodded back and returned the smile.

"Major," Orlov said to Adler as the VIP party moved towards the helicopter. The Army photographer was moving around snapping away pictures on his Nikon insuring that he'd have some good photos to choose from.

"Actually, it's Captain," corrected Haverly, coming up behind her.

"Ah, yes. Thank you," she said to Haverly. To Tony Adler she said, "Sorry to have kept you waiting. I'm afraid we had a side trip into the city with the Ambassador. He wanted to show the Senator the Notre-Dame Basilica."

Adler nodded again, not surprised that they'd gone sightseeing.

"It's an amazing church. Fantastic!" Haverly said, sidling up to her. "The French completed it in 1880, and I don't know if you know this or not, it is one of the reasons why Saigon is referred to as the *Paris of the Orient.*"

"Actually, I didn't," said Orlov. "*Parlez vous francais*, Major?"

"Eh, no, "I'm afraid I don't speak French," said the now red-faced Haverly.

"*Et vous, mon Capitaine?*" she said turning to the Captain.

"*Un peu,*" replied Adler with a modest shrug. "*Mais j'ai peur que mon francais soit un peu rouille.*"

Orlov laughed and said, "Well, your little bit of French you claim doesn't sound all that rusty to me. Defense Language Institute?"

"No, Ma'am. I studied Russian at DLI. What little French I mangle I picked up working with the French Foreign Legion in Chad a while back. Good soldiers, and their English was a lot better than my French."

"Let's hope we fair better here than they did over here," said the Senator overhearing the exchange as he joined them.

"Yes, sir."

"In your frank and honest opinion, and judging from those tabs and patches you have on your uniform," said the Senator, pointing to Adler's uniform, "how do think we're doing over here?"

Adler gave a small smile and then offered a more diplomatic answer. "I think as long as we don't abandon the South Vietnamese and give them the aid that we promised, they'll hold their own. I'm sure the briefing you had at MAC-V headquarters, and what you received from the Ambassador, probably gave you a better overall assessment than what I'd have to offer. Are you ready for the ride to Cu Chi, Senator?"

"And then Tay Ninh, and then Phuoc Van, I believe," said Orlov, checking her clipboard.

"Phuoc Vinh," replied Adler, correcting her. "Camp Gorvad."

"Yes," she agreed, rechecking her clipboard. "The Senator is looking forward to a visit to the Cao Dai Temple later in Tay Ninh."

Adler shrugged. "We're running a little late. We may have to skip the trip to the Temple, if we're to stick to the time table on your itinerary."

At that quickly Haverly stepped in, shaking his head. "Uh-uh, no can do. The Senator would very much like to visit the Temple, so let's do our best to keep that in as well."

"It's a National Heritage site, I believe," said Senator Russell.

"So I've been told, sir, but visiting it will largely depend upon how well you keep to the schedule we have."

"Not to worry, Captain," Major Haverly said, smiling his best *'fuck you'* smile. "I'm sure we'll find the time to fit the temple in and be back here in time for their dinner with the Ambassador."

Haverly's practiced smile didn't last, and as the VIPs turned towards the helicopter he shot Adler an exasperated look.

"Your call, Major," Adler said. "But if that's the case then we need to get a move on. We've got a schedule to try to keep."

Without waiting for a response the Captain wheeled around, raised his right hand and index finger circling it high in the air, visually informing the pilot to 'crank it up'.

The helicopter's Aircraft Commander, Mister Corsi, and his co-pilot, Mister Kehr, began flipping switches and the giant tadpole-like Huey mechanically whirred and loudly whined to life.

With Colonel Bainbridge watching on from the chauffeured sedan, Major Haverly led the VIPs towards the open helicopter bay where Adler stood to the side ready to help each of them into the aircraft.

"My son just told me from that arrowhead patch on your right shoulder that you're a Green Beret? Is that right?" the Senator said, as Adler helped him aboard.

"My last tour of duty, Yes, sir."

"Your last tour of duty? So, Captain, how many does this make for you?"

"Three, sir."

"Well then, I'd say we're in good hands, Major," Senator Russell said over his shoulder to both Major Haverly and his son.

Haverly did the dutiful thing and gave the Senator a *'Yes, sir,'* and reverted to his well-rehearsed smile.

Climbing into a Huey was always awkward, and a helping hand, especially someone with a heavy rucksack, or in the Senator's case, bad knees and slight paunch, was always appreciated.

"Thank you, Captain," said Russell.

Adler smiled, nodded.

When he offered a hand to the Major, though, it was promptly ignored. But then, an interesting thing happened next. The Major hesitated at the open cargo bay, as though momentarily confused about the best way to climb aboard before deciding to go in butt first. Turning on all fours with his hands and knees, he rose to an almost exaggerated crouch and took the seat between the Chief of Staff and the Senator's son.

After those in the VIP party were on board, Tony Adler climbed in and took the far end seat on the left side of the open cargo bay doorway. Satisfied all was ready, the crew chief climbed in and radioed the pilot though his helmet headset all was good-to-go.

The Huey shook and shuddered as it lifted off, which was when Adler noticed that the Major was checking and re-checking his seat belt and looking apprehensive as he did.

Somehow the thought that the Major didn't like flying in the open door helicopter made Adler smile.

He watched as Haverly's eyes grew wide as the helicopter lifted up off its skids for a moment, and then thumped back down as the pilot readied to turn the Huey towards the flight line for take off.

"You want to change seats, Major?" he said over the growing mechanical noise. "Get a better look at the countryside?"

Haverly shook his head and said nothing. A line of sweat that had nothing to do with the rising heat of the day was forming over his brow, as the Major appeared to be taking in several quick short breaths to steady his breathing.

With clearance from the tower the Huey dipped its bulbous nose, raced over the flight line, and quickly gained altitude. It quickly flew up and over Tan Son Nhut and parts of Saigon, and as Adler peered at the excited passengers he noticed that the Major was staring straight ahead, not looking out of the opened doors of the aircraft and gawking at the passing scenery like the others were happily doing.

"Ah!" Adler said to himself as a grin slowly began to form on the corners of his mouth. "Better and better."

Chapter 8

The NVA soldiers that had stopped for their rest break across from the Lurp team had moved on, but they hadn't moved far.

The sound of an unseen someone chopping wood further down the trail told the Americans they were still nearby.

We got commo!" whispered Jonas Warren, handing the coiled-lined radio handset to Sergeant Carey.

The Team Leader nodded, and took the handset, but his eyes and rifle barrel never left the enemy soldiers across the trail.

"Valhalla, Valhalla...Longboat Niner-One, over."

"Valhalla," came the muffled response. "Go."

The latest line of NVA soldiers that had walked passed the team brought the total number to what both what he and Thomas had agreed, was a little over 200.

This was critical intell, so Carey passed it along clearly and distinctly, so there would be no confusion, or misunderstanding the message, nor the team's precarious position.

The nearest U.S. or South Vietnamese military outpost was Fire Support Base Rachel; six clicks away, and in the very direction the enemy soldiers were heading. There could be little doubt about the NVA's line of travel or its intent.

Judging from the number of enemy soldiers that had filed by, and given the heavy weapons and mortar tubes and plates that some of the bicycles were transporting, Rachel was going to get hit with a ground assault after the NVA gave it a miserable pounding barrage with the heavy mortars. The grunts on the remote Fire Support Base were in for a vicious fight.

The heads-up sighting by the Lurps would put the Fire Support Base on an early warning high alert and give the grunts the advantage. Gunships would be scrambled from distant bases, and other air support, and artillery would be shifted and coordinated to Rachel's advantage. It would still be a tough battle, but the odds would significantly move in Rachel's favor. Friendly lives would be saved.

When Sergeant Carey finished relaying the message there was a slight pause on the other end of the transmission.

"Say again," came the inevitable reply. The report had cause a stir.

Carey passed along the message one more time, and once done, the Lurp Team suspected what was coming next.

"Roger, I copy. Wait one," came the cryptic reply from the Ranger Company's TOC after receiving the report a second time.

As Carey waited and held on the line, he took some satisfaction that they had done their job. Now all they needed to do was quietly slip away to a pickup zone and wait for the extraction helicopter before the ground attack at dawn, and the running chaos in the immediate area that would follow.

That satisfaction, though, was dimmed and clouded knowing that the team's primary extraction site was back the way the NVA soldiers had come from. Given that the jungle trails twisted and wound their way through the great green and brown expanse, it was possible that even by staying off of the trails and moving through the brush they'd pop out on another branch of the trail system and bump into more enemy soldiers as they moved to an extraction site.

Considering the circumstances Valhalla's response to '*Wait one*' left the team leader waiting longer than he was comfortable with. Why were they taking their time? The clear and loud sound of the wood chopping told them that NVA weren't all that far away.

The short wait became an eternity, but when Valhalla came back on the line, Carey was relieved.

"Longboat Niner-One actual...Valhalla, over."

"Niner-One actual. Go."

Carey listened but Thomas noticed his posture and demeanor physically changed as he was listening to whatever was being said by Valhalla. His shoulders slumped, his jaw was clenched, and he looked as though he'd tasted something sour.

It was obvious to Thomas and Warren that he wasn't very much liking what he was hearing and the dour look on his face said as much.

"Roger, Valhalla-Six," he said. "I copy. Niner-One out." The Lurp Ranger Team Leader handed the handset back to the RTO as all faces turned to him to hear the message.

"Vahalla-Six says, 'hold in place, *Charlie Mike*," he said, finally.

Valhalla was the TOC. Valhalla-Six was the Company Commander.

"Hold in place, Charlie Mike? Seriously?" said the A-T-L wondering why there was no mention of an immediate extraction. *Charlie Mike* was Army phonetic talk for, *continue the mission.*

"That's affirmative. They want us to see if more NVA are moving on Rachel."

"Like what? Two hundred or more aren't convincing enough?"

Carey shrugged. "They're also sending out a scout helicopter and high bird to verify the sighting. Until then, we hold in place."

"They don't believe us."

Carey shrugged a second time.

"Valhalla-Six does," he said, "but the higher-highers want verification. Could be, too, that Six is trying to figure out how to get us out of here seeing how our primary extraction site is the where the NVA came from."

That was possible, reasoned Thomas with a frustrated sigh at the next obvious problem.

"And they're moving in the direction of the Fire Support Base," he said.

"Roger that," said a dispirited Carey. "Our secondary extraction site."

"Well, ain't that just dandy?" said Thomas, sarcastically expressing what he and perhaps the other team members were thinking about the call. Doc Moore, a quiet religious man, was probably the only member of the team who didn't swear, but nodded with Thomas.

Their primary and secondary extraction locations were now out of the question and no longer viable options. An alternate plan needed to be devised, something both men figured that Six was working on. Any wrinkles in a makeshift scheme needed to be ironed out.

Carey pulled out his map and Thomas moved closer as the Team Leader unfolded it. The two Lurps poured over the section of plastic-covered map searching for other possible extraction sites. The nearest open clearing on the map that could hold a helicopter was ten kilometers away to the east, but that would put them at, or just over, the border in Cambodia, a No-Go.

Because of the large numbers of NVA that had passed their hide site, the North Vietnamese Army and the Viet Cong were sure to have larger bases and congregated forces in hidden camps in the area. From the proverbial frying pan into the fire was never a good transition.

Carey figured if worse came to worst he could request a McGuire Rig extraction, maybe not at their present location, but certainly at another site within their operating area. It could work.

While only one or two others on his team had been pulled out of the jungle using this method all volunteers going through the Ranger Company's training were required to do it. It wasn't the best option, but it was a working one.

During their training they'd been told that the extraction method was the brainchild of Special Forces Sergeant Major, one Charles T. McGuire, who was said to have devised the simple and yet effective method of pulling out a soldier or a small team of soldiers out of a tight, dangerous spot in jungle combat when there wasn't a suitable pickup zone available.

McGuire's solution was to have a helicopter come to a hover over a team's location and have a two-man extraction team aboard the helicopter lower long ropes with D-ring carabineers tied on the ends to those waiting to be extracted below.

Those soldiers on the ground would tie a separate eight-foot long rope around their chests and under their armpits, and use a D-ring carabineer they carried to link into the D-rings and ropes from the helicopter. With a thumbs-up from those on the ground, those attached to the ropes would be lifted up and out of the jungle, dodging tree limbs, and perhaps spitting out twigs and leaves, and scaring the hell out of monkeys and birds in the process.

If all went well the soldiers would dangle beneath the helicopter like puppets on strings while being ferried to a safer location, well out of harm's way.

It was quick, efficient, and for Carey and the other members of Team Nine-One, it could be their exit strategy.

But it was the, '*if all went well*' add on that troubled him. Murphy's Law said that what can go wrong, will go wrong. The military's version of Murphy's Law in combat included heavy enemy machinegun fire, a well-aimed RPG, and a shitload of accompanying trouble.

Given that there were so many enemy soldiers in the immediate area, a hovering helicopter would make for an easy target to shoot out of the sky, with the bonus that the five Lurps dangling beneath the bird would be crushed to death or skewered on the trees as it fell.

It didn't help that the Monsoon storm was taking a nasty turn. If the extraction didn't happen soon, then it was likely that any and all available aircraft would be grounded until the latest round of the seasonal storm had passed.

A sudden finger snap from Warren instantly ruled out a McGuire Rig Extraction; the RTO pointed back out to the trail where another long line of North Vietnamese soldiers began filing by on the trail.

In what was becoming an afternoon pattern of watching a parade, the five Lurps lowered themselves back down, hugged the ground, and peered through the leaves and branches as a new enemy count began.

Once again Thomas had taken up the Claymore's clacker, and once again, kept his eyes glued on his team leader waiting for the nod he hoped wouldn't come.

Heavy rain began pelting the treetop canopy overhead as angry gusts of wind sent trees and branches creaking and swaying. The Monsoon was growing more violent as though to match the war below.

Both heaven and earth were in turmoil.

Chapter 9

The scheduled ninety-minute visit to Cu Chi, with the briefings from various Generals and selected field Commanders, had tweaked the VIP itinerary one more time. The visit had taken slightly over two and a half hours.

With the customary grip and grin photos, the longer than scheduled briefings, basecamp lunch, and of course, the chats with some of the soldiers and photo ops, the VIP party, according to Tony Adler's watch, was an hour and seventeen minutes over the allotted time.

This latest wait had him checking his watch more than a few times, his sighs giving way to a cynical smirk.

Given the flight time to Tay Ninh, more briefings, photo ops, and glad-handing, and the side trip to the Cao Dai Temple, there was no way they could stop in Phuoc Vinh, let alone keep to their time-table to be back to Saigon in time for the Senator's dinner with the Ambassador. That is, unless they hurried, which didn't seem to be in the VIP party's game plan.

It didn't help that a light rain was beginning to fall when they touched down on the flight line of the 25th Infantry Division's Tay Ninh basecamp. The helicopter's rotor wash, aided by growing gusts of wind, pushing well ahead of the heart of the Monsoon's storm, sent a cloud of dust swirling over the tarmac in an orange frenzy.

It was near the end of the wet season, so the latest storm, along with the accompanying high winds and heavy rain that flooded the lowlands, was expected. What wasn't predicted was the Tropical Disturbance piggybacking on the tail of the Monsoon.

Some Meteorologists believed it would probably peter out before making landfall, or just add more wind and rain to the predicted downpour. The prediction was wrong. The Tropical Disturbance hadn't petered out as it came out of the South China Sea. It morphed into a weakened tropical depression, well short of a typhoon, but still with wind gusts pushing over 80 miles per hour.

Weather advisories would be issued for the coast and later for the inland regions, and military aircraft would be grounded until the larger storm had passed. But that was later. Mister Corsi had received the advisory from the Tay Ninh Tower passed the news along to the Captain.

For the time being the storm was a dark and distant backdrop to the Nui Ba Den- the Black Virgin Mountain that overlooked the province and Tay Ninh basecamp. The brooding storm was still well off in the distance and slowly making its way southeast. There was time to stay ahead of it, but not much.

"Storm moving in," Tony Adler said to the Major, hoping to hurry the visit along.

"We're good," Major Haverly said, casually eying the sky and dismissing the Captain's concern. "Just be ready to go once we return."

The Major didn't wait for a reply as he turned towards a party of senior officers and a Military Police escort that was on hand to greet the VIPs.

The helicopter's aircraft commander called out to Adler.

"I'll refuel here while we wait, Captain."

Adler nodded to the Warrant Officer and said, "And I'll see if I can find us a chow hall."

When the helicopter returned a short time later, Adler had a box of burgers and soft drinks waiting for the crew.

"It's the best I could do," he said, by way of an apology.

"No problem," said Mister Corsi, scarfing down a cheeseburger. When Adler hadn't grabbed anything to eat the pilot asked, "What about you?"

"I'm good! I have a C-ration can of Ham and Lima Beans," Adler said, tapping his right cargo pocket.

"Ham and motherfuckers! You are seriously hard core, sir!"

"Old habits," said the Captain, "You think we can beat the storm?"

He was staring off towards the approaching troubling sky as he spoke.

Corsi's eyes followed the Captain's line of sight and the Warrant Officer shrugged.

"If we can get them back in an hour or so and get airborne, we can. If not, then we'll have to sit the storm out in Phuoc Vinh, Captain."

"I believe they're planning on returning to Saigon."

"Then, we may have to scrap the visit to Phuoc Vinh, sir. No way we can do both."

Adler nodded. "Your call," he said. "Let's hope our VIPs aren't dawdling over postcards. Where you from, Mister Corsi?"

"Staten Island, New York, Captain," replied the Warrant Officer. "Home of the best Italian pizza in all of the state, and quite possibly, the entire country. You, Captain?"

"Chicago."

"Chicago?"

"Uh-huh, and later we'll have a talk about who has the best fucking pizza."

"Deep dish pizza isn't pizza, Captain. It's excess cargo weight."

Mister Corsi liked the Captain, and he liked being a taxi for the VIPs. It wasn't a bad gig. The Major, though, seemed to have a stick up his ass, but all in all, this task sure as hell beat combat assaults.

The briefings and sightseeing trip came in under an hour, something that pleased both the Aircraft Commander and his co-pilot. Adler was happy as well.

They were still ahead of the combined storm, and if they blew off Phuoc Vinh, then they might have the VIPs back in time for a delayed dinner. But that plan, too, was put on hold because just as they were climbing back into the helicopter, Major Haverly informed him that there would be an unscheduled stop before they visited Camp Gorvad in Phuoc Vinh.

"A stop? Where?"

"We'll be delivering some mail and sundry packs to the soldiers stationed atop the mountain," he said, pointing to the Nui Ba Den. "So how about you give the PIO photographer over there a hand so we can get started?"

Adler turned and saw the young soldier struggling with his camera gear bag and the large orange bags and packages from one of the escort vehicles. Adler didn't mind helping but he was less than thrilled with this latest change to the itinerary.

"Delivering mail?" he said.

"That's right," Haverly said. "The Senator didn't believe it would be a problem. In fact, he kind of liked the idea when I suggested it. We're heading back in that direction anyway, aren't we?"

"Sort of."

"Then *sort of* shouldn't be too much of a problem. Besides, the Senator is all up for serving the troops."

"Serving the troops," echoed Adler in a less than enthusiastic mutter and the Major nodded.

"That's right. It'll make for some good photos and great PR, and in case you seem to have forgotten what our role is in PAO-Liaison, this is part of the job. It's too good of a photo-op to pass up. The mountain top, with the jungle below in the background, is a good opportunity for us."

It would be, thought Adler, in better weather, but given that some heavy rain would soon be falling, as a prelude to a much nastier storm, it might be a dumbass call as well. His face said as much.

"You don't look too pleased about it, Captain," said Haverly.

"The weather people said we're in for some heavy wind and rain, Major. We could be a bumpy flight from Phuoc Vinh, which is also why he thinks we might have to wait out at Camp Gorvad until the bad weather passes."

"Wait it out? How long?"

"Don't know, but I'll let him know about the mail stop."

Haverly stopped him.

"You grab the mailbags. I'll inform the pilot that we're cancelling Phuoc Vinh and going directly back to Saigon."

Adler guessed that the mention of a bumpy ride might have had something do with the Major's compromise. If he scrapped the trip to the mountaintop, then that might make for a better return flight, but that wasn't in the cards. The Major was gambling they could beat the storm.

By the time Adler returned with the two large mailbags from the jeep with the large, clear plastic bags that was bulging with sundry packs filled with candy, pens, paperback books, and other small items for the GIs, he found Mister Corsi wearing a resigned smirk.

"The Major thinks we should try for Saigon rather than touching down in Phuoc Vinh."

"Yeah, that's what he said. What do you think?"

The New Yorker grinned. "I think ours is not to reason why, ours is but to do and fly. If you can get everybody inside and ready we'll take off and do our best to stay ahead of that bad boy."

Corsi pointed off in the direction of the churning, black clouds.

Adler nodded and started herding the VIP party towards the helicopter.

It was then, too, that the Captain was informed of yet one more change. Because extra space was needed for the bulky bags of mail and sundry packages, the Major decided that the Army Photographer who'd been travelling with them throughout the day, would remain behind at the Tay Ninh basecamp. He'd catch another flight back to Saigon in the morning.

However, to make sure the mail delivery to the scenic mountaintop was captured on film, Captain Haverly had the photographer hand over his camera.

The Army photographer, a Spec-4 with less than a year in service, didn't look too thrilled with the decision, but then as a lowly enlisted man he really didn't have much choice in the matter, either. In the Army, when someone with a higher rank asking nicely for something it generally was followed by a lawful order or direct command, if it was initially refused.

"Not to worry you'll get your photo credit," Haverly said, offering a small concession, and then held out his hands for the camera. "Well, unless I get some better shots."

The Major laughed at his own small joke as he sent the frowning photographer back to the waiting jeep.

What Adler knew, that perhaps Haverly wasn't aware of, was that in 1968 the small base was overrun and that 21 GIs were killed in the attack with several others taken prisoner.

The enemy owned the mountain, as it's many caves and hidden tunnels attested to. Any time spent on the mountaintop needed to be brief.

When he tried to let the Major know this Haverly shut him down.

"Old news," he said. "Besides, we're not staying. We're only briefly touching down."

They would deliver the mail and sundry packages to the mountaintop.

Mister Corsi and the crew chief rightly decided it was time to close the doors to the cargo bay and let the Captain know they'd take off once it was done.

"Warm and comfy works," said Adler and then informed the Senator and others who had no objections. Adler thought that Major Haverly even looked somewhat relieved.

The flight to the Army's small outpost atop the Nui Ba Den was short, as was the mail delivery to those manning the radio relay station camp. The small base was in the shape a giant misshapen boot print that had been hurriedly pressed into the side of the mountain. Its communication bunkers were topped with a series of large antennas that allowed its radio operators to reach across the province and beyond. The radio station was protected by a series of sandbagged bunkers and fortifications ringed with razor sharp concertina and stringed barbed wire, tangle foot, trip flairs, Claymore mines, and a contingent of Signal Battalion and grunts to man and guard it all.

As the helicopter touched down on the outpost's helipad, the crew chief opened the right side cargo bay door, and the off-loading began. Haverly was snapping pictures of a smiling Senator Russell handing the bulky mailbags and sundry packages over to a bewildered looking Second Lieutenant and Private First Class. Quite likely the officer and enlisted man had received word that some VIPs were on their way only moments before before, and that they'd be needed to be at the heli-pad to greet them to find out what the visit was all about.

Just up from the helicopter pad two morose looking GIs were conducting a shit burning detail. The two were standing over four 55-gallon metal barrels that had been cut in half and used as catch basins in an adjacent outhouse.

Every so often the two soldiers churned the JP-4 jet fuel that had been mixed in with the urine and excrement to keep it burning as thermal columns of noxious black smoke swirled and danced in the wind. The soldiers who'd been stirring the rancid mix in the swirling flames stopped what they were doing and stared at the helicopter and the unloading process.

The 'special' delivery mail run made for a brief and awkward event, but Haverly got his PR shots. In addition, the Major and the rest of the party also got another aspect of the daily life on the mountain when the wind that blew over the crest of the mountaintop shifted and sent the stench and smoke from the burning shit barrels towards and into the helicopter's opened door.

The once smiling Major Haverly, who was fully engulfed in the swirling choking smoke, flared his nostrils in disgust, glared at the GIs at the burn barrels, and hurried back to the awaiting helicopter.

Tony Adler smiled as the Major and the VIPs saw another aspect of the *whole Vietnam experience.*

The helicopter hadn't shut down on the mountaintop heli-pad and the VIP bird was soon up and away.

Because of the delay, the edge of the storm overtook them, and the punishing wind gusts, and wind whipped rain gave a precursor to what more was to come.

The flight to the mountaintop and the brief stopover had taken less than thirty-minutes, but it was a critical thirty-minutes for the flight south. The storm had outraced them and they were soon caught in its angry, shaking grip.

The UH-1H helicopter was being bounced around and pounded in by the storm. Crosswinds and violent gusts, at times too, had the flight crabbing its way forward. Even with the closed cargo bay doors it still made for made for a chilly and dismal go.

The battering the aircraft was taking in the storm proved to be the deciding factor for the aircraft commander's next decision.

"We're heading to Phuoc Vinh!" yelled Mister Kehr, relaying the message Mister Corsi had given him. Adler nodded to co-pilot and then turned and passed the news along to the Major and the others.

Outwardly, Major Haverly pretended he didn't like it, but given that he and everyone else inside the aircraft was being badly tossed and jostled, touching down at Phuoc Vinh was a better option than trying to continue on.

Neither the Senator nor his Chief of Staff objected to this latest change, the storm was playing havoc with their stomachs as well.

Oddly enough, the one that wasn't all that worried about it was Tony Adler, who seemed to be taking it all in stride.

Over Normandy, the German anti-aircraft fire pummeled the Douglas C-47 and had torn jagged holes through the airplane's fuselage. The incoming shrapnel injured several of the paratroopers waiting for the green light as they readied to jump. Nearly everyone in the stick made it out of the aircraft and although he was parachuting into enemy occupied France under fire, he was happy to be out of the aircraft that was proving to be a magnet for the enemy fire.

Twenty-six years later, it was another bumpy military ride. At least we're not getting shot at, he thought as glanced around and saw the concerned and worried looks on the faces of the VIPs. Haverly wasn't looking all that much better.

"Good," he thought. Maybe now these Very Important People and the often pain in the ass Major might come to understand that the war isn't an amusement park for their entertainment, let alone something just for public relations photo ops, or political posturing.

"Yeah," he said to himself, shaking his head, and staring out the small window in the cargo bay door, "and maybe if a frog had wings it wouldn't scrape its ass every time it jumped."

Chapter 10

They counted forty more NVA soldiers heading in the same direction the others had taken, only to the Lurp's dismay, the line did the unexpected and halted in place.

An enemy officer, a short bulldog of a man, barked a command in Vietnamese, and the NVA soldiers standing in the heavy rain, broke ranks and dispersed to find shelter.

They took the easy way as soldiers in any and every army often did in combat, and began utilizing the more open and accommodating space on the far side of the trail for ease of comfort and better accessibility. At a glance, and perhaps even a better look, the snare of difficult underbrush, web of vines, and dense bamboo thicket across from the open space held no shelter or practical aspect of comfort. They would avoid it.

Because the ugly storm with its increasing winds had arrived along with them, the NVA soldiers quickly got busy putting up plastic tarps and erecting temporary shelters to shield themselves from the pelting rain.

That they weren't starting fires, weren't making camp, and were huddling together told Carey and the others it was looking to be another temporary rest halt for these latest arrivals.

The closer the main element of NVA moved on Fire Support Base Rachel, the more their tacticians would slow the advance of the others behind them.

To arrive undetected they would need to move slower on their approach. The NVA Commander would call up his officers and senior NCOs to layout the plan of attack and order the positioning of the mortar teams and assault teams. While they had covered it prior to their departure from their base in Cambodia, and each aspect had been laid out on a ground map, the physical terrain dictated modifications. The trail system would only take them so far.

They would need to be set up and ready for the pre-dawn attack and that meant working through the dense jungle.

The difficult terrain and the weather weren't helping the NVA, but it was a lifesaver to the Lurp team.

Carey had purposely picked the team's hide site because of its inaccessibility, believing that even if the Viet Cong and NVA stopped to rest, then they wouldn't give the difficult patch across from the open space any serious consideration.

Any why not? There was room to stretch out and get comfortable in the better open area, with canopied treetops overhead to protect them from any aerial surveillance, and shield them from the growing wind and rain.

The storm that seemed to be gaining in strength over the province was pushing the natural umbrella to its limits. The high winds and violent gusts that had the trees shuddering and decaying limbs and branches breaking in the heavy rainfall were working in the Americans favor, at least for the moment. But moments don't last.

There was no guarantee that the Lurps wouldn't be found out where they were, and that everything could all change in a terrible and furious instant. While the thick underbrush, interlocking leaves and vines, and bamboo provided adequate concealment, it didn't do shit for cover, if bullets and Rocket Propelled Grenades started flying. With that in mind, Carey decided to better use the distraction of the storm to Nine-One's advantage.

He'd move the team from its precarious position and have his people slip deeper back into the jungle.

"Weapons and LBE only," he whispered to his people as Warren, the RTO, began rigging the radio with a carrying harness.

With Thomas still watching and waiting for the signal to blow the Claymores, Carey instead made the motion of a fisherman reeling in his catch while pointing towards the three anti-personnel mines and wiggled his right index and middle fingers to mimic walking back away from the NVA. He pointed to the direction he wanted the A-T-L to go and held a flat hand out and down to show that he wanted him to low crawl.

With a chin up nod, Thomas unplugged the wire from the charging device to the three linked Claymores and began pulling on the wire.

As low to the ground as the mines had been set up on their swivel prongs, the first of the three Claymores was carefully pulled free. The rain that dampened the soil and had loosened the prongs had also made the reeling in maneuver an easier go. Thomas kept pulling and dragging the Claymores back and so far hadn't drawn any undue notice or attention from anyone on the other side of the trail.

All the while he was reeling in the anti-personnel mines, Warren, who had the radio in the carrying harness on his upper back, had his weapon aimed in on the enemy soldiers they could see across the trail. Carey, Doc Moore, and Bowman were widening their field of fire 180-degrees for the other enemy soldiers they could hear outside of their range of vision.

Even without the Claymores they could easily take out a dozen or more of the enemy soldiers in what even young Bowman knew would be an Alamo outcome. Once they opened fire they'd soon be out gunned and over run by the sheer enemy numbers coming from who knows how many directions. Trails twisted and turned in the jungle and that pucker factor kept them cautious.

In theory, and best case scenario outcomes, Lurp teams would surveil the enemy without being compromised, ambush a small patrol, or perhaps captured one or two enemy soldiers to bring back for interrogation. If compromised then they would Escape and Evade a larger force, and if they compromised and couldn't E&E then they'd fight it out until a Quick Reaction Forces came in to assist them.

In theory.

In reality, though, if they compromised by a larger force of Viet Cong or NVA, and if they couldn't make a run for it, then it was also likely the enemy would over run the small teams, and kill every one of the Lurps to the last man well before any Quick Reaction Force help could arrive. There was only so much time and ammunition. For now pulling the team back was the better tactical option.

The second Claymore was soon following the first and both were were steadily coming back from where they'd been positioned. The third Claymore, however, got hung up on a thumb-size branch sticking out of a small brush and held up the string of mines.

Thomas tried tugging on the line to free it only the branch wouldn't give. The last mine was stuck, which meant that all three were stuck.

"Come on! Come on! Come on!" he whispered to himself, and then remembered something that his father had taught him as a kid when he first took him fishing and his hook got snagged in the reeds.

Shifting to his left a foot or so, he held his left arm out low and wide, and tugged again. The fishing maneuver did the trick and this time the last mine scooted around the small branch as all three of the plastic-encased, hard cover book-sized mines eased back towards the much-relieved Assistant Team Leader.

When the first Claymore was within reach, Thomas grabbed onto it, made it safe by removing the blasting cap, and handed it over to Carey.

He did the same with the second Claymore and was just about to pull in the last one in line just a yard or so in front of him when an enemy soldier rose from where he'd been sitting beneath the base of a large tree across the trail and started towards the Lurps' hide site.

Thomas froze.

The NVA soldier was of moderate height, thin, and barely out of his teens. With an SKS rifle slung on his left shoulder, he took three steps into the thick brush this side of the trail and stopped. Staring down at his waist, he unbuttoned his trousers, took out his pecker, and began taking a piss.

Finishing up with a few shakes, the NVA soldier tucked himself back in, and briefly fumbled with re-buttoning his trousers. He was just about to turn and go back to the others when something odd caught his eye just a few yards in front of him.

He didn't seem too worried or all that concerned about whatever it was either, since his rifle was still slung over his shoulder, and he was wearing a curious half smile as he took a few more steps towards the small, dark lump on the ground.

As he was bending over to get a better look he abruptly stopped when he recognized the American anti-personnel mine for what it was, and the thin black wire that was attached to it.

His curious smile disappeared as his surprised eyes followed the line back to the camouflaged face of an American soldier staring back at him from a few feet away. Both of the American's hands were filled with bunched up line.

The NVA soldier started to turn and shout out an alert to his comrades as he grabbed at his shouldered rifle, only before he could do either his ankles were jerked out from behind him by a second American he hadn't seen. His shout and cry were muffled as his face hit the jungle floor with a hard and wet thump.

Like the high school wrestler he once had been, Jonas Warren, leapt on the man's back pinning him to the ground while Thomas scurried in and wrapped his hands over the man's mouth to stifle the scream.

The one-sided wrestling match went unnoticed by the rest of the NVA still hunkered down in the rain just across the trail.

Fighting to free himself the small, but wiry enemy soldier twisted, and turned, and with what little space he managed to find, he head-butted the American who was holding him down.

He felt the bigger man's nose crack under the impact, temporarily causing the American to give up some of his grip. That gave the NVA soldier just enough freed up space to pull out the heavy knife he had sheathed on his belt. When he tried reaching back and stabbing the bigger man, the American pinned his knife hand down on the ground in the mud. However, the natural arena was too wet and slippery to keep it there, and the NVA soldier pulled the knife hand free, and once again, swung it over the big man's back with everything he had. He was desperately plunging and hacking at the American with quick and violent strikes.

He got in what he knew were three hard hits and felt the knife blade stick and hold, only the razor sharp blade didn't seem to have any noticeable effect.

Wrenching it free he struck again and again. The repeated blows from the heavy knife, though, had only cut into the team's radio high on Warren's back. They hadn't struck the man.

When he tried hacking at the big American again, Warren smacked the hand back down and pinned it to the ground while his other forearm slammed against the back of the enemy soldier's neck.

There was a decided *oomph,* but the North Vietnamese soldier still managed to pull the knife under his chest ready to slice and stab at the hands of the man who was covering his mouth when it wasn't being pressed into the wet ground.

As he felt the burly American's hands reaching for his face he inched up the knife ready to strike. With two hands gripping the knife handle, and with one final effort, he used his elbows to push himself up only to have Warren shove all of weight on the man's back forcing him back down.

The soldier collapsed onto the blade of the knife and the blade dug deep into his neck. A second shove hard against the center of the man's back drove the blade in deeper. The knife that the NVA soldier had carefully honed severed his carotid artery. Any fight left in him was dying in gurgling spurts. The enemy soldier's body went limp as his life slipped away in spasms on the wet and muddy jungle floor.

When he was sure the man was no longer a threat, Warren rolled off of the dead soldier's back and stared at the treetops trying to steady his breath from the fight. His nose was broken and seated at an unusual angle. The rain diluted the blood that was pouring from his nose, down his mouth and chin, and spilled down the front of his jungle fatigues as he rolled back over and retrieved his M-16. The blood on his uniform was a mix of his own and that of the dead man's. It should've been a sickening site, but war seldom stopped because of ugliness or brutality. They demanded both.

Across the trail another NVA soldier with a green plastic cape rose with a machete in hand and began hacking at low hanging branches that he handed to several other soldiers who were building a lean-to. After taking down several branches, he eyed the bamboo thicket towards the Rangers' hide-site.

He was just about to start across the trail to the bamboo thicket when one of the NVA soldiers called him back. They had enough branches to frame the lean-to shelter, but what they needed was the green plastic cape he had over his shoulders.

After the soldier with the machete had turned back around Thomas went back to reeling in the third mine. With the last of the Claymores secured, he began covering the dead man's body with leaves and grass only to have Carey motion both he and Warren back.

Warren looked a mess, but shrugged it off.

"I'm good, good," he whispered to his Team Leader, as though a crooked, bleeding nose, and swollen eyes meant all was well or actually good. Considering the alternative, perhaps it was.

Carey nodded and as Warren reached for his rucksack, Carey shook his head. The packs weighed seventy to one hundred pounds. They were heavy, unwieldy, and shouldering them was always a hunched back and burdening load. Dragging them was out of the question, too, since either meant drawing the notice of the nearby enemy soldiers.

They would make do with only what they carried on the LBE harnesses; ammo pouches, grenades, canteen, first aid pouch, bayonets, and rolled eight-foot sections of nylon rope and D-rings for their McGuire Rigs.

"Take out any extra ammo, grenades, and the Claymores you have in your packs. Leave everything else," he whispered to Thomas and then looked to the others making sure, they too, had gotten the message.

"Extra battery," he said to his RTO.

Warren nodded.

He retrieved A Claymore from the top of his rucksack and tossed the sling in its cloth carrying case over his shoulder and back, figuring it might prove useful in a running escape, if they were compromised.

They needed to quickly put some distance between themselves and the NVA soldiers across from them before anyone else came their way to relieve himself or look for building material.

To Thomas he said, "Leave a little surprise for them, Darrell."

The A-T-L nodded and went to work setting up a booby trap. He worked the pins from two *Willie Pete*-White Phosphorus grenades and tied the pins to a short strap beneath the rucksack.

Anyone who shook, bumped, or lifted the rucksack would set off the White Phosphorus grenades in a fiery devastating blast.

Carey covered Thomas as he was setting the booby trap, impressed, and maybe a little frightened by the near joy Thomas seemed to be having as he went about his work.

With the booby trap in place, Thomas picked up his rifle, and nodded to the T-L.

"Done," he said in a low voice.

"Good," Carey whispered to Thomas pointing the way he wanted them to go.

"Go," he said.

"How far?"

"Until it's safe enough to stand without drawing attention and then move 40 to 50 yards east and wait for me. Go!"

Thomas nodded and began his low crawl as Carey motioned for the others to follow. As the Team leader, Carey would remain behind to cover their escape. He'd be the last to leave.

It only took a few minutes for the four Lurps to low crawl through the vegetation and to disappear in the jungle, but for the Team Leader who was left behind, the minutes ticked away like hours.

What does it take to go 40 to 50 yards through thick jungle, ten, fifteen minutes? Carey checked his watch. He'd give them thirteen minutes more before he followed.

It was a tense wait. He was on his own, and there were a dozen or more of hardcore NVA soldiers just across the trail that hadn't yet realized one of their own was missing. What happened if they got up to move on before he made his getaway? Someone was bound to notice that their buddy was gone and then they'd start looking.

The tension amped up when an enemy soldier rose up and out of his plastic tarp, and started to look around for something.

Carey hugged the mud and aimed his CAR-15 in on the enemy soldier. When the soldier went back under the tarp, Carey breathed easier and checked his watch, again.

Seven minutes to go. The NVA were still hunkered down by the rain and the Lurp Team Leader quietly prayed for the heavier rain to continue.

"Keep those bastards down," he said to the Heavens. "Keep the Monsoon right where it is!"

Four minutes more by his watch.

Three.

Two.

Taking one last look at the dead man and a peek at the other NVA soldiers across the trail, and then only when he was sure his people were a good distance away, Carey turned, lowered himself down as low as he could get, and crawled through the small tunnel-like opening the others had left moving through the thick underbrush. It was a slow and steady low crawl. Now wasn't the time to fuck up by hurrying.

Ten yards on, when there was enough of the jungle between him and the NVA to remain unseen, he rose to a crouch, and moved through the jungle at a much better speed.

He'd tried covering the obvious route the others had made as he went, but the disturbed ground with the telltale sign of scuff marks in the soil from boots, turned leaves, broken twigs, small branches, and pulled vines showed their direction of movement. The best he could do was to cover some of it up and not leave any more unnecessary sign. Still, it was no easy go. The jungle was rife with natural barriers; tangling vines, bamboo thickets, fallen trees, and tightly woven dense brush with thorns that fought to slow any interlopers.

He had gone what he estimated to be fifty yards on, and hadn't yet found the others. It was ten yards further on when he heard a barely audible snapping noise that swung him around to his left. Turning his head he found himself staring into a rifle barrel that was pointed at his midsection. It was Bowman, the new guy, down behind the cover of a moss covered fallen tree.

Bowman lowered the rifle and waved him in to the team's makeshift perimeter where they had set up and waited for him to show.

In a cautious and tactical move, Thomas had them step off of their line of travel, move two yards into the brush, and then buttonhook five yards back, parallel to the line of travel they'd taken and the small path they created as they moved. The four Lurps were kneeling in a modified wagon wheel perimeter, ready to ambush any enemy soldiers who might've followed.

They'd made good their retreat and now maybe, they could call in their Escape & Evasion plan to the TOC, and tactically or not-so-tactically run like hell to get to a better location where they could be extracted.

There was, of course, another problem.

"We lost radio contact," Thomas said in a frustrated low voice to Carey gesturing the radio on his back.

"Battery?" Carey said, turning his RTO.

Specialist Warren shook his head as he held up the handset. The lower half was badly damaged. "It broke in the fight," he said. "We can receive, but we can't send."

Carey nodded and frowned, angry at that bit of news, but even angrier with himself for another very good reason. In the commotion and hurry to fall back, he left the URC-10 backup radio behind on or around his rucksack, and was now cursing himself for the costly mistake. Back in Romeo Company he'd get his ass chewed out about that during the team's debriefing, but right now that was the least of his problems.

"Backup radio?" asked Thomas.

Carey shook his head. "Back at our hide site," he said while the Texan gave him a *what the fuck* look.

No back up radio meant no commo and there would be no going back to retrieve.

"Okay then, so what's the plan?" asked Thomas putting words to what the rest of the team members were thinking.

"Time and distance," he said, bringing out his mission map and compass, scrambling to work out a better option. "They may not find the body right away in this rain, but sooner or later, they will."

"We moving to Rachel, then?" asked Doc Moore over his shoulder since it seemed to be the direction they would take.

"No, we can't move to Rachel," Carey said, still studying his map. A worried crease appeared between his eyebrows and stayed. He would have age lines long before they were supposed to appear, and a cynicism born from flipping the safety switch on his assault rifle from SAFE to FIRE.

"The NVA are heading towards the Fire Support Base. My guess is that they'll attack it at first light, which means by midnight they'll have their people in place all around the base."

"And if they find the body?" said Moore.

"No *if* about it, Doc," replied Carey. "*When* they find the body, and hopefully not for a while yet, but when they do, they'll start tracking us, so I want them to think we're a grunt patrol from Rachel..."

"And heading back that way so they'll move to block us," said the Medic, nodding in sudden understanding.

"Roger that, and while we'll be moving further away," added Carey with the next part of his plan.

"Fake left and go right," grinned Thomas.

"Uh-huh, and that leaves here," Carey said, pointing to a small white blob in the mass of green on his map.

The rest of the team members leaned to see where Carey was pointing. The white blob surrounded in a sea of green, that represented a small clearing in the jungle, was a good four to five miles away.

"Looks familiar," said Thomas, while not quite placing why it had.

Carey nodded. "It should. It was one of the potential LZs we looked at on the over-flight we blew off for being too small..."

"Because of an island of trees dead center," finished the A-T-L. remembering why they'd dismissed it the day before the team's insertion.

"Yep, but looking better and better now."

During the pre-mission over-flight searching for viable insertion and exfiltration sites for the mission, they'd spotted the small, thin clearing that was no bigger than a two-car garage leaning out of the floor of the helicopter.

The island was little more than a small mound with a clump of several tall trees in the center of the clearing. The natural hazard left no room for a helicopter to touch down in the small clearing, so they wrote it off. Now though, it could serve another purpose.

"When the TOC doesn't receive any of our SITREPs they'll send a bird to come looking for us. By then, though, it'll be dark, and without a radio, and if the storm gets any worse, we may have to wait it out until it passes."

"But they won't be able to land at the site because of the trees."

It was Bowman, and it was statement of fact, and something of a question.

"No, they won't," said Carey, "so we'll go out by dope on a rope."

"McGuire Rig?"

"Uh-huh."

Heads nodded with a few hopeful smiles. It was do-able.

During their McGuire Rig training when they were strung out on the long ropes beneath a Huey helicopter it was initially all fun and games with some even laughing and yelling, "*ALL RIGHT*!" "*COOL!*" or a very loud, "*FUCKING-A!*" during the training exercise.

The training demonstrated that it was an easy way to get out of a tight spot, but not necessarily a comfortable one. The longer the flight time, the more the ropes that were wrapped beneath the arms and around the chests and backs, tended to squeeze air from the lungs. The pressure of the individual bodyweight too dictated the amount of pain that went with the wrap. A little discomfort, though, was little price to pay when you were escaping and evading the enemy, and more so when the hunters became the hunted.

As Carey was outlining to the team members how they'd get out of the jungle, Jonas Warren had his knife out and prying apart the broken handset. When he got down to the two connection wires in the damaged talk speaker he cut the protective plastic covering away exposing the copper wires. Holding down the talk button on the handset he then began tapping the wires together in a deliberate pattern.

"Yo Jonas, what are you doing?" asked Carey, eyeing the activity.

"Morse Code, hopefully," replied Warren. "And hopefully someone on the other end will recognize it."

"Tell them we're doing an E & E from our last known."

Warren tapped the code but didn't get a response. He tapped it out again.

"Anything?"

Warren shook his head.

"Keep trying."

To the others he said, "It'll be dark soon. We maybe have an hour before the sun goes down. We need to make the most of it and the storm to work our way towards our new extraction point. Let's get...."

An explosion boomed in the distance behind them, cutting him off. Even in the howling wind and rain the booming noise from the blast pierced through the jungle like a lightening strike. The explosion was quickly followed by muted screams and cries from the NVA who'd been wounded when someone triggered the rucksack booby-trap.

"Oh Hell!" Carey said, staring back the way they had come. He was hoping for more time.

"Darrell?" he said to Thomas and when he had his attention added, "take point. Jonas, you're behind him. Doc, you're next, and New Guy?"

"Bowman," said the new guy.

"I know," Carey said. "You're covering me, new guy. I'll take rear scout. Move!"

Chapter 11

They moved out at a quick pace in the direction of the Fire Support Base. They'd gone a quarter mile before Carey signaled Thomas to perform another buttonhook maneuver.

There was no way of knowing if the NVA had immediately figured out what had happened and started after them, let alone how far behind them they'd be.

However, there was one thing the Lurp Team Leader was certain of, the NVA weren't fools. They would figure it out and while they wouldn't alter their plan to attack the Fire Support Base, they would send others to track down and kill the small American patrol.

"They'll be coming after us with a vengeance. Get ready for a fight," said Carey. To Thomas he said, "See what you can do about providing a proper greeting back down the way we came and another one on our right flank. I'll put something out on our left in case they try to flank us from that direction. They'll be more careful this time."

"On it!" said his A-T-L, and Thomas went to work setting out the Claymore mines.

"Cover him, new guy," Carey said to Bowman, who gave him a chin-up nod.

"It's Bowman," he said as the two started to move out.

The Team leader shrugged. "Not yet," he said. "But we'll see. Oh, and take this."

Carey removed the extra Claymore mine and handed it and the carrying case to the new guy.

"You want me to set it up?"

"No, that's Thomas' job. You just hold onto it and cover him. You copy?"

"Copy," said Bowman.

"Good, because we might need the Claymore later, in case we really hit the shit."

Bowman wanted to ask what hitting the shit entailed if this wasn't it already, but decided against asking.

Bowman swung the carrying case over his shoulder and back.

"You ready new guy?" said Thomas.

"It's Bowman," he said, again.

"No, it's that way," said Thomas, chuckling as he turned and made his way out to their previous line of travel. The Texan's chuckle, though, wasn't sustained. There was deadly work to be done.

"Anything with the Morse Code?" Carey said to his RTO.

The broken nosed RTO shook his head

"Keep trying, Jonas."

Warren looked up and gave a low grunt.

"What do you want me to do?" asked Doc Moore.

"Keep your Aid Bag handy, Doc," Carey said over his shoulder and then moved into the brush to their right.

The counter flanking measures were a tactical precautionary move. Carey was certain the NVA were tracking them, and this time around they'd be more guarded in their pursuit, and looking for some payback.

They would just as certainly be following the thin, unmistakable path the Ranger Lurp team had inadvertently left in their wake. They would deploy flankers, too, well to their left and right in a three-pronged attack. It was an effective tactic that both the Viet Cong and NVA used successfully in the past, and what a wise tracking team would use now to their believed advantage following their prey.

When the two Claymores were in place and well concealed, and Thomas and Bowman back in place, Carey had one more trick up his camo sleeve.

"Cover me," he said to his A-T-L, not that he had to ask. Thomas gave a nod and watched over his Team Leader as he crept out and over the cover of the fallen tree and set a concussion grenade with a fake trip wire across their old path. The concussion grenade had been fitted with a blasting cap. There would be no six-second delay.

The fake trip wire wasn't attached to the grenade pin, but was made to appear that way. Instead, the Team Leader attached a fortified wire to the pin that he'd trigger from hide site with a simple pull.

Back in place he was reasonably satisfied the team had some perimeter protection. The fallen log offered cover from their left while a small mound offered something to their front and on their right. If they stayed low, they were good for the attack coming their way.

Wiping the rain from his eyes he lowered the brim of his boonie cap and then looked around to make sure his people were ready. Warren had several grenades out and ready beside him while Thomas had the Claymore clacker in his hands. Bowman, who they screwed with simply because he was new, was down and facing forward. To his right Doc Moore was facing out with his M-16 in hand and his Aid Bag unzipped and ready to use.

Surprisingly, Carey was calm. Alone was one thing, but with his team in place and ready, the fear, for the most part, had subsided. It wasn't just safety in numbers, but knowing just who was to your left and right that made the difference.

It was, perhaps, twenty minutes later when Doc Moore heard the movement on their left flank. There was a brief rustling in the underbrush that had nothing to do with the wind or rain. Branches were carefully being pushed aside and the leaves on those branches were rustling and scraping as the branches sprung back.

The rustling and scraping momentarily subsided before it picked up again. Moore snapped his fingers once, pointed to his right ear, and then in the direction of the sounds he'd heard.

The rest of the team were straining to hear what Doc had heard when there came a distinct sound of a branch breaking under the weight of a heavy foot through the jungle on their right flank. The heavy rain had dampened much of the enemy's approach, but not all.

The enemy soldiers that were tracking the Lurps were close.

Soon, the rifle barrel, right shoulder, and left profile of a stern-face of an NVA point man came into view.

The rain was dripping down his pith helmet and rolling off rounded brim as the hunched over soldier studied the ground as he moved. He was a hunter staring intently and picking out the bent leaves and disturbed ground of his human quarry.

Over his shoulder as he moved, a second NVA soldier was covering the point man tracker, his eyes and AK-47 slowly sweeping the jungle looking for a possible ambush.

The tracker paused briefly in place, causing the second soldier behind him to halt as well and the stoppage earned a rebuke from a third NVA soldier, an officer or senior NCO, perhaps, who wasn't in view. The Lurps heard the NVA soldier angrily whispering and telling the two in front to move faster.

The second soldier took a step forward, while the point man, though, ignored, the order. He sensed that something wasn't quite right which he confirmed when he saw the thin, olive drab trip wire and the black, oblong grenade it was attached to.

There was the distinct and telling metallic click of an Assault rifle being flipped from SAFE to FIRE on their left flank that told Carey they were indeed being flanked and that the flankers were close.

With his A-T-L holding the triggering device to the Claymore and Carey holding the trip wire to the concussion grenade, he gave a nod to Thomas and pulled on the trip wire.

Thomas was a fraction of a second behind Carey squeezing the arming device for the Claymores three times in quick succession triggering the ear-pounding dual explosions.

The concussion grenade brought down the tracker and the two NVA soldiers behind him while the Claymore detonation sent out a massive flying wall of ball bearings from the protective anti-personnel mines with thousands of the buckshot-like projectiles fanning out through the foliage and devastating wide swaths of the jungle and anyone on their old path.

Although they hadn't been caught in the carnage and had the protection of the fallen tree, the Lurp team was hit by the shock wave and overwhelming noise from the blast. The Lurps and any surviving enemy soldiers were briefly stunned as the wall of heat and concussive force rolled back over them like an angry tsunami.

"FIRE!" yelled Carey rising up on one knee and spraying the jungle in front of him. His CAR-15 aimed in at knee and hip level. Thomas, Doc Moore, Bowman, and Jonas Warren followed his lead as they emptied their 20-round magazines, reloaded, and fired again.

"Grenade!" yelled Warren and the team members dropped as he let two fragmentation grenades fly. The explosions brought on screams from those caught up the blast radius and sent more shards of shrapnel whistling through the jungle.

What the Claymore anti-personnel mine, and grenades had failed to tear and shred, the rifle fire did.

A burst of return fire from several Ak-47s came at the team from their left flank and targeted the American perimeter. The enemy small arms fire raked the fallen log and was beginning to find its way over the small mound.

"DOWN!" yelled Carey, reaching for the triggering device to the Claymore he'd set out to their left.

They were still taking fire from the left flank and Warren grunted under the pain of the incoming rounds that had grazed his left tri-cep and skidded across his back.

Carey triggered the Claymore and once again the blast took the place of the thunder from the storm. It also ended the incoming enemy small arms fire. A surviving NVA soldier could be heard making a hasty retreat.

Warren was on his face in the ground, but then lifted himself up, swearing, and saying, "I'M OKAY! I'M OKAY!" as the jungle took on a brief and eerie silence with only the falling rain and wind through the treetops providing the only noise.

The one-sided firefight had been brief and brutal. Because of the physical proximity of their anti-personnel mines there was blowback pressure from the explosions and far-flung debris. Bits of the heavy plastic casing from the Claymores, as well as the swivel prongs the mines rested on came at the Lurps as unintended shrapnel.

A sharp piece of plastic from the mine's casing blew back across Carey's left brow line in a glancing blow that had missed his eye, but left a small trench from the brow to his hairline. The explosion also had sent the scissor-like prongs slicing into the meat of Bowman's right thigh where they'd stuck.

"Ah, fuck, I'm hit!" cried the new guy pulling out the twisted metal prongs and angrily tossing them aside.

Doc Moore, who already had his Aid Bag out, and was bandaging Warren, turned to Bowman. "You okay?"

"Just shrapnel," said the new guy, holding a hand over the bleeding wound. "Nothing big."

Moore tossed him a bandage.

"Put this on and tie it off," he said. "I'll look at it in a minute."

Bowman nodded.

"How about you, Ben?" he said looking at his team leader.

"A scratch," said Carey, probing his fingers into the small, bloodied trench that burned more than ached.

Doc Moore wasn't sure about his team leader's self-prognosis and after he patched up Warren he scooted over to Carey. He wiped away the blood, applied a butterfly bandage, and closed off the small wound with the Sergeant wincing as Moore worked.

The fight was over. The immediate threat was gone. None of their wounds of the team members were life threatening, and the few enemy soldiers left standing returned haphazard and non-directional fire as they hurriedly retreated.

Out on the small path, those caught in the ambush were no longer a threat. The NVA point man tracker, and the second soldier covering him were dead. Both were laying like tossed rag dolls in an ugly display while the third NVA soldier, the officer or NCO that ordered them to move faster, was down as well. He wasn't dead yet, but with both legs gone at the thighs and a hole in his chest, he soon would be.

The tracker's arms were shredded below the elbows and what was left of his torso was hacked meat. The soldier covering him hadn't fared much better. There was no one alive in the NVA's tracker team ranks yelling commands or orders pressing for a counterattack, which told Carey the small patrol trailing them was momentarily leaderless.

"Damn it! They hit the radio!' said the RTO, checking out the shot up backpacked radio.

The incoming rounds targeting Warren had missed him, but trashed what was left of the team's radio. There was no salvaging it.

"Leave it!" ordered Carey. "It's dead weight."

A frustrated Warren nodded.

"Cover me," Carey said to Thomas realizing what he'd forgotten.

Scurrying back over the fallen log and back out to the trail he quickly searched the dead soldier's pockets, gathering up any and all of the documents and papers of theirs as he could find. This was physical intelligence and the Intel Officers would be all over him for those materials and more during the team's debriefing.

Stuffing the papers and a blood stained journal into one of his cargo pockets he turned back to his team.

The documents, papers, and journal would give the Higher Commands a working understanding of which unit or units the enemy soldiers were part of, provided the team could successfully escape and evade any more pursuers.

Time and distance, Carey thought to himself, again, and pointed in the new direction he now wanted Thomas to take.

"Once more into the breach," he said. "New Guy, take my Claymore."

"What breach?" asked a confused looking Bowman as he retrieved Carey's extra Claymore from the ground.

"As in, we few, we proud, we very, very lucky band of dumb sumbitches," said Thomas.

"Henry Five," Doc Moore said to the new guy. "Well, sort of."

"Who?"

"A team member of Sergeant Shakespeare's," said Warren.

"Really?"

"No."

"Sarge, you want your Claymore back?" said Bowman.

"No, you carry it, in case we hit the shit, new guy."

"It's Bowman," Bowman said tossing the Claymore's carrying sling over his shoulder.

"Naw, it's a Claymore," said Thomas. "You don't need to give it its own little nickname, new guy."

"We good to go?" Carey said, interrupting their nervous small talk. The team members nodded or said they were, but the Team Leader was mostly directed to the Medic.

"We are," said Moore.

"Good. Then, let's move!"

And the five Lurps, now without Morse code, slipped away one more time while the NVA tracking them, or what was left of them, would need time to recover their wounded and dead, and reassess their strategy.

Sixty yards on Carey had Thomas change the team's direction of travel once more. They would now head southwest towards the small clearing that would hopefully be their new pickup point. They moved on, pausing only for compass headings and a realignment of their map.

It was hour later when Carey called for a halt. From his pace count he figured they had gone a difficult mile. This latest halt would give them time to catch their breath, steady their nerves, and listen for anyone still following as their hearing readjusted to the jungle.

All was good, or seemingly so, and they moved on.

During their run they'd broken out to a few more small trails and a seemingly deserted jungle bunker complex that they'd carefully skirted while staying hidden in the heavy vegetation and shadows. There was still more ground to cover.

The day, or what had passed for it in the black and tumbling sky, was done. Night was setting in and their going had slowed. The rainfall had increased and the treetop canopy couldn't even loosely shield them from the heavy downpour anymore.

The wind had picked up too, and was howling as the Monsoon storm that was hammering the jungle, straining tree limbs, and cracking and breaking others, was masking any sounds of movement the Americans were making. Thunder and distant lightening brought an angry fight to the heavens, if only to match the one on the ground.

On the next temporary halt Carey pulled out his red filtered flashlight and used it to take a new compass heading. Marrying up where he figured they were on the map and where they still needed to go, Carey turned in the direction he's taken on the compass. Then, taking over point from Thomas he led his people through the saturated jungle in determined silence. Not dead silence, thought Carey. No, not yet anyway.

They were wet, cold, tired, and pushing the limits of their adrenaline rush, and they kept moving. If they weren't happy about the heavy rain, then they begrudgingly welcomed it as an ally.

Carey was thinking that if their luck could hold, then the enemy soldiers that'd tracked them and who'd survived the ambush would retrieve their wounded and dead, and maybe give up the chase.

It could happen, thought Carey and then gave a cynical chuff knowing that there was no such a thing as luck. Luck was what you made it. There was only chance.

So far there hadn't been any artillery fire peppering the jungle, which told him it was possible the NVA believed he and his team were a small patrol from the Fire Support Base that for some reason hadn't alerted Rachel to the pre-dawn attack heading their way.

The Ranger team leader was counting on the NVA to hedge their bet and, instead of pursuing the team they'd move to block all approaches to the Fire Support Base to cut off any retreat from the Americans manning the Observation or Listening Posts.

It was already a lot to count on, but he was also counting on the NVA to send two to three-man teams to cover any open areas in the jungle that might serve as possible landing zones for an in-bound helicopter. They would adjust their tactics to meet any new threat, but they also had to contend with the massive tangled weave of the jungle that dictated time and distance.

The gamble was to move to the unlikely exfil location that the NVA might not waste the time or manpower to cover. Open stretches of jungle tended to attract the attention of roving helicopter gunship patrols. The storm would ground most until it passed, and it would pass.

With the bad weather there'd be no way they be lifted out anytime soon, even if the TOC could somehow learn where Nine-One was heading, and there was still the possibility of being hit by Friendly Artillery Fire, if the team didn't move out of the immediate area after the pre-dawn attack of the Fire Support Base, and if the helicopter gunships and fighter jets didn't turn the jungle into a meat grinder targeting the dispersing NVA elements in their retreat.

There was much to mull over and there were one, too many *ifs* for Carey's liking. He needed to keep the team moving. The small clearing was still two to three miles off. The working strategy was still time and distance.

The torrential rain slowed the going as it saturated the rain forest floor and the once dry ground squished beneath their jungle boots turning to slippery mud.

With no radio contact the Romeo Company TOC, let alone anyone else, would not know of the team's predicament. The TOC would still believe the team was huddled down in the recorded ambush position they'd called in earlier.

Carey knew that position would be marked on their TOC's situation map. It might even be protected from artillery or gunship fire following the ground attack on Rachel while the ground around that position would be fair game. But that all ended because one enemy soldier had to take a piss.

Everything had changed and their E&E was a race they had to win. There would be no trophy for second place. It was all or nothing, and the nothing meant dying in the jungle, or worse, being severely wounded, unable to move, and hearing the grunts or growls of something slowly working its way through the underbrush towards you to finish the job.

There were worse ways of dying in a jungle war than being killed outright, and the natural predators were just as vicious as any army.

Chapter 12

The *'Hold in place. Charlie Mike'* order MAC-V had relayed for Team Nine-One hadn't sat well with the Lurps in the field, nor with their Ranger Company Commander, for that matter.

Along with the order that had been relayed to Robison, came a command to report to Camp Mackie's Tactical Operations Center, the BIG-TOC, for a briefing regarding the Lurp team's enemy sighting.

The report of several hundred NVA heading towards Fire Support Base Rachel, hauling heavy weapons and mortar tubes, had the BIG-TOC abuzz with concern. Contingency plans were being drawn up, but not yet implemented. They had not been implemented because there was a certain amount of skepticism from some of Camp Mackie's higher-highers regarding the sighting, as it hadn't yet been confirmed.

Fire Support Rachel had sent out additional OPs and LPs-Observation Posts and Listening Posts, along with a platoon-sized reconnaissance patrol for verification, but no enemy soldiers or unusual activity had been encountered or reported. And that gave rise to doubt.

As the Ranger Company Commander entered the BIG-TOC he was met with cooled enthusiasm and a host of questions from several higher-ranking officers, foremost among them Mackie's Intel Officer. The Intel Officer, who was a veteran Major, wasn't exactly Torquemada, but his cynicism carried that impression and feel. For Robison it was hard deciding whether the Intel Officer was playing Devil's Advocate, or if he was just being an asshole. The Ranger Captain suspected it was a little of both.

The Intel Major questioned the Ranger Company Commander on the reliability of the sighting and wanted to know how the enemy numbers had been counted. Was the direction of movement correct? And, if so, why hadn't anyone from Rachel heard or seen any enemy activity?

Robison bristled, and other than an occasional twitching with his jaw muscles, he hid it well. In a calm, professional, and unlike Ranger voice and style, he responded, "*Yes,*" to reliability, direction of movement, and the approximate numbers counted, and calmly stated that he had no explanation as to why the OP's, LP's, and reconnaissance patrol hadn't heard or found any signs of enemy activity. However, he did have a few questions of his own and rattled them off to the Major, who was Ranger school qualified, but who had likely never served on a long-range patrol.

Were the OPs and LPs were set up further than their 100 yards or so? How far out did the Recon platoon go? Was a Pink Team, consisting of a Cobra attack helicopter and an OH-6 low bird Scout helicopter, sent out to have a look anywhere near the coordinates where Team Nine-One reported the sighting?

Robison wasn't done, but he was conciliatory to a point.

"Of course, Team Nine-One's sighting would need to be verified," he said. "Where are we at on that, sir?"

"Not where we need to be," said the Intel Officer. "If you think I'm busting your balls then keep in mind there's a lot riding on this. You roger that, Captain?"

"Yes, sir," said the Ranger Captain, thinking he'd give the Major the benefit of the doubt provided his tone and demeanor changed.

Robison knew there was a lot riding on the veracity of the sighting. Once Nine-One's sighting had been confirmed, then a series of critical steps would be set in motion. The OPs and LPs at Fire Support Base Rachel would be called back in, artillery tubes would be lowered and adjusted, flechette beehive shells stockpiled and readied, and extra sandbags, trip flares and additional Claymores would hurriedly be set up and in place. Helicopter gunships, Air Force jets, and other critical assets would be diverted and redirected from other combat missions, briefed, prepped, and placed on stand-by.

More than that Robison knew that the reputation of the new Ranger Company was riding on the accuracy of the sighting. The uncertainty and doubt he was confronted with at the Mackie TOC questioned the integrity of the unit. The sighting had to be confirmed and when Robison asked again what was being done to make that happen, the answer he received wasn't helpful.

"A Pink Team was sent out but they never made to the location site," said the Intel Officer. "The helicopters were forced to turn back because of the storm. We'll send up a Mohawk as soon as possible, but that might take awhile."

The fixed-wing Mohawk airplane had SLAR capability; the side-looking-airborne-radar that could scan through foliage and pick up enemy movement but getting the plane airborne was also subject to better weather conditions. Until the worrisome storm passed there would be no aerial confirmation, and without confirmation, the doubts would remain. Serious doubts.

Captain Robison returned to the Ranger Company more than a little annoyed. Coming through the canvas tarp his TOC used as a curtain to screen the dust as well as to hide the inside light, he found Sergeant Cantu monitoring the wall of AN-77 radios while Specialist Taras was listening in on another frequency with a smaller PRC-25 radio. A small, hand-held URC-10 radio lay on a reused ammo box beside him that now served as a footrest.

Taras, who was Cantu's shift replacement in the TOC, was an hour early reporting for duty. At eighteen years of age he was the youngest Ranger in the unit and had a much older voice that carried a surprising calmness and control in a tone that some said made him sound like a benevolent Johnny Cash, only with a distinct South Philly accent. Never mind that his 'you' came across as 'Youze' or that the G's at the end of some words seemed to be missing in action, Taras was good at his job; a job he technically stumbled into.

He'd injured his right knee on his second mission, but not from a stumble of his own accord. When the insertion helicopter couldn't touch down on the side of a hill, it was forced to hover. Against the Team Leader's shouted protests, he and his fellow team members were forced to jump ten feet down to the hard-packed ground below.

When it was his turn to go Taras leapt from the helicopter skids, and when he hit the ground, it was on the balls of his feet, both knees, and finally, his face.

As he hit the ground the seventy pounds of his filled rucksack, along with the team's backpacked PRC-25 radio were shoved hard against the back of his neck and head. The ten-foot drop and the combined weight what he carried drove his face into the dirt. The face plant came with nasty bruise to his right cheek just below his right eye when it hit a small flat rock. Had it been a rock with sharp edges he would've been gushing blood. As it was there would only be a nasty welt. But that wasn't all.

When he tried to stand something in his left knee gave way and he stumbled-stepped and limped into the tree line following the others who were just inside the wood line, *laying dog*.

Laying dog meant the team was hunkered down, waiting, watching, and listening to see if they'd been detected.

"You okay?" asked the Team Leader.

"Screwed up my knee on that jump."

"That was no jump, that was a fall," said the Team Leader. "Doc, check him out."

When the medic went to work he found that Taras had little to no lateral movement in the knee. The pain was crippling and he swore as the medic probed and twisted the injury to better assess the damage. When Doc was done he applied an Ace bandage and recommended to the Team Leader that Taras be medevac'd out.

"He's done," said the medic.

"No, I'll keep up," said the young Ranger.

"You sure?" asked the Team Leader.

Taras nodded, the medic shrugged, and the team moved out. Taras limped through the first day of the mission on a badly swollen knee. There was no way he was going to medevac'd unless he was seriously wounded or dead. To his credit he didn't bitch or moan about the injury, and performed his RTO duties surprisingly well in spite of it, even during a brief firefight on the second day of against a Viet Cong patrol. He'd proved himself at a cost.

Back at Camp Mackie the Aid Station medics iced the now softball-size swollen and damaged knee and sent him to the 45th Field Hospital in Tay Ninh for X-rays and a formal evaluation. There, several Orthopedic Doctors determined that Taras had torn his ACL in his left knee, and although it wasn't enough to get him medevac'd to the States, it was enough to keep him out of combat. The Doctors put him on permanent profile, meaning there would be no more field missions for the novice Ranger. That presented a problem.

"What do we do with him?" the Captain asked his First Sergeant, when Taras came back from Tay Ninh on crutches and with the medical evaluation in hand

"His team leader said the kid didn't rattle under fire and was great on the radio," said First Sergeant Poplawski, not wanting to toss the kid to the dogs.

"I'm told he had no quit in him, either," said the Captain.

Poplawski shrugged. "We can always use someone like that in the TOC."

The Company Commander agreed, and there it was. Taras was assigned to the Operations Center and like Cantu, proved indispensible to the Ranger Company's field operations.

The young Ranger nodded to the Captain and handed him a towel as he came back into the TOC. Drying himself off Robison returned the nod.

"Have we heard from Nine-One?" he asked.

"No, sir," Sergeant Cantu said. "They've gone quiet in their hide-site. Taras is setting up to monitor other frequencies."

"Try the team again and see if you can get them to break squelch, if they can't talk."

"Yes, sir."

"Where's the First Sergeant?"

"Checking on the McGuire rigs, sir," said Cantu.

Captain Robison nodded as Cantu went back to the bank of radios. The Ranger officer turned his attention to the coffee pot on the hot pad.

He poured himself his fourth cup of coffee for the long day, figuring the caffeine would carry him into an even longer evening and night, or at least until they'd heard from Nine-One that all was well, or were in a running gunfight, and needed immediate fire support, or a QRF, A-SAP.

Coffee cup in hand, he turned to the plastic-covered operational map posted on the TOC bunker's wall to the left of the bank of radios. Each team's current, or last known locations in the field were circled with red and blue grease pencils, colored coded to show insertion and extraction sites, last known locations, and routes of travel. He found

Nine-One's insertion point, route of travel for the two previous days, and the circle where Nine-One had set up their ambush site, and had called in the NVA sighting.

He followed the enemy's line of movement across the map towards the only potential U.S., South Vietnamese, or Allied target in the immediate area, which was Fire Support Base Rachel. It was a little over a mile away from Nine-One's hide-site.

An OP/LP from the Fire Support Base might only go out a 100 yards into the tree line to watch and listen for signs of enemy movement, while a platoon doing a recon sweep might venture out a few hundred yards further to conduct a broader search, but that might be the extent of it, especially in the bad weather.

Captain Robison took a sip of the coffee and frowned into the coffee cup.

"I take it the First Sergeant made the coffee?" he said to Cantu.

"Yes, sir."

"Of course, he did," agreed Robison.

What was in the coffee pot would last another hour or so before a new pot was made. The First Sergeant had a standing order that his coffee pot was never, *"I say again, never!"* to be scrubbed out and cleaned. Poplawski maintained that like an old iron skillet, an occasional simple sluicing of the coffee pot was good enough.

Good coffee, some claimed, was the nectar of the gods, and while the First Sergeant's coffee had what some might say was "*a more earthy flavor*," a more discerning critic might categorize as, "*Damn near sludge!*"

Robison spooned several hefty helpings of powdered coffee creamer into the cup, along with a steady stream of sugar that he poured from a restaurant-style sugar dispenser. Stirring the mix with a plastic spoon from a box of C-rations until the sugar and powdered creamer had blended in, he tried another sip.

Serviceable, he thought, turning his attention back to the wall map. He listened as his Operations Sergeant tried, and failed, to raise Team Nine-One.

"Gotta be the lousy weather, sir," the NCO said in a tone that said he probably didn't believe it himself.

"Could be," said the Captain, noticing that the Sergeant's coffee cup was half-filled.

"You need topping off?" he said, holding up his coffee cup and nodding towards the Sergeant's cup.

"Yes, sir," said Cantu. "I could use one. And three helpings of the creamer, please?"

"Creamer? Seriously?" said First Sergeant Poplawski picking up on the last part of the conversation as he came through the entrance of the TOC and was stopped in the doorway by the coffee order request. "Jesus, Cantu. You call yourself a Ranger?"

"Pretty sure we both did because of his keen ability to apply the appropriate course of action in any troubling situation when we selected him for this job," said the Company Commander coming to his defense. "Specialist Taras too, for that matter."

"I...I don't drink coffee, sir," said Taras.

"Can't blame you, Ranger," the Captain said, holding up the coffee pot. "How about you, Top? You need a cup?"

Poplawski nodded.

"Cream and sugar?"

Poplawski snorted and frowned.

"Not fucking likely, sir," he said.

Cantu chuckled as Captain Robison was pouring the coffee.

Taking the offered cup from his Commanding Officer, Poplawski watched as the Captain added the powdered creamer for Cantu until the sergeant said, "That's good, Captain."

"Sugar?"

"Yes, sir."

"Say when," said Robison, pouring the sugar as the TOC sergeant stared back over his right shoulder overseeing the measuring process.

"When!" said Cantu, signaling him to stop. "That's good, sir."

Jesus, thought Poplawski, he's making a fucking candy bar. He was just about to say something to Cantu when he noticed that the officer was adding more of the powdered creamer to his coffee cup as well.

"Horse piss, is it, Captain?"

Robison shrugged. "More like a Clydesdale with a slight kidney problem, that is, if you use the right amount of powder creamer and say, a sack full of sugar."

"Tis an insult and slam, sir, against my fine Italian coffee maker."

"It's possible your fine Italian coffee maker isn't the problem, First Sergeant. By the way, what's the deal with it? Why is so special to you anyway?"

Poplawski shrugged. "Technically, it was a gift from my second ex-wife," he said, studying the coffee maker and giving it a thoughtful nod and half smile.

"Technically?"

"Well, sort of..."

"Sort of?"

"Sort of because she threw it at me after she'd found out that I was sleeping with her sister, so it was the last thing of mine she hadn't tossed out the window when she decided to toss me out."

"A gift, was it?"

"Well, I caught it in time, so technically, yes, sir."

The Ranger Officer shook his head, chuckling. "You think there's a lesson to be learned from that, First Sergeant?" asked Robison.

Poplawski brightened. "Yes, sir," he said. "Never marry a woman with good looking siblings."

An incoming radio transmission interrupted their banter. The Sergeant turned his attention to the radio and responded to the call. Both the Company Commander and First Sergeant caught the end of the call through the radio's speaker. It wasn't Team Nine-One.

"Yes, sir, I copy, wait one," the TOC Sergeant said, passing the radio's handset it over to the Captain.

"Swordman-Six, sir."

Robison nodded.

Swordman-Six was the call sign for a full bird Colonel decision maker at the Camp's BIG-TOC.

Robison listened, said, "*I copy*" a few times, and then ended it with "Valhalla Six, out."

To First Sergeant Poplawski he said. "The weather people say the storm should pass by 22:00 hours. The 25th Infantry Division will send up a Mohawk out of Cu Chi for a look-see shortly afterwards."

"Hmm? I take it they still don't believe Nine-One's sighting?" Poplawski said as though he'd tasted something sour.

"Looks that way."

"Just a thought, sir," said Poplawski. "Maybe we should perhaps ask Swordman-Six or any of those other fine minds around him if they'd like to join one of our teams on a mission in the field. Maybe make it n open invitation?

"Not a bad thought at that," replied the Captain before turning his attention back on the Area of Operation's wall map. His eyes were locked on Nine-One's last known position that was circled in red.

The red grease pencil circle stood out in sharp contrast to the map's sea of green that was the heavy jungle and the browns, blues, whites, and blacks that defined everything else. A circle in dark blue grease pencil showed the team's insertion site as well as its primary and secondary exfiltration sites.

Closely studying the map, Robison saw the problem. If the NVA were moving on Rachel and were between Nine-One and the Fire Support Base, then the primary extraction or pickup point was out. And, if they moved towards the secondary exfil location, then they would be heading in the direction the NVA had come from, and most likely, still controlled.

The veteran Captain scanned the wall map looking for other natural openings or clearings that could serve as potential pickup zones before finally settling on a few that could work.

"Anything?" Robison said, back to the two Rangers working the radios.

"No, sir," said Cantu.

"SIR!" said Taras, excitedly. "The Signal Battalion relay up on Nui Ba Den reported they picked up part of a Morse Code message that 'somebody dash-one are E&E-ing east of their last known. I've got the Signal people on the horn."

Taras held out the radio handset and the Officer took it.

"Who's on the line?" he said to Taras before pressing the push to talk button. "Who am I speaking with?"

"Echo Three-Two."

Robison nodded. "Echo Three-Two," he said into the handset. "Echo Three-Two. This is Valhalla Six, over."

The reply came back immediately. "Echo Three-Two. Go."

"Status of the partial Mike Code message, over."

The radio relay station operator atop the Nui Ba Den Mountain told the Ranger Company Commander what he'd passed along to Taras moments before.

"That's it? Nothing more?" said a hopeful Robison.

"That's a negative at this time, Valhalla Six."

"Roger Three-Two. Much appreciated," Robison said, ending the transmission. "Valhalla Six, out."

Staring back at the wall map one more time, he checked his watch.

"Get me someone at the 1st of the 9th TOC. Let's get a bird ready to roll," he said to Sergeant Cantu.

"Roger that, Captain," said the Sergeant.

To Taras Robison added, "Stay in touch with Echo Three-two, in case there's anything new to report."

"Yes, sir."

"I'll be ready to extract the team on your say-so," said Poplawski.

"Good," Robison said. "Let's find our people and get them out of there."

Chapter 13

The Typhoon-like storm, that had piggybacked on the seasonal Monsoon downpour and doubled its intensity, had overtaken the VIP helicopter. Gale winds and unrelenting rain had turned their helicopter flight into a roller coaster ride off its rails.

The roiling, angry sky had swallowed up the remainder of the day, and the punishing tail and crosswinds had the helicopter bouncing and trembling over the whine of its engine.

Both the Aircraft Commander and his co-pilot were doing everything they could to keep the helicopter airborne and struggling when a massive knock sent the jet engine screaming as the Huey plunged into a jolting descent.

Adler could see a momentary panic on the co-pilot's face as he turned to the Air Craft Commander, who was hurriedly flipping switches and yelling into his headset. A loud and piercing audio alarm was reverberating through the cockpit and the RPM warning light came on indicating a potential engine failure.

Mister Corsi lowered the collective pitch to reduce lift and drag, all the while fighting the force of the storm trying to keep the aircraft from plummeting into the canopied jungle below. It was a losing battle.

"MAY DAY! MAY DAY! MAY DAY!" he yelled into his radio headset, the cry loud enough to carry to the cargo bay behind him. "Blade Master Three-four going down! Three-four going down!"

They were dropping altitude at a critical rate.

"GOING DOWN! GOING DOWN!" shouted the co-pilot turning to the passengers seated in the cargo bay unable to hide his fright.

"What's happening?" cried Orlov, the Senator's Chief of Staff, grabbing at Adler's arm in panic.

"BRACE YOURSELVES!" he yelled to her and the others. "DO IT!"

The Senator was holding onto his son and the frame of the seat as others clutched or grabbed onto anything that looked stable or solid, which wasn't much in the open cargo bay. Major Haverly's hands were gripping his seat belt as tight as he could hold it, his eyes flitting in terror.

Dark as the day was Corsi spotted a small clearing in the jungle through the heavy curtain of rain and turned the helicopter towards it. The small clearing was maybe four hundred yards away and he prayed he could keep the Huey in the air long enough to reach it.

If they could make it to the clearing then they'd stand a better chance of surviving upon impact. If not, then they'd crash through the treetops and pinball down to the ground, the aircraft likely buckling and breaking apart as they went. He'd seen one too many helicopters go down in the jungle and had flown out the bodies of his friends in body bags afterwards. It wasn't pretty.

"Come on! Come on! COME ON!" he yelled over and over again more to himself than anyone else.

He needed eighty-knots an hour to keep the Huey from rotating out of control, only the forward speed wasn't there. In a sudden, sinking realization, Corsi knew they weren't going to make it. They were well short of the clearing. They would be going down through the trees.

"OH SHIT!" said the co-pilot, realizing their fate, too, seconds later.

"BRACE FOR IMPACT! BRACE FOR IMPACT!" yelled Mister Corsi just as the helicopter slammed into the tops of the trees tail boom first. The smaller tail rotor sliced through the treetops, hit something solid, and sheared away. The aircraft bucked forward, and as it did it sent the spinning main rotor blades chopping into the tops of the trees until they too broke and spun away in splintered pieces.

What was left of the helicopter, that hadn't shattered or broken away, began to crumple and fold as the Huey continued its fall through the dense green and brown mass. There was a loud metal-wrenching rip as the tail boom cracked and then bent at a skewed angle.

The right side door was next to go, wrenched away as a spike-like splintered tree limbs jabbed at the Huey and those inside like terrible spears before what was left of the helicopter finally dove nose first into the rain soaked ground. The cockpit and cabin of the Bell helicopter dug a small trench, did a half roll, and then teetered on it's right side against a large tree before it finally toppled back over right side up.

As it rolled, Tony Adler felt something slam into the left side of his head with the force of a well-swung Louisville Slugger. He wasn't knocked unconscious, but his vision was blurred, his head was pounding, and he was reeling and woozy to the point of feeling like he was going to puke. He also found himself fighting to keep from passing out. Losing consciousness, though, might've been a temporary blessing.

Someone was groaning to his right. When he turned to see who was making the noise, a lightening bolt shot through his neck and spine. A thousand electrified needles stabbed him behind his eyes and sent what felt like sparks blowing out his ass. He winced, shut his eyes, swore, and then willed his eyes back open.

His left arm and leg were tingling and went momentarily numb, the feeling slowly returning without conviction.

The pain was slow to yield, but there were more immediate concerns. He could smell leaking fuel. He and the others trapped inside the wreckage needed to move.

Dark as the sky had been above the trees in the storm, the jungle was bathed in a gloomy twilight fitting for the dark turn of events.

The crippling pain he felt when he'd turned had been overwhelming, so much so that he hadn't noticed that a broken shard of the helicopter's windshield had grazed his left sleeve and tri-cep. There was some minor bleeding that was more annoying than serious, but his possible spine injury was the real problem. If he hadn't broken his spine, then a few vertebrae high up near his neck were badly tweaked.

The chilling fear and prospect of being paralyzed kept him from twisting or turning his neck and head again. When he'd move he knew he needed to turn his whole body to keep the injured spine better in alignment. As his vision improved and he found better focus, he saw a steady stream of blood spreading out across the cargo bay's metal floor beneath him.

Christ! Had he missed another wound?

In alarm, he hurriedly began checking his thighs and legs only to discover that the growing stream of blood wasn't his. Any sense of relief was short-lived and greedy.

The blood was from the helicopter's crew chief that had been sitting in the door well just over Adler's left shoulder. Managing a half turn and keeping his head, neck, and back in line he saw that the upper half of the crew chief's right leg had been brutally torn away high on the thigh in the crash. A severed femoral artery was spurting blood at a deadly rate from the ugly, gaping wound.

Both of the crew chief's hands were squeezing what remained of the thigh in a desperate attempt to stem the blood loss, but it was too late. He wasn't dead, but he soon would be.

Adler grabbed at the young man thinking he could do something to somehow save him, but there was little he or anyone else could do other than witness the young soldier's final moments as the light in his eyes was rapidly fading with each heartbeat spurt of blood.

"But, I...I go home next month," said the crew chief in wide-eyed bewilderment and then died.

The frustrated Captain's attention was drawn to a low moaning cry that was growing into wail that was coming from outside of the wreckage. The storm hid some of the human noise, but not all of the mounting hysteria from the one making it.

It was Major Haverly. He was seated with both legs stretched out in front of him on the ground in the rain and mud, cradling a badly broken right arm. His lower lip was quivering between cries.

Adler couldn't see any other serious injuries with the Major that warranted the noise.

"You okay, Major?"

Haverly shook his head as he held up the arm that was in the shape of a horseshoe. It was serious, but it wasn't catastrophic.

"It's only a broken arm. You'll be fine, so keep it down out there!" said the Captain and when Haverly hadn't complied, Adler said it again, this time with considerably more force.

"SHUT THE FUCK UP!" he growled.

When the now startled, more senior officer looked up he found a stern-faced Captain glaring back at him.

"We don't need to draw the attention of any enemy soldiers who might've seen the helicopter go down and who maybe are nearby searching for our crash site," Adler said, glancing at the surrounding dark jungle.

To the other survivor's he said, "Who needs help?"

"My...my Dad," said Zack, the Senator's son, standing outside of the aircraft cabin where he too had been thrown. The teen had been banged up and bruised with a walnut size knot on his forehead and a few small facial cuts from the crash. Like the Major, the injuries were not life threatening. However, it wasn't his injuries that had his young face drawn and pale.

As Adler turned to the Senator he saw that Russell had his hands gripped around a splintered tree limb the size of the fat end of a softball bat that had speared him through his stomach. A closer look showed that the splintered tree limb exited out his back, and had pinned Russell to the transmission wall behind him.

Horrific as it was, there was little Adler could do to help the Senator. Worse still, he knew it and that there were others in the wreckage he could help.

Stephanie Orlov, the Chief of Staff, who was seated next to the Senator, had her head lowered in her hands. She was dazed and holding a bleeding and badly broken nose. Blood was dripping through her closed fingers and she was dazed and groaning. There was a small cut above her left brow where she too had taken a header against the co-pilot's seat.

"Hey! You okay?" Adler said, tapping her forearm to get his attention.

Orlov turned and looked at him, but hadn't responded.

Besides the broken nose and a small cut over her right brow, she showed few outward signs of anything more serious.

"What?" she said, staring at him very much stunned and confused.

"Can you move?"

"I...I think so," she said, finding some focus, "a little woozy."

She looked a mess, but she wasn't whining.

"Woozy's good," replied Adler and then to the Senator's son said, "Zack? Can you help her out of here? I'll see to your Dad."

"Yes...yes, sir."

"The Senator!" she cried when she got her first real look at Russell, which was another reason why Adler wanted her out of the wreckage.

"I'm on it," Adler replied. "Help's on the way," he added, trying to reassure her, the others, and maybe even himself.

"Right now I need you and everyone else who can move to get clear of the aircraft. It's leaking fuel. It could go up at any second."

She hesitated. She was reluctant to go, but Adler was adamant.

"Go! I need you to move outside to a safe distance," he said, and to the boy added, "Zack? Give her a hand."

The boy helped Orlov out of the tangled wreckage and led her several yards away from the crash site. However, once they were clear of the wreckage, they both slowly began to make their way back to the dark and battered cargo bay.

"How can I help?" said the Senator's son, uncertain what he should do and looking to the Special Forces Captain for guidance.

"I need you all to set up a perimeter," Adler said, over his shoulder.

"Perimeter?" echoed the boy, hesitantly. "But..."

"It's okay, Zack," said the Senator in a surprisingly calm tone, given the ugly nature of his wound. "Listen to the Captain. Go and help keep watch out there."

"But my father..."

"Will be fine," said the Senator, trying to reassure his son. "Help Stephanie and any of the others who're injured. Can you do that for me?"

The Senator glanced towards the pilot and co-pilot as his son nodded.

"Yes, sir."

From where he was pinned in his seat, the Senator couldn't see the lifeless expression on the dead pilot's face. As the helicopter tumbled into the trees the nose of the aircraft had been violently shoved into the right side of the cockpit.

The instrument panel had crushed Corsi's ribcage and chest. His flight helmet was hanging at an unnatural angle and when Adler reached inside to try to find a pulse in the Aircraft Commander's neck, it wasn't there.

Mister Kehr, the co-pilot had fared better. His right boot was trapped inside a bent rudder pedal, and he was struggling to free himself. The instrument panel was hissing. A thin line of smoke was coming through the face of a broken switch and there was the smell of plastic wiring melting. He needed to get out of the helicopter. They all did.

Just before the helicopter hit the treetops Kehr had crossed his arms in front of his face and lowered his head. The arms and his flight helmet bore the brunt of the damage. Small tears in the arms of his Nomex flight suit were blotched with blood, but luckily nothing significant. Any sense of relief or joy he had of surviving the crash, though, quickly faded as he caught sight of Mister Corsi.

"Oh Christ, Mike! Sweet Jesus. No, no, no," he cried, finally kicking away the bent metal and wrenching his boots free as he, too, reached for the pilot only to realize what Adler had already figured out. The co-pilot turned to the Special Forces Captain in disbelief and sorrow.

"He's gone, Mister Kehr," said Adler, and when Kehr didn't respond, he said it again. "He's gone but how about you? Can you move? Are you okay?"

"I...yes. Wrenched my ankle. Bad sprain, but I don't think it's broken. I'm okay."

"Good," he said, "I need you to climb out and help the others set up a perimeter around the crash site."

The odor of the leaking JP-4 jet fuel had permeated the cargo bay, and the small wisp of smoke rising out of the badly damaged instrument panel, along with the occasional sputtering sparks, only gave the order more urgency.

"Get it done."

"Yes...yes, sir," said the reluctant co-pilot, as he climbed out of the damaged helicopter door, steadied himself, and then reached back inside to retrieve a short, stubby looking weapon.

Adler was surprised to see that it was a M-3 Grease gun. The short-barreled sub-machine gun was a Tanker's weapon that got its nickname because it resembled an auto mechanic's tool. It was heavy, had limited range, but it held a 30-round magazine that fired .45 caliber rounds that could knock down a brick wall, if the shooter could manage to keep it from rising as it fired.

Mister Kehr had carried it with him on every flight in the event the helicopter went down. He had it because he didn't want to be on the ground in the jungle with nothing more than his Survival vest and a standard issue, six shot, Smith and Wesson model-10 .38 caliber pistol. Another reason he had the M-3 was because it gave him a swaggering look slung over his shoulder to and from the aircraft. It was also something he secretly hoped he'd never have to use in close ground combat. Any swagger gone as he limped away.

"Tim? Petey?" he said, limping as he called out for the crew chief and door gunner, hoping to find them still alive.

"The crew chief's dead," Adler said to the co-pilot and before he could say anything more a voice called out behind the injured Major.

"Out here, Mister Kehr," came the voice of the second crewman.

Other than some small scratches and a mud-stained, disheveled Nomex flight suit that sported a few leaves and twigs, Petersen, the door gunner, also appeared not much worse for the ordeal.

He had somehow survived after being thrown out of the aircraft well above the ground as it bounced down through the trees. He was lucky, something that became abundantly clear as he made his way to the side of the wreckage and peered inside.

"I'm okay," he said, coming to a startled halt. "I..."

The door gunner's mouth made a stunned and silent 'O' as his eyes went from the dead pilot to the Senator who'd been speared to the back of the cabin, and then to the dead crew chief.

It was Adler who drew him out of the quiet revulsion.

"Son, I need you to find your machinegun and as much ammo as you can retrieve," he said to the rattled door gunner.

"S...Sir?"

"We need to set up a working perimeter. Let's get it done."

Petersen nodded, turned back to the jungle, and went searching for one of the helicopter's two missing machine guns. Meanwhile, the

Major was still seated in the dirt and mud, holding his broken arm, and loudly blubbering.

"Major, you need to get it together and calm the fuck down!"

Haverly stared at the Special Forces Officer with a mix of shock, hurt, and anger. He started to say something, but Adler spoke again.

"It's broken, for Christ's sake. You're not going to fucking die," he said, reaching into his left pant leg pocket and pulling out a small cardboard box the size of a pack of cigarettes that he tossed to the sniveling Major.

"Here! There's a cloth sling inside you can use to hold it in place. When you're done, find a weapon."

"I'm..."

"Find a weapon. Do it!"

The rear area staff officer, who was sorely out of his element, gave a brusque and bitter nod.

"What about you, Captain? You need to get clear of this mess as well?" said the Senator in a disturbingly normal tone.

"I will, sir," he said. "Later."

The Senator stared into the face of the Captain realizing what the *later* implied, and all that was left unsaid. Russell was a realist. He had a five-inch round tree branch sticking through him, he was trapped inside a mangled helicopter that was leaking fuel, and he could hear electrical sputtering from the damaged instrument panel.

"Please get my son to safety," he said to Adler, his eyes pleading the case. "I need you to do that for me."

Adler wasn't all that certain if any of them would get to safety and skirted the question. "A Quick Reaction Force is on its way, so we'll all be out of here soon. Until then, let's see if we can make you a little more comfortable. Can you move your arms and legs?"

The Senator tried, only his feet and legs never budged in the attempt. There was no movement in his arms either. He could move his neck, but just barely.

Needing to get a better look at the extent of the Senator's wounds, Adler slowly leaned over to check the exit wound and balked at what he saw.

The splintered tree limb had plunged through Russell like a giant javelin. It was shoved through his lower abdomen and groin and tore out bits of bone and splintered shards from his spinal column before it came out jaggedly through his left hip and back.

No wonder he couldn't feel his legs or arms, thought Adler. It was a wonder that he could even speak, let alone breathe! To add to matters, the Senator's bowels had vacated. The stench of his emptied bowels was lessened to by the falling rain, and all but overpowered by the more ominous odor of the leaking jet fuel.

"Some mess, huh?" apologized the Senator getting a whiff of himself.

Adler shrugged as he tried to hide some of Russell's embarrassment.

"I think I might've pissed myself a little too," he said. "You, at least, have a better excuse. Don't worry, we'll get you out of here."

It was another hopeful, optimistic response that he didn't quite believe, but said anyway. Words had medicinal value even when they were only placebos.

The truth was there wasn't a whole hell of lot he could do for the Senator. It would take a chainsaw, a pry bar, and a damned good doctor or medic to free him, and they didn't have the tools or medical help to even make an attempt.

"The Cavalry's on the way," he said, still wanting to believe it himself only this time maybe his voice didn't convey the certainty of his words. "Help's coming."

Chapter 14

The Senator's wound was horrific, but terrible as it was, there wasn't much blood seeping from either the entry or exit points. The circumference pressure from the splintered tree limb had temporarily sealed the wound, holding in the bulk of the blood and whatever else that was ripped, severed, and torn inside by the giant spike.

Adler had seen something similar to it once before, back in the Central Highlands, during his first tour of duty, working with the 'Yards.'

While he and most of his Special Forces Advisory team were working on shoring up the team bunker in their camp his medic and several others from the team were conducting a MEDCAP mission in the nearby village.

The SF medic was inoculating the Montagnard children against measles, mumps, and rubella while those accompanying him and the local villagers, were providing security.

Adler's group had almost finished filling and stacking sandbags when gunfire erupted in the distance and a frantic radio call came in that the Viet Cong were attacking the MEDCAP team. Rifle in hand, Adler led a Quick Reaction Force to the beleaguered village. It was an all-out race and they joined the fight on the run.

With the addition of Adler and his people bringing additional firepower to the fight, the Viet Cong began their retreat. The VC had lost ten dead and were seen dragging away two more of their wounded.

Seven villagers had died in the attack. Three women who were weaving mats were gunned down, as was a pregnant woman and her two-year-old toddler who were walking nearby.

Two scrappy Montagnard fighters were shot when they charged the intruders with only machetes. The machete-wielding Montagnards bought enough time for the rest of the MEDCAP Team and other Montagnards fighters to join the fight. The defenders were soon greeted with RPG fire from the enemy attackers in the vicious give and take.

Adler's Team medic was temporarily blinded in the fight when one of the exploding Rocket Propelled Grenades sent hot metal splinters and rock fragments into his face and eyes.

The medic wasn't the only one wounded by the RPGs. A 66-year-old man, who'd served in the village militia, had also been seriously wounded. The old man had been hit with an RPG round that had speared his body, drove him to the ground, but had failed to detonate.

The nearly three-foot long armed missile that hadn't exploded and hadn't activated the four-second self-destruct fuse was instead thrust into the man's lower back and lodged in his ribcage. The coned-shaped warhead of the missile was pushing out the front of his chest. There was little bleeding then, too.

The trouble was, the team medic was in no shape to treat the man, and no one else immediately wanted to step in to try to help, in case the Rocket Propelled Grenade round finally did explode. While the deciding minds were locked in discussion about how best to proceed, it was the village headman who decided to act.

Calmly walking over to the old man who was sitting up and moaning, the headman squatted, and whispered something to the wounded man.

The injured man nodded. Then, in a slow and steady motion, and with an audible sucking sound, the village headman began pulling the deadly projectile out of the old man's chest. It was a painful process and when the three-foot long missile was finally pulled free, the headman gently set it aside. Before he turned back to treat the old man's wounds, the man went into a series of violent convulsions and bled out in a flood of gushing blood.

Later, when Adler was waiting for the Medevac helicopter to arrive to take out the team's wounded medic and several injured villagers, Adler told him what the village headman had done.

"He probably would've been better off it the projectile had been left in place," said the blind medic.

"What? You saying the RPG round could've been removed in surgery?"

"No," said the medic. "They never would've allowed the old man into the hospital, let alone on the evacuation helicopter. The hard truth is they most likely would've left him to die..."

"Seriously?"

"Uh-huh, with it still in him," he said, "EOD would've removed it, afterwards."

"Yeah, but he still would've died if they left it where it was."

"True, but less painfully, I'm sure. Did anyone give the old man morphine?"

"I don't think so."

"Jesus, then definitely less painful, if they left it in him," said the medic. "If you ever see something like that again, give him some damn morphine, tell everyone to stand clear, and leave it alone."

There was no risk that the splintered tree limb that had gutted the Senator would explode, but removing it would certainly produce the same dismal outcome. He'd be just as dead as the old Montagnard.

"Try not to move. Help's on the way. We'll get you safely out of here," Adler said, again to Senator Russell, only to have his face giveaway another possible truth.

At that the Senator did the last thing the veteran Special Forces soldier expected, he laughed.

"I've been in Congress long enough to recognize bullshit when it's in session," he said, "I'm dying and we both know it."

Adler started to say something when the Senator's Chief of Staff, who was standing just outside of the wreckage, interrupted him.

"Is there anything I can do to help?"

Her nose had stopped bleeding and while she'd tried to wipe away most of the blood there were small streaks mixed with rain dripping down the right side of her chin and neck. Her eyes weren't swollen shut, but it was close. They had narrowed from the swelling. Not sure what she could do to help, she still wanted to do something useful.

"Ma'am, I need you to get clear of the aircraft. But, if you'd really like to help, I need to know if you can handle a weapon?"

"What?"

"A rifle or pistol? If I give you one will you know how to use it?"

Orlov nodded and the Senator chuckled, again.

"Go ahead, tell him," Russell said to the woman prompting her for the punch line while offering Adler a clue. "Her father was a Marine."

Orlov nodded and said, "That's what? A seven round, 1911, .45 caliber, Colt semi-automatic sidearm, probably with an eighth round chambered in the holster on your hip?"

Adler smiled. "It is indeed. Here you go, and *Semper fi*," he said, handing the woman the handgun.

"Where do you want me?"

"I need you to stand guard over there," he added, pointing to several large trees just south of the crash site. The trees offered both cover from the rain and ground cover in case of an attack. "Find some cover and take a knee in case we get any uninvited guests."

"Guests?"

"Yeah, enemy soldiers; North Vietnamese Soldiers or Viet Cong that operate in the vicinity and who might've seen, or heard the helicopter go down. I doubt it in this weather, but let's not take any chances."

To the Major he said, "Haverly?" and when the distressed-looking officer turned to him he added, "Hey, Major? How are you doing?"

"How in the hell do you think I'm doing?"

"Better than some, so I'd appreciate it if you find some cover as well."

The Major, who was adjusting the cloth sling to his arm shot the Captain a scowl, but managed to keep what he was thinking to himself.

"Take the north side," he said, pointing in the direction he wanted Orlov to go. "Find a place to try to keep out of the rain, take a knee, and find some concealment."

"Concealment?"

"Yeah, hide. Just in case."

The *just in case* didn't need to be explained.

"You said, help's on the way?" Orlov asked, turning back to Adler.

He nodded and immediately wished he hadn't. The small head move sparked the damaged nerves again. His eyes slammed shut in the blinding pain as he tried to steady himself and get through it.

"You okay?"

Adler shrugged. "The May Day call went out," he said, not knowing if it was true or not, but giving both she and the trapped Senator some verbal comfort. "Someone must have heard it."

That, too, might've been another lie.

If there were enemy soldiers nearby, then they might've heard the crash and were already moving towards them, but Adler was hoping that the heavy Monsoon storm had hidden, or at least disguised the noise from both the helicopter and the crash. For the time being they were still in the proverbial game, and it was in the early innings.

To the badly limping co-pilot he said, "Is there a First Aid kit in this thing?"

"Yes, sir. There is...was. I'll find it."

"Any morphine?"

"Mike had the medics add a few Syrettes in case we ever went down."

"Find them," he said, giving a sidelong glance to the badly wounded Senator.

Mister Kehr began rooting through the damaged cockpit area searching for the 1st Aid kit, found it, and then came to an abrupt and troubling pause at the sight of his dead friend slumped in the pilot's seat.

It was the Captain who brought him back to the task at hand.

"Any luck with the morphine?"

"Yes, Yes, sir," said Kehr, retrieving the Syrettes and handing them to the Captain.

"Thanks," Adler said and turned back to the Senator.

"We'll have you feeling a little better in a minute. This should hold you over until help arrives," he said in a damn near convincing tone.

"You ever think about going into politics?" asked Russell in a chuckle that sounded like a wet cough. "You sound pretty convincing, even when you're lying."

"Sir?"

"We're what? A half hour out of the last base we were at? If help is actually coming in this lousy weather, which isn't likely given what happened to us, then I'll probably be dead before it shows up. Not certain how to respond, Adler kept his thoughts to himself before the Senator reiterated his earlier plea.

"All I ask is that you do your best to get my son and the others to safety, Captain," pleaded Russell. "I don't want them to die out here, too."

Adler told him he'd try everything within his power to make it happen. "We're getting you some morphine. Hang in there. I'll be right back," he added, and then oh so carefully moved to check on their thin and shaky perimeter. It was a slow go, but then, it needed to be.

Once outside of the wreckage, he surveyed the crash site and those who were supposed to be standing watch in their makeshift perimeter. The door gunner, Orlov, Haverly, and the Senator's son, were standing in a poor definition of what it took to adequately guard the site. Mostly, he suspected because they were a little uncertain how to go about it.

Just as troubling, they were all still way too close to the helicopter for safety. Rain or no rain, if the highly flammable helicopter jet fuel went up, which was a distinct possibility, given the sputtering instrument panel, then they'd all be caught up in an explosive inferno.

The rain was still falling, but the overhead canopy had saved it from being a deluge. Those standing the closest to good-sized trees enjoyed a little extra cover. The worst of the storm seemed to have passed and the dark veil that accompanied the Monsoon storm had lifted.

The sun that was still hiding in the storm was going down would soon set and then the scene would become an exercise in shadows.

The one good thing Adler noticed was that Petersen, the much too young looking door gunner, had managed to find and retrieve one of two M-60 machine guns the Huey carried. The machine gun, that had been attached to a bungee cord anchored to the aircraft and had been ripped away on impact, still looked to be in good working order. It was a welcomed gift that would add firepower to the defense of their weak perimeter, if push came to enemy shove.

The second M-60 that the crew chief had manned, though, was bent in half and stuck under the bulk of what was left of the helicopter. Other than making a lousy paperweight, it would be of no practical use.

One M-60, though, was something, if it came to a fight, and young and skinny as Petersen was, he had a hundred rounds locked and loaded dangling from the feed tray ready to go.

He also had four hundred to five hundred belt-fed rounds wrapped like crisscrossed bandoliers over his shoulders and thin chest. Anyone who had caught a glimpse of him would have to agree that he looked like a painfully white and scrawny Poncho Villa.

"Any smoke grenades?" Adler asked the young soldier.

Door gunners generally carried a few smoke and fragmentation grenades with them stored beneath their seats in ammo boxes. The smoke and fragmentation grenades could play a critical role in any perimeter they had if the enemy suddenly showed up.

"No, sir. I couldn't find any. The box we had must've gotten flung out when we went down. I'll keep looking."

Adler started to nod, but caught himself, only not before the slight move he'd begun out of habit, pinched a few of the damaged nerves or whatever the hell it was that he'd injured. The blinding and radiating pain was followed by numbness in his arms and hands.

"Never mind for now. It's going to get dark soon, well, darker, anyway," said Adler. "We'll search at first light. You just take that 60 and use it to cover the crash site out in front of the nose of your bird."

"Yes, sir."

"Specialist Petersen, right?"

"Yes, sir."

"How long you been in-country, soldier?" Adler said, trying to take his mind off the pain. He was clenching and unclenching his hands to get them to find function again.

"Five months, sir. You, Captain?"

"Forty-one, so far."

"Damn, sir! You looking to vote in their next election or something?"

"Something," he said, rubbing the back of his neck and wincing as he did.

"You okay, sir?" said the door gunner watching on.

"Okay leaves a lot to interpretation," Adler said. He took in a deep breath as the numbness and pain subsided. There would be no more craning his neck, or twisting his torso without additional pain or worse, paralyzing damage.

He kept telling himself that when he turned, he needed to shift his whole body while doing it, and slowly too, but well understood that telling himself to do something, and actually doing it were two separate and very distinct things, especially when it came to everyday habitual gestures.

Because Petersen and the others in the VIP party were still too close to the wreckage if it suddenly went up in flames, he told them to move further away and spread out a little. When they hadn't moved far enough, he waved them further on.

"Further," he said. "And watch the jungle, not the helicopter."

He doubted they had ever seen a helicopter explode and burn from a fuel leak. If they'd had, then they certainly would've moved further away without having to be told.

When they still hadn't moved far enough away for his liking, Adler used hand gestures to keep them moving. "More!" he said. "Keep going. Okay...okay...now stop. All right, now keep your eyes and ears open for any unnatural noise or sign of movement in front of you."

Mister Kehr, the surviving pilot, had found the 1st Aid kit and came back to Adler with several Syrettes of morphine in his hands. The two small injection packets looked like mini-toothpaste tubes with attached needles.

"Good-to-go, Captain," he said, handing them over. "Also, retrieved these."

He was holding Mister Corsi's pistol and an M-1 carbine that the Aircraft Commander kept on board the helicopter.

"Thought we might need these," he said.

"Good call," said Adler. "Give the carbine to the Major and the pistol to the kid."

"Roger that."

Kehr started to turn to go when Adler grabbed him by the elbow. In a low voice, he said, "Did you get a response on the May Day call before we went down?"

Understanding the implication of exactly what the Captain was asking, the twenty-year-old Warrant Officer glanced at the others to make sure they couldn't him before he spoke.

"No, sir," he said, in a low voice, warily eyeing the others and feeling guilty as he did. "I don't know if anyone heard it."

"Then, what say we keep that to ourselves for now? Once MAC-V realizes they've lost a serious VIP, they'll have everybody and his brother out searching for him, and the rest of us in the process. Make no mistake, the Cavalry is coming."

"Yes, sir."

"Until help arrives we need to keep a good perimeter. I'll stay with the Senator, so I'll need you to take charge out there."

"What about the Major?"

"He's, eh...injured. Broken arm, so give him the pistol and the carbine to the Senator's son. The kid is in military school, so he probably knows how to use it. If not, then give him a quick point-and-shoot lesson."

"Roger that," said the Warrant Officer, hobbling off.

Once the weapons were handed out and a semi-working perimeter was in place, the Captain slowly and carefully worked his way back into the wreckage and back to the Senator's side.

"This should help some," he said, rolling up the left sleeve of the Senator's jungle fatigues and plunging the small needle of the morphine Syrette into his arm and then squeezing out its contents from the tube.

The effect was instantaneous. Relief washed over Russell's face in a warm, soothing breaking wave. His grimace was replaced with a surprisingly placid expression that bordered on tranquility.

"Help's on the way, you said?"

Adler started to nod one more time, but stopped himself in time. Old habits died hard, and if he needlessly kept nodding or twisting his body to see who was doing the talking or needed his attention then he might need the second shot of morphine.

"Yes, sir," he said only the Senator wasn't convinced.

"Just get my son and the others out of here and safely back. Again, that's all I ask."

Adler said he would, with a host of uncertainties hidden behind his reply.

Thanks to the morphine the Senator's pain had diminished enough to make him feel somewhat comfortable, or as comfortable as the drug allowed with all things considered.

"I need you to try to remain as still as possible," he said, ignoring the Senator's obvious paralysis while trying to offer him a little bit of hope.

"Not to worry," Senator Russell said with a drug-induced smile as his eyes went to the heavy wooden spike that had impaled him and he managed a pun. "I'll stick around."

He chuckled, as did Adler, who was thinking God bless morphine.

Christ! I hope I'd have his composure if something like this ever happened to me and I hope to God it never does.

"You hang in there," said the Captain, patting the Senator's shoulder. "Help's on the way, sir. I need to see how the others are doing. I'll be right back."

Climbing out of the wreckage in a crouching squat took a little more doing. There was more tingling. This time, though, it was his legs that were growing numb and when he tried to stand up straight for a look-see he had to steady himself against the damaged helicopter.

"God damn it," he said, partially because of what was happening to his body, but also because while the others were down behind trees or on one knee watching the stretches of jungle in front of them, Major Haverly was still standing in the open, facing the wrecked helicopter, cradling his broken arm, and looking pitiful. He wasn't bothering to help safeguard their makeshift perimeter as he had been told to do.

The only thing worse than a soldier sleeping on guard duty in combat was one who wasn't paying attention to his combat surroundings. The crash site perimeter was basically little more than being on jungle Red Alert. Haverly's injury wasn't life threatening, but his inability to cover the sector of the jungle he'd been assigned, especially after he'd been told what to do, was.

Adler suspected that yelling at him wouldn't do much good, so instead, he turned his whole body back around to have the co-pilot to babysit the arrogant sonofabitch to get him to better cover that sector when Haverly let out a terrified scream behind him.

The frightened cry that had Adler and the others quickly turning to see what was the matter, found the terrified PAO-Liaison Officer trying to bring up the small handgun to fire only to have Mister Kehr violently shove it back down as a frightening looking apparition with upraised hands stepped out of the shadows and into their imagined secure perimeter.

"Don't shoot!" said the apparition. "We're friendlies! Everybody stay calm. Friendlies coming in! Don't shoot!"

Chapter 15

"Oh, thank God!" cried the much-relieved Major, believing that help had finally arrived.

Haverly wasn't alone in that reasoning. The initial surprise and fright showing on the faces of the crash survivors as the camouflaged face-painted, armed intruder stepped out of the jungle, gave way to nervous smiles and palpable relief by his upraised hands and surprisingly calm demeanor.

A second, just as frightening looking, but somewhat confused soldier, followed him out of the jungle, with a third and a fourth trailing moments later. After a quick survey of the crash site, a fifth soldier, turned and took a knee facing back the way they had come.

The Major's surprise was matched by an equally shocked and surprised co-pilot and door gunner that hadn't heard or seen any of the new arrivals either until the one in the lead stepped out into the crash site and announced himself.

Both still had their fingers on the triggers of their weapons and barely held their fire. Their adrenaline was racing, but then so were their spirits at the thought of being rescued.

Adler, on the other hand, wasn't so sure it was a QRF rescue team. QRF teams didn't generally wear camo face paint or camouflaged uniforms that were stripped of rank or unit patches. Their bandaged wounds, too, spoke volumes.

"I need to speak to your officer in charge," Haverly said, confronting the soldier with the upraised arms who appeared to be their leader. "Where is he?"

"My Officer-in-Charge?"

"Yes."

"Back at Camp Mackie, sir."

"Camp Mackie?"

"Yes, sir, but I'm the Team Leader."

"You? You're in charge of the QRF?"

It was preposterous to the Major that this important rescue mission would be given to a Second Lieutenant as young as this.

"Sir?"

"We need to get to the rescue helicopter, Lieutenant? Which way to the landing zone?"

"It's Sergeant, sir. I'm not an officer. There's no landing zone, but I've located a possible PZ..."

"A what?"

"A PZ, a pickup zone. It's not big enough for a helicopter to touch down, but it might offer a way out by rope. We were heading there before we ran into you."

The now confused Major kept turning to and from Adler and the five soldiers like a worried metronome.

"Well then, Sergeant, we need to get going. Take us to it. NOW!"

"Sir?" Carey said, more than a little confused at what the officer with his broken arm in a sling was suggesting.

"You have a team medic or Aid Bag?" asked Captain Adler, stepping in and interrupting Haverly. The Major started to protest but the Captain commandeered the conversation.

"Both, sir."

"Good..."

"Where are the rescue helicopters?"

"Wait one, Major," he said to Haverly, who wasn't happy about being interrupted. Adler, though, didn't give a hoot whether he was happy or not.

To the face-painted Lurp team leader, he said again, "I need your medic now."

"Yes, sir," said the Team Leader.

"We have a critically injured man pinned inside the helicopter who needs some immediate assistance."

"I don't understand. Where...where are the others?" blurted Haverly, still not comprehending who these Lurps were, if they weren't part of a rescue force.

"We're all here, sir."

"But there's only five of you!"

"They're not a QRF," said Adler.

"No, sir, we're Lurp team Nine-One."

"Lurp what?"

"Not now, Haverly!" Adler said brushing the Major aside. "Your medic?"

"Doc?" Carey said over his shoulder to one of his people. "You're up."

Carey then called over Thomas.

"Darrell, head back the way we came, maybe 20-yards out, and keep a good lookout. Take the new guy..."

"Bowman," said Bowman, the new guy.

Carey nodded, "Yeah. I know." To Thomas he added, "Take the new guy with you."

The A-T-L and a now smirking Bowman, moved swiftly into the heavy brush. They were silent as they went and soon disappeared with little more than a minor rustling of brush.

With the medic following, the Special Forces Officer led him to the wreckage and pointed out an older, gray haired man inside the darkened crumpled cargo bay. The man appeared to be sleeping upright.

The medic climbed inside the helicopter dragging his aid bag behind him. As his eyes adjusted to the thin light, Doc Moore saw the problem and reared back. The man wasn't sleeping. His head was slumped down and facing the long pike that had impaled him where he sat.

"He's..."

"Yeah, he's injured," said the Captain looking on. "He needs a good medic."

To the Lurp Team Leader standing beside him, he said, "You're a Staff Sergeant, I take it?"

"Buck Sergeant Ben Carey, sir," he said. "R Company- Ranger."

"Do you have team radio, Sergeant Carey?"

"Had sir, it was damaged. But that's not our immediate problem, Captain."

"Say again?"

Carey explained the situation to Adler; the NVA Battalion they encountered, the loss of radio contact, and that they had done an E and E when they were compromised.

"We're being tracked, or were until we set am ambush. It's possible we're still being followed."

"Followed?" said the Major, listening in.

"Yes, sir, we blew a hasty ambush on an NVA team that was tracking us."

"How long ago?" said Adler, taking back control of the conversation and questioning.

"A good while out. No more than two hours ago, Claymores stopped a few and slowed down some others, not sure if they gave up the chase."

His tone suggested they hadn't, something that Adler picked up on it. From bad to worse was seldom a long journey in combat.

"The larger main body of the NVA appears to be heading in the direction of Fire Support Base Rachel."

"You sure of the count?"

Carey nodded. "Yes sir, and we called it in before we had to Di-Di-mau from our hide site."

"Which means they'll probably hit the Fire Support Base at first light."

"Yes, sir. That's my best guess as well, minus the ones that were tracking us."

"My God! You mean you led the enemy right to us?" cried Major Haverly in a barely controlled panic.

"At ease, Major!" said Adler.

"We...we need to get out of here!"

"What we need is for you to back away from here and get back to help guarding our flimsy perimeter until help arrives for the Senator. And how about you keeping a better watch this time?"

Haverly was grumbling as he trudged back over to where he'd been standing and should have been on guard.

"He has two people out in front of you so don't shoot them!"

"Senator?" said Sergeant Carey to the Captain. Doc Moore had heard it, too, as his eyes went from the Captain to injured older man and then back to the Captain.

"And right now just someone who needs your help. He needs you, Doc."

"Yes, sir," said the medic, taking in a deep breath as he dried his face and hands as best he could, opened his aid bag, and grabbed at tape and gauze bandages.

"There's a fuel leak," he said, when he got a whiff of the ruptured fuel tank. There was no mistaking the more immediate odor or threat, let alone his worried tone.

"There is," said the Captain.

"Then we need to get him out of here, as soon as possible."

"Agreed," said Adler, not sure how soon the *possible* was in terms of an actual timeline. "I just wasn't sure about the best way to do that. I'm hoping you'll give me a few workable options."

"Just the one shot of morphine?" Moore asked, staring at the empty Syrette tube pinned to the man's collar.

Adler nodded. "It seemed to help," he said. The medic turned back to the Senator.

"Sir? Sir?" Doc Moore said, nudging the injured man's hand and when that didn't produce a response he moved closer to his face.

"Sir?" he said, again.

This time Russell lifted his head, opened his eyes, and gave a half smile.

"You the doctor?"

"Combat medic, sir. How you feeling?"

"Been better," said the Senator, offering the second half of the smile.

"Yes, sir, I imagine so. Can you move your legs and arms for me?"

Russell took in a short breath, slowly blew out the air between his teeth, and tried to do what the medic requested.

Nothing moved. There was slight movement in his neck and head, but that was the best the Senator could do.

"I'm afraid that's it," he said.

The paralysis told the medic that, in addition to the severe internal injuries, there was possible significant spinal damage. Grabbing a small flashlight from his top right pocket, Doc Moore switched it on and used the light to check the exit wound.

The beam of light glistened over the shards of splintered and broken bone from the Senator's lower back confirming the spinal damage, and the thick tree limb that had speared and pinned him to the helicopter's back wall.

Moore then checked Russell's eyes, ears, and head before he began searching for additional injuries or wounds. He didn't want to concentrate on treating the wound he could see and miss another troubling one he missed because he hadn't bothered to check for it. Fortunately, thought Moore, there aren't any additional wounds and then wondered if a word like *fortunate* even applied in this instance.

"Any sharp pain when you breathe?"

"Some pressure in my throat, but to be honest, I can't feel much. The morphine's working for the moment."

Doc Moore nodded. "Good," he said. "Let me know if that changes."

"Trust me, son. I will."

The splintered tree limb that had speared and trapped the Senator limited the medic's treatment options.

The tense looking medic studied the predicament from several angles and then turned and gave a frustrated look to the Special Forces Captain and the Lurp Team Leader who were watching him work. The facial expression said it all.

The physical damage wasn't pretty and while he had treated everything from combat wounds to the clap, this was something frighteningly new to him. He doubted the Senator would survive, but kept the thought to himself.

"Would it be safe to move him, I mean, if we can cut the branch free?" asked the Captain.

"Sir?"

"We're running out of time and options," Adler said. "If we cut the tree limb from the back wall and leave what's inside of him in place, will it be okay to move him?"

The medic considered the question. "Maybe," he said, warily. "But it's also possible it might cause even more damage."

"I'm worried about the leaking fuel."

"Yes, sir. Me too."

It was Senator Russell who ended the debate.

"Cut the damn thing," he said, taking charge of the plan. "That'd be better than all of us being burned alive because you didn't want to leave me here. Do it."

The decision was made.

"You heard the Senator. Let's get it done," said Adler. Over his shoulder he said to the Ranger Team Leader who'd been leaning in the cargo bay, watching on, "You have a machete?"

"No, sir," replied Carey, "but I have this."

His *this* was a larger and better version of the fixed-blade survival knife the pilots carried on their survival vests. Carey's knife had a deadly eight-inch blade that was razor sharp from its point down to its heel. Better yet, the spine of the knife had a deep, serrated edge that was practical for sawing.

"Good, then we're in business," Adler said. The knife wouldn't have been his best choice, but you make do with what you have. Adapt and overcome. To the medic he added, "I'll cut. You let me know if I need to stop."

Doc Moore nodded.

As the Captain shifted from where he was crouched to find a better working angle he reared back in staggering pain.

Doc Moore couldn't see the Captain's face, but Carey could. The Lurp Team Leader quickly moved in, lent Adler a steady hand, and offered another suggestion.

"If it's all right with you, Captain, what say I do the cutting?"

Adler gave a reluctant *yes,* greatly appreciating the offer. His hands and arms were tingling and quickly going numb, again. He was losing the dexterity in his hands.

"That might be best," Adler said. "Go ahead, Sergeant."

When Adler handed him back the knife Carey scooted in and took over. Holding the tree limb steady with one hand, he carefully began sawing through the thick limb with the serrated edge of the knife with the other.

"Doc? Can you give me some light here?"

"Can do," said the medic, using the flashlight shine some light on where it was needed.

In the cramped and confined space there wasn't much room to work with, nor was there room for error. With the built-up fumes from the leaking jet fuel, Carey was careful not to have the metal blade scrape up against any other piece of exposed metal. Even with the rain, one spark and the helicopter might erupt into a fireball; something Carey kept in the forefront of his thoughts as he continued sawing in a slow and steady rhythm.

The sawing took some doing, the serrated blade slowly and methodically making progress through the tree limb. He was about halfway through the thick spear when the blade caught in the green, wet wood.

It was stuck and when Carey tried to work it free by twisting the knife blade, the reverberations brought on a gurgled groan from the Senator. The spike in him was shifting.

"Stop!" cried Doc Moore and Carey did.

"I'm almost there," Carey said, by way of an apology as he freed the blade. "Doc, is there anything you can do for him?"

There was a small amount of blood trickling down his mouth to his chin. Moore wiped it away.

The Senator, who they thought was paralyzed from the chest down, apparently wasn't. Not all of the nerves to his upper body had been severed. His face was pinched in pain.

"Sir," the medic said to the Senator. "How about I give you another shot of morphine to take away that edge?"

"That...that would be much appreciated," replied the Senator. "I may not be able to feel much in my arms and legs, but everything behind my eyes is screaming."

The medic dug into his Aid bag and found the morphine syrettes he carried for the team. Unbuttoning the two top buttons of the Senator's jungle fatigue shirt, he peeled back the shirt from Russell's left shoulder, and stuck the small tube-like syringe and squeezed out its contents into the Senator's right arm.

It took a long moment for the drug to take effect as it worked its way through Russell's system. It wasn't long before the Senator was smiling once more, his disposition calm within the confines of the morphine.

Checking the entry and exit wounds, Moore noticed a small trickle of blood seeping from around the base of the splintered tree limb. The sawing motion and twisting knife blade had loosened the surrounding pressure.

"Take it slow," he said, cautioning Carey as he reached back into his Aid bag to grab a roll of gauze.

"The more the tree limb moves," he said, "The more it risks a bleed out."

With the roll of gauze in hand the medic began stuffing the gauze in the bleeding edges of the wounds until the bleeding stopped, front and back.

"We're good," said Moore. "Keep sawing."

Carey gave a solemn nod, shifted his left knee beneath the tree limb he was cutting to better steady the spike, and gripped it tighter. The limb hadn't moved as he finished sawing through the wooden spear. As he made the last cut through the wood there was a slight, but decided give from where it had been trapped against the cargo bays back wall.

"Whoa! Whoa! Whoa! Hold up!" said Doc Moore, holding up an open hand to add weight to his words. Using his flashlight to get a better look behind the Senator, he turned back to the others and nodded. "We're good in back, too. It's okay."

Carey held the spear in place as he shoved the rest of the thick branch out of the side of the damaged aircraft.

The medic said, "If we can slowly scoot him forward, I think we can move him."

"Do it," said the Captain.

"I'll need you to ease him forward while I hold onto the branch in back to keep it from moving," Doc Moore said looking to his team leader. "Slowly."

"Got it," Carey said, taking in a deep breath, settling himself, and then taking the Senator by the hips and gradually began sliding him forward. The two worked in cautious unison until Russell was at the edge of the seat.

"We're good!" said Moore. "Now, we need a few more hands to make a seat when we move him out of the helicopter."

The last was aimed at the Captain who'd moved to just outside of the open cargo bay door.

"Can we get a hand here?" Adler said to one of the other Lurps standing guard.

"Jonas! New Guy!" called Carey to his team members who rushed over to assist.

"Where do you need us, Captain?" asked Warren.

"Here," Adler said. "Once we move him to the floor and over to the edge of the cargo bay doorway, I'll need you two to lock arms and make a seat for him to lift him out. From there we'll move him to wherever the medic think's best."

"We'll need to keep him stabilized," cautioned Doc Moore. "Follow my lead."

Heads nodded and when they were in place and ready, Doc Moore said to Russell, "Ready, Senator?"

"I'm dying to get out of here," said the injured VIP, chuckling. The second shot of morphine was working well.

Doc Moore looked to Sergeant Carey.

"On three," he said as they readied themselves.

The count began, and on three, the two lifted the Senator up from the edge of the bench seat and gently set him down on the cargo bay floor before easing him to where the others were waiting to help.

The Senator was lifted out and away from the wreckage and over to the base of a large tree. The tree that rose several hundred feet in the air and was six feet around had an exposed root system above the ground that fanned out like protective wings.

Doc Moore had picked out the tree for two obvious reasons. First, the overhead canopy made the base of the tree a little dryer than the surrounding ground, and secondly; the large exposed root system a foot or two above the ground wound allow the Senator to sit up in place without causing what was left of the spear inside him to shift or move.

After they set him down Doc Moore removed a small section of poncho liner and draped it over the VIP's head and shoulders to better shield him from what rain had worked its way down through the canopy cover above them.

As the others went back to their positions in the perimeter Adler called over the woman and the Major.

"Miss Orlov? Major? Doc, when you get a moment, can you check these two out? They were injured in the crash as well."

Moore nodded. Since the woman had taken a nasty header into the back of the co-pilot's seat when they crashed, the medic checked for a possible concussion. The broken nose would have to be reset later.

"We got you out of the helicopter, Senator," Major Haverly said to Russell, as he waited his turn with the medic. "Now we'll get you to a hospital." Turning to Adler he added, "We need to leave."

"We do, Major, but right now it's one thing at a time, so take a breath, and get it together."

"Excuse me?"

"I said, take a breath. Right now I need you to keep it together. We don't have any radio contact to the outside world, and it's possible nobody knows we even went down, or if they do, then they won't be able to put any aircraft in the air to search for us until this storm passes. It's letting up. It won't be long."

"But you heard what these people said. They have enemy soldiers chasing after them. We need to get out of here."

"Again, take a breath."

That proved to be too much for the angry, frustrated, and embarrassed Major. He'd had enough.

"AT EASE!" he cried, which was the Army's way of saying, *shut up.* "I'm getting a little tired of your condescending attitude, Captain. You seem to have forgotten who the ranking officer here is."

"No, I haven't forgotten," said Adler, directly challenging the higher-ranking officer. "Unless you have some sort of actual combat experience, or have served in a leadership position in the field, other than in a Public Affairs capacity, then I'm assuming tactical command here..."

"But..."

"No buts, Major. I'm in my element, and you're sorely out of yours. If you'll stop grumping and whining and start helping, that would very much be appreciated," Adler said, stepping to within inches of the senior officer to emphasize the point of the exchange. "Do you copy, sir?"

When he didn't get an answer from Haverly who was angrily staring at him, Tony Adler held the stare, and asked a second time.

"I said, *do you copy?*"

"I *copy* all right, Captain," the Major said, sarcastically emphasizing the command he'd been given. "And you better believe I'll deal with you later, Adler. Your career is over!"

Adler shrugged off the threat.

"What say you and I both worry about the later, later?" he said. "For the moment, for the here and now, we need to concentrate on the critical priorities here and now. Once the medic takes a look at your arm, I need you to move back and cover your part of the perimeter while the Ranger sergeant and I plan our next move. That is, unless you have a better tactical idea on how to get us the hell out of here?"

Haverly had nothing to say to that, and after Doc Moore had treated his broken arm and retied and readjusted the sling for a better fit, the brooding Major stomped back to where he'd been standing and once more pretended to be guarding the crash site's perimeter.

"He reminds me of my ex-husband," Stephanie Orlov, staring at the back of the Major as he walked away, only before he could ask how he reminded her of her Ex, she added, "He was an asshole, too. Anyway, just to let you know, I appreciate all you're doing for the Senator and the rest of us. I doubt I'm alone in that."

Adler managed a small smile.

"Much appreciated," he said. "We're all in this together."

"Some more so than others," she said, glancing back at the still grumbling Major.

"Oddly enough, he's actually good at what he does."

"I take it that this isn't it, though?"

Adler smiled and the smile slipped into a smirk.

"No, it isn't," he said, and then pointed to her bruised face. "How's the nose?"

"Sore. I feel like I stepped into the wrong ring and can't throw in the towel."

"You're doing fine," he said. "We've taken our hits, but we're still moving forward."

"One round at a time, huh?"

"And we don't let our guard down."

"Don't take this the wrong way but you seem to be handling all this surprisingly well, calm even. You don't even look afraid. How is that possible? How in the hell do you get used to this?"

Adler shrugged, with a brief sigh. "You don't," he said. "The fear comes later. Everything else is training, experience, and then more training, so that at times like this, you have a better working understanding of what needs to be done, and who's best able to do it."

"Like the old saying; Lead, follow, or get the hell out of the way?"

"Uh-huh, and no doubt it came about for good reason."

"Without sounding too much like a pain in the ass, what is the next plan?"

Adler shrugged. "We're still working that out," he said with a half smile.

Orlov nodded but looked like there was something more she wanted to ask.

"Something else on your mind, Ma'am?"

"There is," she said. "Is it okay if Zack spends a few more moments with his father? I'll take his place watching the jungle."

Adler locked eyes with the woman understanding what was being left unsaid. He glanced over at the teen that was guarding his section of their small perimeter while every so often sneaking worried looks back at his father. The kid had reason to worry about his Dad.

The addition of the five Rangers tightening up their security made it an easier decision for Adler to make.

"Sure, send him over."

"Thank you," Orlov said.

Adler scanned the dark sky as best he could through the small openings above the canopied treetops. The rain was easing up. A window to the stars had briefly opened through the clouds. "Even if the May Day call wasn't heard, help's on the way. The storm's moving on, so it won't be long before the sky's going to be filled with every kind of aircraft imaginable searching for our crash site," he said, giving her some hope and maybe bolstering a little of his own as well.

Orlov nodded, gave a hopeful smile, and then made her way over to where Zack Russell was standing.

Because of the Senator's political clout, Adler knew help would soon be coming, but then, one way or another, so would the enemy, before or after they attacked the Fire Support Base. The real question was, which of them would show up first?

With that in mind he quickly came up with a backup plan, something that would get all but two of them up and moving. Moving the Senator, though, was out of the question.

He was in a bad way and jostling him through the jungle would only make it worse. If he were to have a chance at all, Senator Russell would need to remain in place until a Medevac helicopter could come in for him.

That meant someone would need to remain with him at the crash site to watch over him, and since his own injuries had left him moving a little precariously, Tony Adler knew who that someone would be.

"Sergeant Carey?"

"Sir?" said the Ranger making his way back to the Captain.

The wind and rain were easing up, the Monsoon storm moving its fury elsewhere. Adler was about to glance up through the trees, caught himself, and rubbed his neck instead. The winds were no longer shaking the treetops, and the heavy downpour had eased to a much lighter shower.

"The storm's losing its punch," he said to the Lurp team leader.

"Yes, sir, it is," Carey said, taking a quick glance skyward, then lowered his gaze and wiped away what had dripped down through the trees.

"The wet brush should keep down the noise as you move."

"Sir?"

"I'll need you to lead the others out of here just prior to first light, Sergeant."

"Sir?"

"Even if those NVA trackers trailing your team have given up tracking you, then after the main body hits the Fire Support Base, those who survive will bombshell out in smaller groups before heading back across the border."

"Roger that, sir. I understand that's their usual SOP."

"Which means we're bound to be getting some company heading this way. Got your map?"

"Yes, sir."

Carey brought out the plastic covered map along with his red filtered flashlight. As the Captain unfolded the map and laid it out on the cargo bay of the helicopter, the Lurp Team Leader moved in closer and gave it some light.

"Okay, since you and your team were patrolling this sector, I take it you have a good idea where we are. Show me."

Sergeant Carey looked to the Captain and then to the map. Retrieving his compass, he shifted the map around to align it with the compass needle.

"Here," he said, after a brief moment and pointed to where he believed was their present location.

"All right, okay," said the Captain, studying the map and quietly looking for options.

It took a moment, but he found what he was looking for, figuring it would do. It would have to do.

He pointed to where they were on the map. "So, if this is approximately where we are," he said and then dragged his finger across the face of the map. "Then this is where you need to be."

Carey's eyes focused on the spot on the map the Captain was pointing to. He nodded.

"It's a good hike, but when you move these people to this location, you should be good."

The area the Captain pointed out was a large opening in the rain forest that looked like a par-5 hole on a shitty golf course. It must have been a few hundred yards long and just as wide, with another fifty yards of open space that doglegged to the left. The map face showed a lot of open ground with sparse woods and foliage. With so much open area the NVA couldn't, and wouldn't, go anywhere near it, at least, not after attacking the Fire Support Base. It presented too much of an easy target from the air.

"There's plenty of open ground there, which will make it easier for rescue aircraft to spot you from the sky, when you lay out a marker. If you find a place to hunker down inside the tree line you should be good."

"Yes, sir."

The site was five clicks, five thousand meters, and roughly three miles. An otherwise easy go of it for Rangers in flat, open ground, but through the rugged, inhospitable jungle, in enemy held territory, three miles might as well be thirty.

It was indeed a *'good hike,'* although *good* might not be the way Carey would've described it. Something more like *fucking difficult* came to mind. Still, the young NCO saw the Captain's reasoning.

They could hold up inside the tree line, drop an orange flash panel out in the open on the ground in a small depression, and maybe make an arrow with sticks pointing to their location.

Placed in a natural depression or one they'd dig out, both the orange flash panel and the makeshift arrow could easily be from the air, but wouldn't be noticeable from anyone on the ground.

There was just one problem that Sergeant Carey could see with the Captain's plan. "The Senator's in no shape to travel, sir," he said, airing it.

"No, he's not."

The Ranger team leader went quiet for a moment, as he quickly comprehended the rest.

"Just so you know, Captain," he said, "Rangers don't leave anyone behind."

Adler smiled. God bless this kid and the others for that kind of ballsy, courageous loyalty that told them they could always achieve the impossible, only this had nothing to do with courage or loyalty. It had to do with survival for the others. Practicality weighed over sentimentality, and you couldn't always save everyone.

"Which is why I may have to give you a Direct Order to get those survivors to safety."

Leaning in to the Lurp, he lowered his voice. "The move will kill the Senator, so that's a no-go. Like it or not, I need someone to lead everyone else out of here, and that's you. If anyone can get the job done, that's you and your people. Rangers lead the way, right?"

Carey didn't like it, but he'd carry out the order.

"Yes, sir."

"Good, however, I could use one those Claymore mines of yours, if you could spare it?"

Carey nodded. "New Guy?" he said to PFC Bowman.

"Yes, sergeant?"

"You still have the Claymore I asked you to carry?"

"Yes, sergeant."

"Good. Give it to the Captain."

The young Lurp pulled the anti-personnel mine, and its attachments in the olive drab carrying case from across his back, and handed it over to the officer.

"Thank you," said Adler and Bowman nodded.

To the Captain, Sergeant Carey said, "I have a few grenades for you, too, if you need them."

Each team member on Team Nine-One carried at least three fragmentation grenades in a canteen pouch on their web gear. When Carey handed several to the Captain, Tony Adler was happy to have them.

"You sure? Don't want to leave you short."

"No, sir, we're good," said Carey, shaking his head.

Adler checked his watch.

"I got 18:20."

Carey checked his watch, saw that it was running a few minutes slow, and then adjusted it to the Captain's time. "Check, 18:20," he said, locking in the minute hand.

"Get some rest. I want you ready to move them out by 0-500," said Adler. "That'll give you a good head start on anyone coming from Rachel. Until then, I want a good eye on a perimeter in case whoever was tracking you hasn't given up the search."

"Roger that, sir."

"As soon as you make contact with the QRF give them our location."

"No need, Captain. I'll lead them back."

Tony Adler chuckled.

"You ever consider re-enlisting?"

"Thinking on it, sir. Maybe go Airborne."

"Airborne?" said the surprised Captain. "I thought all you Rangers were jump qualified?"

"No, sir, the Ranger Company takes any and every volunteer who can make it through the in-country training and who they think will make a good Lurp."

Adler shook his head and chuckled.

"Well then, after doing what you do over here in the jungle, leaping out of a perfectly good airplane with a parachute the government purchased from the lowest bidder won't seem all that scary."

"Yes, sir, which is also why I'm thinking about getting out of the Army and going to College."

Chapter 16

The heavy storm had stalled over the province and lingered well into the early morning hours. Shortly after 0-400 hours when the weather had finally cleared, the bank of radios in the Romeo Company TOC came alive with call signs and activity.

"Sir!" Sergeant Cantu said over his shoulder to Captain Robison noting the unusual activity over the airwaves. "Helicopters and fixed winged aircraft all across III Corps seem to be scrambling to get airborne."

"Outstanding!" said the Captain. To Poplawski he said, "Looks like someone, somewhere, finally believed Nine-One's sighting about the NVA moving on the Fire Support Base."

"The team's last known location was here," Poplawski said more to himself than the Captain as he thumped his right index finger at a grid square on the TOC's wall map.

Robison eye's followed his First Sergeant's lead as he too studied the map with renewed intensity. The team's radio contact was lost, but if the team leader had held to his E&E plan that had been relayed to the mountain relay station by Morse Code, then barring capture or worse, he'd still be moving his people east, but where?

"What was the direction of movement for the NVA?" Robison said to Sergeant Cantu, who checked his logbook notes.

"West from their last known, sir."

Robison nodded. "Which means they probably crossed the border here or here," he said, pointing to the sites on the wall map while the First Sergeant nodded in agreement.

"And which is too close to the secondary extraction site, so Sergeant Carey wouldn't head in that direction."

"No."

Both he and the First Sergeant were trying to figure the Team Leader's plan of action. The grid squares on the map made for a strategic chessboard, and Carey and his team members weren't pawns.

"And since the primary extraction site was the Fire Support Base..."

"That's about to be hit..."

"Then he wouldn't lead his team there, either."

"And the last word sent was they're heading east."

Robison agreed. Of course, that all rested on the premise they'd effectively evaded the NVA and had gotten away. The Ranger Company Commander and his First Sergeant were scouring the wall map searching for the next most likely extraction location or locations that team on the run led by a team leader smart enough to use it.

"I doubt he'd take his people here, if they were doing an E&E," Poplawski said, pointing to a good-sized natural opening in the jungle. "The NVA would look at their own maps and realize it's the only site close by that could serve as a pick-up zone. They'd be all over it."

"Hmm," said Robison, mentally working through the possibilities as the two scanned over likely sites that they thought Sergeant Carey might consider, fallback sites that might hold some promise.

"My best guesses would be here or here," he said, locating several smaller clearings. Neither are large enough to accommodate a helicopter, but both are open enough for a helicopter crew to make out who they were and drop some ropes, if need be. "What do you think?"

"Possible," said Poplawski. "And, depending how old or outdated these maps are, decent enough for a quick McGuire Rig extraction, too."

Robison agreed. Even with the latest maps the jungle was good at reclaiming its own. Once open clearings could be overgrown and no longer open. Still, there would be no way to be certain until you had eyes on the sites. Turning to Cantu he said, "Let's line up a bird to get our people out."

"Roger that, Captain," said the Sergeant.

Close as the Ranger Company was to the Camp's flight line they could hear the whine of turbine engines and whirring rotor blades as helicopters cranked to mechanical life. There was also the unmistakable sound on an in-bound helicopter touching down. The Huey's main rotor blades and the whop-whop-whopping they made produced an all too familiar sound.

Poplawski was just about to head out of the Mackie TOC as Lieutenant Ryan Marquardt, the Detachment's Executive Officer, was hurrying in.

Marquardt was holding a backpacked radio in one hand and an M-16 in the other. His once ironed and dry Tiger fatigues wrinkled and soaked from the short run to the company in the rain.

"Got Team Nine-Two inserted. They're good to go. Sorry I'm late, but I got stuck in Cu Chi by the storm," Marquardt said, laying the radio down and propping the rifle against the bunker wall. "What's up? The flight line is going crazy."

Robison held his hand up cutting him off. "Wait one!" he said, and then turned his attention back to his First Sergeant.

"I need you to head over to BIG-TOC and lock one in one of the helicopters."

"Yes, sir, on it!" Poplawski said and gave a quick nod to Marquardt on his way out.

"We have a situation," the Ranger Commanding Officer said to his Lieutenant, and explained all that happened and what they were doing about it.

The situation didn't improve any when Poplawski returned from the Mackie-TOC ten minutes later frowning and swearing under his breath.

"BIG-TOC's saying there are no aircraft presently available," he said, sullenly.

"Say again?' said the irritated Ranger Company Commander.

"When I told them we needed an extraction helicopter for one of our teams, they told me that there were no aircraft presently available. Apparently a VIP helicopter went down in our A-O in the storm."

"VIP?"

"Some big wig, I heard. No name yet. They're putting every available aircraft in the A-O in the air. For now, they said, we're on stand-by."

"Stand-by?"

Poplawski nodded. "I saw a 1st of the 9th CAV Huey on the flight line getting ready to join in," he said. "Saw them warming up their bird getting ready to join the search."

"Which Troop?"

"Big yellow triangle. Bravo Troop, I think."

"Apache Troop, First Sergeant," said Specialist Taras. "Bravo Troop has a yellow square."

"And that's another reason why we keep you around, Taras."

Not that the clarification really mattered anyway since Romeo Company worked with Alpha, Bravo, and Charlie Troops on a frequent basis. The 1st of the 9th CAV pilots had the reputation for having brass balls and stellar reliability; the reputation well earned and respected by Romeo Company.

On two specific occasions the 1st of the 9th pilots had ignored warnings that it wasn't safe to go into a hot LZ for a team extraction. Each time they roared in and made the pickups under enemy fire.

In one standout extraction a Charlie Troop Huey that was almost on site when they heard that the Lurp team they were picking up were in a nasty running battle with the NVA. The Lurps had two wounded. The pilot was warned off with the report that the team was taking heavy fire at the extraction site. One of the wounded Lurps was critical with a sucking chest wound.

When a third Lurp was shot through the legs in the pickup zone, Somebody Six suggested that the Lurps should try to E&E to another location. That's when the pilot cut into the radio conversation with, "We're already on our short final! We're going in!"

A cobra gunship dove in to cover the extraction with rocket and mini-gun fire, as did a low bird Scout helicopter flying just above the treetops to draw fire away from the pickup zone. The two helicopters allowed the Huey to roar in, flare at the last moment on the edge of the jungle clearing and touch down. With their engine running, rotors spinning like they were caught in a whirlwind, and door gunners providing close machinegun support, the Rangers began dragging their wounded over the deadly ground to the Huey.

The Rangers were firing back over the shoulders, and struggling to reach the aircraft. When the team leader, who was carrying one of the wounded Lurps, took a round to his left calf and stumbled, the Aircraft Commander climbed out of the helicopter, yelled at the co-pilot to take off if he went down, and then raced out the help the two Rangers.

With his .38 caliber pistol firing and hitting an enemy soldier who had stepped out to fire on the Rangers who'd fallen, the pilot scooped up the wounded Ranger under his arm and helped the staggering team leader carry him back to the helicopter.

All the while this was happening the door gunner and crew chief were spraying the surrounding jungle tree line with continuous machinegun fire. Even with controlled short bursts their machinegun barrels were taking on an orange tinge. They were still firing and keeping the determined NVA soldiers ducking for cover as the co-pilot pulled pitch, did a pedal turn, and roared away.

That night after visiting his wounded men at the Field Hospital Captain Robison wrote the team members up for medals for valor. It was valor, the finest kind.

He also wrote the helicopter pilot up for a Silver Star for Gallantry, and saw that the co-pilot, crew chief and door gunner received medals as well, along with the gunship and scout helicopter crews. In another, less formal ceremony both he and First Sergeant Poplawski paid a visit to the Helicopter Troop and presented black berets and company Ranger scrolls to the pilots and crews, informing them that they were now honorary Romeo Company Rangers.

The pilot and crew were overwhelmed with gratitude by the gesture, and that gratitude, that night, led to a bout of heavy drinking.

Word spread, and with that in mind, Captain Robison figured that the 1st of the 9th CAV pilots might be willing to help them out, yet again.

"Convince them to let us go along in the search, more eyes on the jungle to help spot the downed VIP bird, and maybe even suggest they look east of Niner-One's last known coordinates."

"Roger that," said the First Sergeant, but it was Lieutenant Marquardt, who said he'd do it.

"I know a few of the Apache Troop pilots, bought them beers a few times at the Officer's Club, and since I've lost some serious MPC to them playing poker. They'll be happy to see me, again, so let me try."

"All right," said Robison. "Take some Company scrolls to help along the request."

"Company scrolls, sir?"

"Everybody loves swag, Lieutenant," said the Captain. "Get us on that helicopter. Get it done."

"Yes, sir!" Marquardt said, hurrying out of the Company's TOC. With the Mackie flight line less than fifty yards from Romeo Company's TOC, they'd soon have an answer. Robison and Poplawski were putting on their LBE web gear and going through their ammo pouches checking magazines, grenades, and necessary kit when the Lieutenant returned. His wide grin gave away the confirmation even before he spoke.

"We're in!" he said. "They said they're happy to have us along for company. Happy to have the scrolls, too."

All of twenty-two-years-of-age and weighing in at maybe a buck-fifty, the Lieutenant was grinning like his high school prom date had placed his hand on one of her boobs after the dance in the backseat of his Mom's station wagon in the darkened parking lot.

"No *us* involved," said the Captain. "It'll be the First Sergeant and me."

"Begging your pardon, sir," said the XO. "But I think you need to be here in the TOC in case we get hit and go down."

"Say again, Lieutenant?"

"Sir, if we run into trouble out there then we'll need someone with clout who can get us some help, P-D-Q, and that's you."

It was good thinking on Marquardt's part and had Poplawski shrugging in admirable agreement.

"I hate to say it, Captain, but our young Lieutenant is right," he said. "We can handle it."

Robison didn't like it, but realized they were right, although anything P-D-Q, pretty damn quick, arranged by a lowly Captain might take some time.

"I'm disappointed to think that you think I have that much clout, Lieutenant Marquardt, but I see your reasoning. All right," he said, giving in, and then tilted his head towards the backpacked PRC-25 radio the Lieutenant had brought in with him and set aside. "Change the battery and take the radio. If we can't get them out, then we can drop them a radio, and at least we'll have radio contact."

"On it!" said Marquardt, grabbing his web gear, rifle and radio. He started towards the doorway and then stopped.

"What's the freq for the bird on site?" he asked Cantu and the TOC/NCO gave it to him.

"Thank you, Sergeant," Marquardt said, and was gone.

"Upper Hudson's got enthusiasm," said the First Sergeant.

"Ah, that again! You mean our fine new West Point Lieutenant?"

"Yes, sir. Geographically, that's what I said," grinned the First Sergeant.

"Anyone ever tell you that you're tough on new Lieutenants?"

"Yes, sir. I view it as my calling. We Non-Commissioned Officers are the backbone of the army."

"That you are. And I suppose you view new Lieutenants as being a little further down."

"Well, only until they find their fighting hearts and minds, and say, become god-like Captains."

"God-like, huh?"

"Small G, your worship. Lesser miracles."

Robison chuckled, as did Cantu and Taras who were facing the stacked bank of olive-drab radios and trying not to laugh.

The humor quickly ebbed as Captain Robison's tone shifted with critical purpose. "Find our people, bring them out."

"Will do, sir."

"Oh, and look after Marquardt, too. Young as he is he has some good potential."

"A genuine wonder boy!" said the First Sergeant and hurried out of the TOC towards the flight line.

"How old are you, Sergeant?" Robison asked Cantu.

"Twenty-one, sir."

"Twenty-one?"

"Yes, sir. Last month."

"And you?" he asked, turning to Taras.

"Eighteen, sir."

Robison nodded, thinking that they were all genuine wonder boys aging quickly in this goddamn war, in this demanding and stressful job, and hoping they were fortunate enough to continue aging at all.

He turned back to the First Sergeant's coffee pot.

"Coffee, Sergeant? Specialist?"

Both Rangers shook their heads.

"No, sir. I'm good," said Cantu.

"And..."

"That's right, you don't drink coffee," the Captain, said turning to Taras and remembering the young soldier's previously take on the matter.

Robison reached for *the Brick's* Italian Alfonso coffee maker, grabbed the half-filled coffee pot, and refilled his cup. Doctoring it with the powdered coffee creamer and sugar, he took a tentative sip, and gave a head tilting, *meh*. It was hot, it had the required caffeine, and it was drinkable. It would do.

The increased radio traffic from the many aircraft out in the A-O searching for the lost VIP bird turned him back to the bank of radios.

"Turn up the volume on the speaker boxes," said the Captain. "All of them. Let's hear it in stereo."

"Yes, sir," came the dual response.

More aircraft were taking off and soon the skies would be crowded and that greatly improved the odds of finding the missing team, provided they hadn't been captured or killed.

That Nine-One had been compromised by at least a battalion-size enemy element, and that they were running for their lives without a radio left a dark shadow over his thoughts. He said a quick, almost silent prayer for their safety.

"You say something, sir?" Cantu asked turning back to the CO.

"Talking to God," Robison said, realizing that maybe the prayer hadn't been as silent as he'd thought, but hopefully loud enough for some much needed divine intervention. "I'm told he listens to officers."

It was partially a joke, but having been raised by his grandmother, who was a devout Christian, she'd tried to insert the value of hard work and prayer to him early on. Time and again she cautioned him never to discount the power of prayer and the necessity of hope.

The caution, of course, waned in his teenage years, and once, when he came home pissed off about something that hadn't gone his way, he'd questioned her about her take on praying.

"Faith is all some of us had back in my day," she said. "It brought us through some hard trials and tribulations. Never lose faith, Johnston."

"Maybe Nana, but God doesn't always answer your prayers," he remembered saying to the old woman at the time.

The grandmother stared at her grandson, and after a long, patient moment, she smiled.

"He answers the ones you should've asked, but didn't," she said. "The Lord always gives you hope. In difficult times the smart young man is the one who puts that hope to work."

His grandmother had long since passed, but her words had stayed with him. Long afterwards, even if his practice in religion was questionable at times, the advice was still sound. The Army even had its own version of it. "Plan for the worst and hope for the best."

It was probable that Team Nine-One was now in one of the worst spots a Lurp team could find themselves in, and Captain Robison and his people would do their best to find them and bring them back safely.

Romeo Company Rangers were putting hope to work.

Chapter 17

Adler's modified Escape and Evade plan for the Lurp team leader, and the walking wounded crash survivors, evaporated when the buzzing sound of a low bird helicopter broke through the darkness just north of their position.

The steady, rhythmic pops of the helicopter's rotor blades grew louder with each passing second telling them even in the predawn morning that the aircraft was heading towards the crash site.

"That's a rescue helicopter! They've found us!" cried the Major, getting to his feet, his head searching the small openings in the canopy with furtive eyes.

"That's a Loach!" said Petersen, the door gunner, buoyant with the sound of the approaching small three-man Scout helicopter. Even with the poor and limited views, heads turned skyward, but there was little to be seen.

Sunrise was still a while off, and all that any of them could make out of the sky through the trees were slivers of pale orange and purple fade of the post storm pre-dawn sky. With the trees dripping rainwater no one could say for certain when the rain had stopped, but it had. Their hopes were bolstered with the coming of a brighter day and more so, by the in-bound helicopter. They were going to be rescued.

Their joyful buoyancy sank when the low bird, flying at tree top level, was suddenly targeted by enemy small arms fire from what sounded to Adler like four to five AK-47s. It sank further as the muted sounds of the mortar, rocket, and heavy machine gun fire from the direction of Fire Support Base Rachel reached them.

The Fire Support Base was under attack.

With the attack on the small Scout helicopter, and the Fire Support Base getting hit, any approaching aircraft would be skittish about any movement sighted on the ground.

Although the dense jungle offered brief views of the skyline the glimpses they could catch showed a steady stream of opposing tracer rounds less than a hundred yards away. The trail of green tracer rounds from the enemy machine gun fire that arced skyward trying to knock the helicopter out of the sky was met with the flickering orange/red tracer rounds from the Loach's machine gunner's return fire.

If they were hitting the small helicopter, then they hadn't caused enough damage to bring it down as the Loach pilot veered away like an agile and adept bullfighter in another just as deadly arena.

The enemy small arms fire was no doubt from the NVA trackers that were still on the trail of the Lurp patrol. Those enemy soldiers who initially seemed bent on bringing down the small helicopter went quiet and scurried off as the Loach once more maneuvered away and a Cobra attack gunship took over the fight with rocket and bursts of thousands of rounds of automatic mini-gun fire.

The Cobra gunship was attacking at a steep dive before it too swung around and peeled away in a high, wide arc as it readied to roll in for another go.

The wide arc pass brought the attack helicopter in the direction of the crash site. Noise carries in the dark and in the predawn before the jungle comes to life, something that the much alarmed Major with the broken arm didn't seem to be aware of.

"My God! They're going to fire on us! Do something! Toss out a smoke grenade so they know they know we're friendlies!" cried Haverly to Adler.

"That gunship is turning to make another run on the NVA, not on us. Besides, the wet brush will keep the smoke beneath the trees, and if it somehow does rise, it'll draw the attention of the NVA who're firing on the helicopters, and have them running our way before the pilots in the helicopters can even figure out who in the hell we are."

"But..."

"So, I say again, calm the fuck down unless you want that NVA patrol to find us before our people do, Haverly! You copy!"

"I...I copy," said Haverly as his frightened eyes turned to the surrounding jungle.

To the Ranger team leader the Captain said, "Must be the ones tracking you, but that low bird just bought us some time. Give me that flashlight of yours, Sergeant."

"Yes, sir," Carey said tapping the top left pocket of his camouflaged jungle fatigues and brought it out.

"If we can use it to get the low bird's attention we just may get all of us safely the hell out of here."

Adler was thinking that the flashlight might be their best chance of signaling the aircraft.

"Low bird is circling in our direction!" Petersen said, pointing towards the direction of the oncoming aircraft and the growing din of its rotor blades.

The small clearing that the VIP pilot was aiming for and had missed was less than thirty yards away. It was the same small clearing the Lurp Team had been heading for when they broke through the brush and found the crash site along the way. Now, instead of hiding in the brush until sunlight at a distant clearing and hoping to attract the attention of a passing aircraft with the flash panel, Carey had another bold move that would get the low bird's immediate notice.

Carey suspected what the Special Forces Captain had in mind with the flashlight, but figured his own idea offered for a better outcome for getting the helicopter's attention. It was a tough decision to make since it also would draw the notice of the enemy. The Ranger reached into one of the four canteen pouches that he used for extra magazines for his rifle, grenades, and other ordnance and brought a trip flare.

A smoke grenade wouldn't work in the dark and a flashlight, even with a red filtered lens, might be mistaken as enemy rifle fire.

"How about this?" Carey said, holding out a trip flare and then explaining why.

The Loach pilot or one of the other two crew members would easily spot the bright burning light of the trip flare against the dark backdrop of the rain forest and recognize it for what it was. There would be no mistaking the trip flair for gunfire. The blinding white light from the burning magnesium ground flair would certainly get the low bird's attention, as well as the attention of any nearby enemy soldiers.

"Good call, Sergeant. That'll work," Adler said. "Hand it over. I'll do it."

"No, sir. You're injured," said the Sergeant. "Besides, I'm better dressed for this dance."

Adler knew Carey was right. His neck and back were screwed up, and putting on a game face didn't mean he was up for the play. Reluctantly, he nodded to the Lurp Team Leader, who then made his way over to his Assistant Team Leader to explain what he was going to do. "I'll take Jonas with me. You keep a tight perimeter and hold down the fort."

"Will do, boss," said Thomas.

Carey checked his map, took a compass heading, and then oriented the map in the direction he and Warren would need to find the nearby clearing. The two moved out quietly and just a few yards into the bush disappeared leaving Adler impressed at how quickly and how quietly they moved.

At the edge of the small clearing, but still hidden inside the wood line, the two Lurps took a knee and did a cautious look-see around the tree and brush-covered edge of the small open area. A good portion of the clearing to the east was under water; the clearing little more than a natural sump, but what was left was solid enough ground.

There were no enemy soldiers in sight, which didn't mean they weren't there. They may have been taken out by the gunship fire or machinegun from the Scout helicopter, or they were just biding their time.

Reasonably satisfied all was quiet in the immediate area Carey gave Warren a quiet nod, set his M-16 down beside him, and then readied the trip flare.

"Keep your eyes on the far tree line," he said to his radioman. "Anything moves, you shoot."

Looking skyward to avoid damaging his night vision, he armed the flare, and then tossed it out in the clearing well out in front of him as the low flying helicopter began its next wide sweep of the jungle at treetop level.

Carey reached into another pocket and retrieved a flash panel, that small piece of brightly colored cloth- as the Scout helicopter spotted the bright burning light and roared into the small clearing.

Now comes the what in the fuck was I thinking part of my plan, he thought as he took in a slow, steady breath, stood, and stepped out into the clearing. Holding the brightly colored cloth flash panel up and over his head, he stood still and hoped to God that someone in the helicopter would recognize the flash panel for what it was and not shoot him.

The mistake, he figured, would be popping the panel, which to the helicopters pilot, Observer, or machine gunner, might be mistaken for gunfire in the now pale, pre-dawn light. He stood still, holding up the flash panel in the growing light of the not yet sunrise and from the burning trip flare, and waited.

As the three-man observation helicopter edged closer to a hover, Carey had his eyes locked on the Scout helicopter's machine gunner, the *Torque*, who had his eyes down behind the iron sights of his M-60 machinegun ready to fire.

"Please, please don't shoot," he said to himself, willing the machine gunner to hear him.

It was a desperate and critical moment before the machine gunner recognized the soldier standing in the open as a friendly. The machine gunner raised his head above the gun sites, gave Carey a thumb's up, and said something to the pilot and observer through the radio comms in his flight helmet.

The round, clear, and bubbled face of the low bird turned and faced the soldier on the ground, the observer next to the pilot waved, and Carey, shaking in relief, laughed, and waved back. He was also thinking he really needed to take a piss.

Chapter 18

"Sir! A low bird has a visual on our people!" Sergeant Cantu yelled over his shoulder to Captain Robison.

"We got radio contact?"

"No, sir," said Cantu. "The call was relayed from the low bird to the Extraction bird. Niner-One were compromised and they did an E&E."

"They still being chased?" Robison asked with the foremost of them.

"Yes, sir. The NVA tracking after them shot at the low bird near their location. They can't get to a workable landing zone."

"Then radio the extraction helicopter and tell them to McGuire Rig the team out."

"Sir, there's more," said Cantu, hesitating over the word, *more*.

"Say it."

"The low bird also found the downed VIP helicopter. Niner-One's with the survivors. There are casualties."

"Ours or theirs?"

"The VIPs."

Robison now saw the latest problem. Lieutenant Marquardt and First Sergeant Poplawski only had five ropes on the extraction helicopter. One for each member of the team, and since the helicopter couldn't land, or hover low enough for anyone to climb aboard; the others would have to be left behind on the ground. The others, he knew, would be his people, his Rangers.

"You on the freq for the low bird?"

"I'm on it, Captain," said Taras.

With a twist of a knob the small speaker on the radio monitoring the helicopter activity buzzed with radio traffic. The pilot on the Huey was radioing in that they were moving in to attempt a rope extraction.

The pilot's voice came in loud, clear, and tinny, like some talking through an empty coffee can.

"Two minutes out," said the pilot. "Getting ready to drop the ropes."

Another *somebody* Six, a higher-higher Colonel, but more than likely a General, broke in on the frequency and gave the order for the immediate extraction of the survivors from the downed VIP bird.

Robison's dog in the fight may have been his Rangers, but a much bigger dog in the pack was leading the snarl. The Colonel or General's Command and Control helicopter would be immediately in the air and racing to the scene. Other aircraft were quickly being diverted to the crash site. The cavalry had arrived, even if they weren't necessarily all from the First Air Cavalry Division or even riding horses.

The C&C helicopter would be accompanied by a rescue Quick Reaction Force, a Medevac helicopter, and what Robison guessed would be a shitload of Cobra gunships, and as many pairs of Air Force F-4 jets scrambling out of Bien Hoa that they could get in the air.

Until the parade of rescue aircraft showed up on station Marquardt and Poplawski would take the lead in the rescue operation. The First Sergeant was lying on his stomach in the helicopter bay at the helicopter, staring down at the ground as it moved into position. 80-feet below, Sergeant Carey was staring up at him waiting for the Huey to hold to a hover.

Carey was using hand signals with the to crew chief to guide the helicopter in to where it needed to be as Poplawski and Marquardt were readying to drop the ropes.

The first rope the First Sergeant carefully lowered had a PRC-25 radio tied to it to one of the radio's carrying handles. Carey retrieved it and did a quick radio check.

"Commo's good to go!" he yelled to Adler, who'd moved most of the crash survivors to he clearing while leaving the Ranger medic and another Lurp to safeguard the Senator.

"Good," he said. "Let whoever's on the other end know we need a rescue basket stretcher for the Senator."

Carey nodded, the extraction ropes were dropped, and as the helicopter steadied its hover Captain Adler gave an order.

"Hook 'em up!"

"Two long ropes and three short ones," Carey said, informing the Captain of what was in play.

"Good enough!" said Adler, much relieved by the turn of events and more so, knowing they now had commo.

"Gotta love you Lurps," he said to Carey.

"Why aren't they landing?" said a still worried Haverly.

"They can't," replied Adler. "You're going out by rope."

"Rope?"

The Major wanted to object to the extraction method, even as the painfully young looking Lurp was wrapping the eight section of nylon rope around the officer's chest, but he was afraid he'd lose his chance to get out of the jungle.

"Don't they have a rescue basket or something? A metal stretcher thingy?" he said, as the Ranger was making sure the rig was snug beneath his armpits. "With my broken arm this is going to be difficult for me."

Adler ignored the Major.

"You," he said to the Lurp. "What's your name?"

"Bowman, sir, Private First Class."

"Major, why don't you try thanking Ranger Bowman for offering you his own life line?"

Haverly still appeared to have more to say only Adler didn't have time for it. There wasn't the time. To those in the harnesses he said, "Once you have the ropes secured in place, move out into the clearing."

"They'll lift us up to the helicopter, right?"

It was Haverly, again.

When Adler ignored him, it was Bowman who replied.

"Sort of," said the young Ranger as the Captain smiled at the semi-accurate response.

Sort of was right. Those on the tethered end of the McGuire Rigs and ropes would be lifted up above the trees as the helicopter gained altitude, where they'd be left dangling beneath the helicopter as they were ferried to the safety.

Gravity, body weight, and the ropes would yank and pull on their chests and backs. The longer they were strung out beneath the helicopter in flight, the more sore and miserable they would be when they eventually reached their destination, that is, if they weren't shot out of the sky in the meantime.

There was always that, but Adler saw no need to point that out to the Major, or the others.

While Carey was double checking each of the ropes on the Senator's son, and the surviving pilot, it was Warren, who was having an issue hooking up the woman. He wasn't sure just how to wrap the rope under her arms and across her chest without making contact with her breasts.

"No need to be shy, young man," she said. "It's one thing for my tits to fall out of a bra, but another for me to fall out of the sky. Just make sure the rope's secure, okay?"

Jonas Warren blushed and nodded. "Yes, Ma'am," he said, making certain the rope was tied tight and that the D-ring was securely fastened in place above her breasts.

Doing the math with the five sections of rope and accompanying D-rings, Petersen, the surviving door gunner, announced he'd remain behind with the others.

"You can go in my place, Captain," he said to the injured Special Forces Captain, only Adler wasn't having it.

"Thank you, Specialist," he said, "but I think I'll stay here with that M-60 of yours. I appreciate the offer, but you're going out with them now."

Adler held his hands out and there was a look of relief in the young soldier's eyes as he handed the machinegun and several hundred belt fed rounds to the officer.

"You know how it works, sir?"

Adler smiled. "I've used one a time or two," he said. "I'm good to go."

The door gunner slipped into the McGuire Rig and quickly took his place among the others who were rigged and ready. With a check of the ropes around their chests they were ready to be hooked up to the ropes from the helicopter.

Three of the team members for Nine-One had spread out and took defensive positions with the Captain passing the M-60 machine to

Ranger Warren while he and Sergeant Carey were supervising the extraction.

Just as those on the ropes were off of the ground three over eager NVA soldiers popped out of the jungle at the far reach of the clearing and began firing on the helicopter. They didn't worry about those dangling beneath it and hadn't noticed the others on the ground. Knock out the helicopter and those beneath it wouldn't be a problem.

"TAKING FIRE! TAKING FIRE!" came the excited cry from the Aircraft Commander of the Huey over the radio airwaves.

Before he could pivot the helicopter to bring his crew chief's machinegun on target, Warren and Carey opened up and took out three enemy soldiers, who were focused on the more vulnerable helicopter. The three NVA hadn't seen the camouflaged Ranger kneeling off to their left.

On the rifle and machine gun range the closest and easiest pop-up target for any GI to hit was at the 50-yard line. At less than 50 yards Warren made quick work, with the M-60 machine gun, of the real life targets. The three NVA soldiers were down before the helicopter's door gunner could open fire.

"Jonas, secure the Pick-up Zone," Carey yelled to Warren, who skirted the water sump to get to where the three enemy soldiers had fallen.

Warren checked for signs of more enemy soldiers in the immediate area, and when he neither saw nor heard any, he turned and gave the team leader a thumbs-up. He then began flinging the dead soldier's Ak-47s into the murky, pooling water of the nearby sump.

"You're good to go!" Adler radioed to the rescue helicopter.

To the crash survivors on the ropes he yelled, "Link your arms together as you lift off. Otherwise, you'll bounce off each other like well-smacked billiard balls."

Those linked in nodded nervously like ticket holders lined up for a sketchy carnival ride while staring at a few loose nuts and bolts lying on the ground nearby.

Zack Russell, Stephanie Orlov, and Petersen, were on the shorter 90-foot ropes linking arms as the hovering helicopter began to rise while Haverly and Mister Kehr, attached to the two long ropes. Ten feet below the three others, Kehr was helping Haverly, who was having trouble because of the broken arm.

Even before they'd been lifted off of the ground Haverly was visually apprehensive about the mode of extraction and looked like he was about to cry. Still, he looked to be more than a little relieved to be getting out of the jungle. Had he been a better man he might've even been thankful.

When all five were clear of the treetops, the extraction helicopter dipped its broad nose and flew away. For a moment, and because they were attached to longer ropes than the others, the surviving pilot and the Major found themselves dancing across the tops of several trees before the chopper finally gained altitude and rapidly climbed to a few thousand feet.

"Sir," said Sergeant Carey, handing Adler the radio's handset. "It's for you."

"Adler, go," he said into the handset, and then listened to whoever it was with considerable rank on the other end of the transmission. There were a few "*Yes, sirs*" and "*I copy's*" on the Captain's part.

"Be advised to make that happen we need an immediate Medevac, A-SAP, and two body bags. Do you copy?"

When whoever it was on the other side of the radio transmission responded in the positive to the request and with something more, he ended the conversation.

"Roger that," he said. "Adler, out."

Deep in thought the Special Forces Captain handed the radio handset to the Lurp team leader.

"What's the plan, Captain?" asked the Ranger sergeant. "A QRF coming in?"

Adler shook his head, and when he did he grimaced as a bolt of lightening shot up through his spine, and radiated above his eyes. He could feel his left arm growing numb again. Clenching and unclenching his hands into fists a few times as he had earlier when it happened, the arm slowly returning to normal. This time, though, the relief was much slower in happening. A piercing headache, too, had him wincing, and when he began step-staggered to keep his balance, Carey reached out to steady him.

"You okay, sir?"

"I think I may have fractured my back or neck when the helicopter went down," he said. "If I don't twist, turn, or nod, I'll manage."

He gave a small laugh to the less than convinced Ranger Sergeant.

The Captain said, "Thankfully, there's a Medevac bird ten mikes out and judging from the radio traffic on the net, the bulk of the Cavalry is on the way."

"The 1st Cavalry Division?"

"Them, and the 25th Infantry Division, the Air Force, and damn near everybody else in-country with wings and wheels racing in and on their way to this location."

"For the Senator?"

"And the rest of us as well. So, let's get the bodies of the pilot and crew chief out of the helicopter. The Medevac will be dropping body bags soon."

Carey nodded.

Loading the dead into the body bags would be a grim but necessary task, and hopefully wasn't an omen of things to come.

Chapter 19

Tony Adler was right about the extent of help that was on its way. Soon the sky around them began to fill with an array of combat aircraft of seemingly every tactical shape and size. What they couldn't see, they could hear. The loudest of which were the pair of Air Force F-4 Phantom jets out of Bien Hoa that blew in at close to 1,500 miles per hour with thunderous roars that were punctuated by the bombs they were dropping on the main force of the NVA unit that had begun their ill-fated attack on FSB Rachel.

Several of the fast movers were working dangerously close to the Fire Support Base with others flying in loud and low hitting areas leading to the crash site. The jets, dropping their ordnance less than a mile away, were steering away any large clusters of enemy troops that were, or might be, retreating in that direction. The bombs the jets were dropping blew splintered trees and debris geysers high into the sky and left swimming pool sized craters dotting the jungle.

Closer to the crash site more Cobra gunships and low birds than Adler or any of the others for that matter, had ever seen in action were ringing the immediate area and securing the small clearing for the inbound Medevac helicopter.

The ripping, staccato bursts of machinegun fire and thumps and tremendous booms from the exploding rockets and bombs muted much of the noise of the rotor blades of the Medevac helicopter coming in over the trees. The air support was well orchestrated, but then it would be, given whom the Medevac helicopter was there to pick up. There could be no room for error. Careers were riding on it.

After the bodies of Mister Corsi and the crew chief were removed from the wreckage and brought out to the edge of the clearing for evacuation, and when the Medevac helicopter was on its short final, it was time to bring out Russell.

"Let's move the Senator," Adler said to the Ranger medic, as the Medevac's rotor blades grew louder with its approach and the Huey prepared its hover in the growing light of the morning.

Sergeant Carey nodded and joined Warren and Bowman with guarding the extraction site as Doc Moore and Thomas carried the badly injured Senator to the clearing.

With Adler coordinating the evacuation over the PRC-25 radio, the Medevac helicopter's crew chief dropped the requested body bags just before he began lowering the metal stretcher on the hoist for the wounded Senator.

Thomas and Warren secured the body bags, and with Bowman's help, the Lurps loaded the dead men into the now bloodied rubber body bags, and waited for the word to send them up.

When the rescue basket was three-quarters of the way down to the ground, Doc Moore and Thomas carefully carried the Senator out to meet it.

Because the thick spike was still sticking through him, they couldn't lay the Senator down in the metal stretcher, so Doc Moore secured him in the stretcher sitting upright. When all was ready Adler radioed the Medevac to haul him in.

"Ask them if the basket will hold two?" Moore shouted to the Captain. Moore's intent was to go up with the Senator to make sure the spike didn't shift in the process.

Adler got what the medic was asking and radioed the question to the helicopter. The answer came back immediately.

"That's affirmative," Adler said to Moore. "Go!"

Back into the radio when the Senator and the medic were in place in the basket, Adler said, "Take them up."

The metal stretcher, with the Senator seated in it, and the Ranger medic keeping him upright and stabilized, began a slow ascent. The rescue basket twisted and swayed at the end of the cable as it rose up to meet the helicopter. When it was within grabbing distance, the Medevac's medic pulled it into the open cargo bay. Russell and Moore were safely on board.

As those on the ground were waiting for the metal stretcher to be lowered again, the helicopter's nose dipped and the rotor blades changed pitch.

"Sir?" said a confused Carey turning to Adler, who was on the radio again and listening to someone on the other end of the line.

Adler held up an open hand signaling the team leader to hold on. The Captain was doing more listening over the radio than talking before the transmission ended and the helicopter flew away.

"Roger, out," the Captain said, blowing air through his puffed cheeks and teeth the way a young mother might when the first word her baby utters in public is *fuck*.

"The Medevac is being told by someone Six higher-higher to get the Senator to a Field Hospital, A-SAP. They're sending in another bird for us. It's on its way. We'll set up our perimeter here."

"Roger that, sir."

Adler handed the radio to Lurp team's RTO.

"Keep me apprised on what's going on overhead," he said to Warren.

"Will do, Captain."

Six was the numerical designator for a Unit Commander with the *higher-higher* RTO slang for some Commander with considerably more clout. Adler wouldn't have been surprised if even General Abrams was on one of the birds.

Adler didn't necessarily like what he'd been told, but he well understood what was actually in play. The critically injured VIP was the priority. They weren't.

With the Medevac helicopter climbing to better altitude, a 360-degree perimeter was put in place and they watched the jungle.

"We wait," Adler said as the jets, gunships, and low birds helped them maintain a better perimeter.

The wait was only in minutes.

"Captain?" Warren said, holding out the radio's handset. "They're not calling us, but some serious people are in a serious discussion because the Senator's telling them he won't leave without us."

"Break in, and on my word, tell them to thank the Senator for us, but that it's okay to go. There's another in-bound bird coming soon. We're good."

Warren transmitted the Captain's message and then gave a "Wait one," as he made his way to Adler and handed him the handset.

"Sir," he said. "Quarterback Six wants to speak with you."

"Who's Quarterback Six?"

Warren shrugged and held out the radio handset. "Somebody who got everyone else off the frequency pretty damn quick when he spoke," he said, with a second shrug.

Adler reached out and held the handset up to his ear.

"Ground team six, go," he said into the handset.

He wasn't talking much this time either, or when he did, it was once again with a handful of *"Yes, sir's"* and several *"I copy's"* before handing the handset back to Warren.

To the Lurp/Ranger Team Leader he said, "Looks like some of the NVA are moving away from the Fire Support Base and are heading in our direction. The new plan is to bomb the hell out of the crash site with napalm, once we're out of here. A second Medevac helicopter is in-bound. The gunships will cover our extraction. Until it shows up, we need to gather up all the dropped ordnance and anything else we can't carry and set it all in the center of the downed bird's cargo bay."

"Yes, sir," said Carey and then called Thomas and had Bowman over to get it done.

"Oh, and I'll need one of your smoke grenades," added the Captain, but it was Thomas, the Assistant Team Leader who handed him a purple smoke grenade from his web gear.

"Grape," said Thomas.

"Then grape it is, thank you," he said to the A-T-L who nodded a *you're welcome.*

"Once we get the body bags and the rest of you on board the Medevac, I'll mark the crash site the smoke grenade for a few of the F-4's to target. They're going to turn this whole stretch of jungle into a bar-b-que pit."

Even if the F-4 Phantoms scored a near miss on the wreckage, with the napalm and leaking jet fuel, the damaged helicopter and everything surrounding it for fifty to a hundred yards would still erupt in a conflagration of superheated smoke and flames.

"What say I pop the smoke at the crash site, sir?" the Ranger sergeant said to the Captain, once again with a minor change of plan. "No offense, Captain, but you need to get on that Medevac. Besides, I was a starting pitcher for my baseball team in high school."

"Medevac's two minutes out!" called Warren, listening in to the radio's handset.

The kid had a point, again, thought Adler. *My hands and arms are still a little numb and my legs aren't all that much better, which doesn't bode well for being the last man out at a quick run.*

"Starting pitcher, huh?" said Adler.

"Honorable Mention. All-City."

"Which city?"

Carey smiled. "One in East Texas that only had two high schools, but we had scouts from UT-Austin and TCU looking at us from time to time. I didn't have any real heat and couldn't throw a curve worth a hoot, but I can still bean that sucker from ninety feet away."

"Get it done."

"Yes, sir," said Carey and over his shoulder called to one of his people.

"New Guy?"

"Yes, Sergeant?"

"After we send the body bags up, you're coming with me and covering my six."

"Roger that," said Bowman, wondering if they were ever going to use his actual name as he went about the assignment.

All was set. The Air Force jets and Army gunships that were hammering the jungle just east of them were receiving heavy return fire from the ground, which told Adler and the others the NVA were still moving in their direction.

With the wonderfully recognizable sound of a helicopter's rotor blades growing on its short final, the second Medevac helicopter came into view over the trees to begin its hover. When it was set, a metal stretcher was lowered by cable for the final evacuation to begin. The first of the two body bags had started up when Carey made his way towards the crash site with Bowman in tow.

Once he was within throwing distance from the wreckage, he looked up through the thin opening in the trees and waited until he could see the rescue basket being lowered a second time. Then, when he heard the Captain shout the command to send the basket up, Carey pulled the pin on the smoke grenade, and made a decent toss. The smoke grenade landed a foot in front of the broken nose of the wrecked helicopter. He didn't want it anywhere near the leaking fuel.

Carey waited until the smoke grenade began to spit and sputter purple smoke before he and Bowman made their way back to the clearing.

"Sir?" the Ranger Sergeant said to Captain when the basket had once again been lowered. "You're next. We got this."

This time, though, Adler wasn't having it. "That's a negative, Sergeant. Send your people up and I'll follow."

The fact that the Captain wasn't smiling told the Sergeant there would be no arguing the point. Carey nodded.

"New Guy, you're next. Get ready," he said.

"Yes, Sergeant. And it's Bowman, Sergeant."

"Jonas?" Carey said to his radioman. "You're going up after the new guy."

"Bowman," said Bowman, over his shoulder.

Adler chuckled at the exchange. These five Rangers, these young Lurps, scraped and scuffed up were truly a rare breed. They'd quite literally saved the day, bad as it had been, and had seen that the VIP party and the air crew were safely lifted out before them. The survivors wouldn't have fared well without them.

As the rescue basket came down a third time, the FNG Lurp climbed inside and gave a goofy grin and started up. Warren, the RTO, was next to go and when it was his turn, he handed the radio over the Captain.

Their once tight perimeter was growing dangerously thin. After Bowman and Warren were in the hovering Medevac, Carey sent his A-T-L up on the lift.

When the basket came down, again, Carey reluctantly took his turn.

Just before reaching the skids to the helicopter Carey saw the purple smoke working its way up through the canopied covered treetops. The bright purple column would give the soon to be inbound jets a definable target.

The vivid smoke cloud was clearly visible as the sun broke over the horizon and Tony Adler was lifted up and out. As he was being pulled into the cargo bay, Adler tapped the helicopter crew chief on his helmet to get his attention.

"Tell your pilot he can give the jets the okay to begin their run on the grape smoke once we're clear!" he yelled over the noise of the helicopter. "The smoke is purple!"

The crew chief nodded and relayed the message through his helmet's headset.

Message received, the Medevac pilots wasted little time gaining altitude and moving well away from the A-O, as did the helicopter gunships and low birds that were quickly peeling away before the first F-4 Phantom did a wide arc and began its run on the targeted purple smoke.

The Medevac helicopter was well away when the first dropped bomb scored a direct hit on the crash site. The once placid looking sea of green jungle erupted in a deafening explosion. There was a rising tumbling cloud of smoke, flames, and burning debris that rose and fell in a terrible instant.

Like the others in the helicopter the napalm strike drew the attention of those on board the Huey, including Tony Adler who'd craned his neck to watch another jet go to work. It was another simple, natural reaction on his part, and a serious dumb one at that.

The gaping turn toward the noise shot crippling pain from the base of his neck all the way down to his toes. He tried bracing and supporting himself against the back of the pilot's seat and the raised lip of the metal rescue stretcher, but his arms weren't working anymore, and he collapsed back down inside the metal rescue basket in a helpless heap.

"Oh, Christ!" he cried. A thousand pointed bayonets repeatedly stabbed at any, and every exposed nerve they could find, and they found them all.

Believing that he'd somehow been hit by a piece of shrapnel from the violent explosion, or perhaps by an enemy bullet through the open cargo bay doorway, the Medevac medic scrambled over to the Captain's side.

"Where you hit, Captain?" shouted the medic, probing for wounds.

"Not...hit! No wound," shouted Adler. "It's...it's my upper back or neck. I think it's fractured. Can't feel my arms or legs."

The Medevac medic reached back into his kit and brought out a neck brace that he applied before taping the Captain down inside the rescue stretcher so he couldn't move. The medic followed that up with a shot of morphine to the still grimacing officer.

"This should help," shouted the medic.

It only took a moment for the morphine to kick in and take hold, and as it did, the pain behind his eyes subsided. Adler's scrunched up face began to settle and relax. However, he still couldn't feel anything in his arms or legs.

"How you feeling now, sir?' asked the Medevac medic after a while. He was speaking loudly over the din of the aircraft noise.

"Tolerable. Thank you."

The medic nodded as Adler did his best to hide his fear at the thought of being paralyzed. But the gut-wrenching pain told him he hadn't lost the use of his arms and legs just yet, well, at least as long as he didn't try to turn his neck and head. Still, there was one more task to be done.

To Sergeant Carey, he said, "Get me the full names and ranks of everyone on your team, including Bowman, your new guy, and tell your CO to get them to me at whatever Field Hospital they drop me in."

Carey nodded and said he would. Bowman smiled. Someone had finally remembered his name.

To his relief, sensation was returning to Adler's arms and legs, but when he tried to push up on his elbows while he was talking, the medic reprimanded him.

"No! No! NO!" said the Medevac medic, placing a hand on the Captain's chest and forcing him back down. "Try not to move, Captain."

When Adler frowned the medic gave him a disapproving scowl.

"Roger that," said Adler, thinking that was perhaps the best plan of action and non-action.

The extent of all that had happened, and the Morpheus effects of the drug, had him feeling very tired and giving in to some much-needed rest. His eyelids were drooping and finally closing as the booms from the exploding bombs that had been dropped in the distance gave way to the rhythmic popping of the helicopter's main rotor blades through a more peaceful morning. The cadence of the rotor blades lulled him into the embrace of a morphine-induced slumber.

Adler was thinking all was good or seemingly so, but even that, he knew before he drifted off to sleep, was only temporary.

Chapter 20

The Halo Brace that he'd been fitted with at the 3rd Field Hospital in Saigon to immobilize the spinal fractures in his neck and upper back was a necessity, and the necessity was driving him crazy.

But for Tony Adler there was little choice in the matter since the damage he suffered dictated the cage-like device.

"You have damage to the lower cervical vertebrae in your neck and to the Thoracic vertebrae in your back where they connect," explained the Surgeon after the brace had been installed and his patient had come to well after the operation. "A bad turn or twist could've easily left you paralyzed."

The cloth nametag on the Doctor's jungle fatigues read: Christoun. Bronze oak leaves on his collars showed that he was an Army Major. Major Christoun was well over six-four, stocky, broad shouldered with a slightly bent nose, and a heavy New England accent.

"Boston?"

The Surgeon shook his head, looking very much affronted. "Lowell," he said. "We like to see ourselves as a better class of blue collar Brahmins, only without all the bull."

"Boxing?" Adler said, pointing to Christoun's crooked nose.

"Close," said the Surgeon. "Hockey."

Still trying to nod, without success, in the device, Adler said, "How long will I need to be in this damn thing, Doc?"

The *damn thing* was the brace that Adler thought of as a *medieval birdcage.*

"Seven to eight weeks, minimum," Christoun said, checking the rods and adjusting the padded shoulders on the brace for better comfort. "Provided that there are no complications."

"And then, all's good?"

The Surgeon's frown gave away what came next. "We'll see," he said, cryptically. "In layman's terms, you banged up your neck and the top of your spine pretty badly, not to mention, we noticed more than a few compacted disks in your lower back, from what, bad parachute landings, I take it? You one of those fools who think jumping out of perfectly good airplanes is a good idea, are you?"

"I think Buddy Holly and Otis Redding might disagree with you about that whole perfectly good airplane reference, Doc, and any parachute landing you can walk away from is a good landing."

"Well then, maybe that explains the rest."

"This from a hockey player?"

Christoun laughed as he checked the space between the pads on the brace supports and Adler's shoulders, and the tweaked the fitting.

"How do the pads feel? Comfortable enough?"

"They're about the only thing in this birdcage that's comfortable. I can't move very well and I feel like I'm trapped."

"Good, then the brace is working."

Adler's *birdcage* consisted of a lightweight metal band around his forehead held in place by four pins fitted into his skull. The four pins were connected to four firm metal rods that ran front and back, down to a fleece-lined, heavy plastic jacket with padded shoulders that limited and restricted his movement, just as it was designed to do.

"In a few days, give or take, we'll move you over to the Evacuation Hospital in Long Binh," Christoun said, "From there, you'll be airlifted to Camp Zama, Japan, and eventually Walter Reed in Maryland. However, for the time being, you'll remain here until your neck and spine are better stabilized. The first 48-hours are the most critical. You're not out of the woods yet."

"Well, out of the jungle, anyway."

"There's that."

No stranger to military hospital surgical wards, Tony Adler knew they were also the most uncomfortable, if not physically, then mentally for certain. He'd been in one too many and had seen some of the living nightmares of war painfully convalescing in combat surgical wards, nightmares he was certain would never appear on recruiting posters.

Earning tabs and combat patches came at a high price that those who've never been in combat might not readily understand.

"Other than maybe feeling a little confined, how're you feeling overall?"

"Mostly tired," replied the Captain, "and I don't imagine I'll be getting much in the way of a good night's sleep wearing this contraption."

"It'll take some getting used to," Christoun said, "but we'll make a few adjustments with it, and to your hospital bed. That'll help you rest better sitting up."

"Much appreciated."

"We'll also give you something to help you to sleep."

"Even better. Thank you."

The Surgeon nodded, a simple gesture Adler now envied. "Get some rest. You've been through quite an ordeal with the helicopter crash and now you need to take the time to heal and get better," he said, making notations in his hospital chart at the foot of his bed. "And oh, I'm on my way to have a talk with the Radiologist and go over a few things. He's leaning in favor of a medical retirement and I'm not sure he's wrong. We'll need to take a look at the rest of your medical history, so why do I suspect this ain't your first wake-up call?"

"Ain't?"

"Like I said, I'm from Lowell. What we lack in proper grammar we make up for with good looks, charm, and amazing fucking talent. Get some rest."

"Will do. Thanks Doc."

"You're welcome," Christoun said, waving goodbye over his shoulder. "Go Bruins!"

The notations in his hospital chart called for pills for the pain and medication to help him rest. Combined, the two brought on a much-appreciated restful sleep at least for the next four to six hours.

He awoke to the smell of fresh clean sheets in a near empty, hospital ward and a medic delivering a tray of hospital food.

"Thank you," he said to the medic and lifted the metal dish cover to find a veritable treat of scrambled eggs, toast, and bacon.

Eating with the Halo Brace proved to take a little doing, but then so did the cube of lime Jell-O with a lone green bean on the dinner tray.

"Uh...no," he said, pushing it aside and then having trouble trying to drink a cup of coffee.

With his stomach happy, he placed the food tray on his nightstand, did his best to brush away the crumbs of what he'd eaten in the Halo Brace. With a second round of medication he drifted off to sleep, again.

He awoke a while later to a smiling nurse who was sliding a Blood Pressure cuff up his left arm and attaching a small clock-like gauge.

"Good afternoon, Captain," said the raven-haired twenty-something Lieutenant duty nurse. The nametag on her starched jungle fatigues read: Price.

After she had the cuff wrapped in place on the bicep she began pumping up the pressure by squeezing the rubber bulb at the end of the long tube. After adjusting a stethoscope in her ears, she slowly released the pressure valve, and took the reading as the blood pressure ticked on the metered gauge and finally settled.

"How are you feeling?" asked Lieutenant Price, removing the BP cuff and setting it aside before sliding the Stethoscope down around her neck. "How's the pain?"

"Better," he said and maybe actually believed it. With the Halo Brace and with enough pain medication still in play, it was better, if only in a loose definition of the word.

"Any pain radiating in your arms or legs? Any numbness?" she asked as she jotted down the blood pressure numbers on his chart.

"Enough to remind me maybe that I'm still alive, but I'm good," he said. "I mean, all things considered."

The nurse nodded as she adjusted a pillow on his lower back that provided a little more comfort for him.

"You're the talk of the ward, Captain," she said. "I overheard the Surgeon and the Radiologist a little while ago saying that judging from X-Rays you're lucky you're not paralyzed."

"The luck of the Irish."

"You're Irish?"

"No."

The duty nurse chuckled. "They were also surprised that you were missing a lung."

"It's not missing," he said. "I'm pretty sure it's somewhere up in II Corps, along the border near Laos."

"That would explain the substantial looking surgical scar on your chest they were talking about, along with a number of old bullet holes on your chest. There's a few other jagged scars that has them wondering, too."

"Shrapnel from a German grenade."

"German?"

"It's my third war. If I ever get bored I figure I can always take off my pajamas and play connect the dots?"

Adler smiled and the nurse stared back at him for a moment with a sad smile before she returned his smile.

"Don't take this the wrong way, Captain, but you've done more than your share of the fighting, so have you ever thought about, maybe taking up a new line of work, I don't know, something a little more sedate?"

"More and more, lately," he said, wistfully.

"Can I get you anything?"

"A shot of Jack Daniels would be nice."

Nurse Price laughed and shook her head.

"I'm afraid that's not the menu, but how about some fresh orange juice or say, a soft drink? We have Ginger Ale and Dr. Pepper."

"Doctor Pepper sounds great."

"And better yet," she said, patting his shoulder. "It's ice cold."

Tony Adler was happily sipping the soft drink through an elongated straw and was thinking how small treats loomed large at times like these.

Any feeling of general well being or comfort, though, was lost when, out of the corners of his eyes, he caught his dour-faced boss, Lieutenant Colonel Bainbridge, coming down the hospital corridor towards his hospital bed in what Adler thought of as an executioner's stride.

Bainbridge was in his usual Public Affairs short sleeved, impeccably pristine Class-B khaki uniform; however, he was looking even more dour and formal than usual. Adler sighed, thinking, *he's probably not here to find out why the hospital's kitchen thinks lime Jell-O with the piece of green bean is a treat.*

The duty nurse, who was bringing Adler the soft drink, trailed the Colonel by a few steps. When she arrived at Adler's bedside shortly after he had, Bainbridge looked annoyed with her company.

"This won't take long, Colonel," she said to the senior officer.

She placed the soft drink on a nearby nightstand, pulled out a thermometer, and told her patient to '*Say ah,*' as she stuck it under the Captain's tongue when he did as he was told.

The duty nurse smiled at the Colonel and stared at her wristwatch watching the second hand. When she removed the thermometer a minute later, she added the reading to the patient chart clipped to the foot of the hospital bed.

"Could you leave us alone for a minute, Lieutenant?" said the Colonel with a forced smile.

Realizing it was more than a social request, Nurse Price acquiesced.

"Of course, sir," she said, and then back to Adler added, "I'll be back later for the bedpan."

"Thank you," he said.

"I need you to stay hydrated," she said, pointing towards the Dr. Pepper and then with a curt nod to the senior officer, she walked off to attend to another patient.

Bainbridge waited until he and Adler were finally alone before he got to the point of the visit, which the veteran Captain suspected wasn't a '*How you doing? Can I get you anything?*' hospital visit.

"The Senator passed away this morning," Bainbridge said, bluntly.

"I'm sorry to hear that. Unlike some out there, he proved to be a brave man."

The Colonel stared at him for a long moment unsure what to make of the remark. After the stumbling pause, he went on.

"There is no easy way to say this, so I'll just say it. I think we both know that your career is over."

Adler was pretty sure Bainbridge wasn't referring to his fractured vertebrae, and said as much.

"Because the Senator died."

"Under your watch."

"Well, that's a stretch, Colonel, and I think you know that as well as I do."

"Perhaps, but I've spoken with Major Haverly, who had more than a few unflattering things to say about you regarding all that happened after the crash. It's all on the record."

"Yeah well, Haverly's a pompous asshole. Hope that's on the record, too."

"I'll kindly remind you to watch your language, Captain."

"You're right, Colonel. I should have said, *anus,*" replied Adler, enjoying watching Bainbridge becoming even more agitated.

The agitation turned to anger and Adler's joy watching it turn made it almost a perverse pleasure.

"I don't like your tone and that's enough of your smartass remarks, do you hear me, Captain?"

"Loud and clear, Colonel, but then, it could just be a slight echo. Hospital corridors tend to do that, sir. They make for good soapboxes and rants. Do go on."

"You were the officer in charge of transportation, for Christ's sake. You should never have allowed that helicopter to make that unscheduled mail delivery trip to the mountain. You and the pilot should've known better."

"It wasn't the pilot's call either, sir."

"That's not what I gather from Major Haverly."

"I say again, Colonel, the Major's an asshole."

"AT EASE!"

Tony Adler settled back, as best he could, against the hospital bed with as much actual ease he could muster in the restrictive Halo brace.

"How about you go away, and we take this matter up at another time?" he said, with a heavy sigh.

"Excuse me?"

"The thing is, I have a broken neck and back, so my military career actually is over. Also, I'm on some pretty serious medication, so it's doubtful about my being held accountable for what I'm saying now or what I might say. More to the point, I'm not really well

210

enough to be having this conversation, here and now. I'm pretty sure the Doctors here will agree with me. So if you'll excuse me, I need my rest."

"I'm not done with you!" barked the outraged Bainbridge.

"Yeah, you are," replied Adler. "And since you didn't bring flowers, let alone ask how I'm doing, I'm guessing the only real reason you're here is that you're looking to assign fault."

Bainbridge's open-mouthed fluster and momentary silence confirmed it.

Because a U.S. Senator had died on the VIP visit, MAC-V was looking for a scapegoat, and judging from the Colonel's confrontational approach, and Haverly's trying to shift the blame, Tony Adler knew that he and the dead pilot would be offered up for sacrifice.

Enlisted men had a saying for situations such at this; '*Shit rolls downhill*,' and the mustang officer wasn't that far from his hard-earned enlisted stripes to have forgotten one of the military's truest maxims.

"There'll be an official investigation, so you may want to try to get your ducks in a row without any more insubordination or wise crack comments. As I've said, I've already spoken with Major Haverly, and, quite frankly, I trust his judgment more than I trust yours. You're not going to fare well when the C-I-D investigators come calling on me for an interview and my assessment of the matter."

Adler smiled. There was little more he could do.

"Well sir, since you weren't there, I'm not all that worried about your assessment of the situation, let alone any investigation."

"Is that right?"

"It is. Major Haverly's performance was less than stellar after the helicopter went down, as any interviews with the other survivors that any competent investigator will conduct, will most likely discover and confirm. As for the unscheduled mail delivery to the mountain, that was Major Haverly's and the Senator's call, not mine. It was a PR stunt. I protested it and was overruled, all of which I expect to see in the investigation report. Any idea when I can expect the C-I-D people to come calling?"

Bainbridge sidestepped the question.

"You were the more experienced officer in the field," he snarled. "And both you and the Aircraft Commander, should've been aware that the flight during the Monsoon storm would've been questionable at best."

"We were, and as I said, we were overruled. By the way, the pilot's name was Michael Corsi and he died doing everything he could to try to bring that helicopter down safely. Don't scapegoat him."

"Do I need to point out that with the pilot and the Senator dead, there's only your word against Major Haverly's?"

Adler sighed, again. If that was Bainbridge's best card to play, then he was wrong.

"Go fish, sir."

"What?"

"It means you baited the wrong hook, Colonel."

"What?"

"There were pilots, as in plural," said Adler. "There were two, Mister Corsi, the Aircraft Commander, who was killed in the crash, and Mister Scott Kehr, the surviving co-pilot, that were flying the Huey. I suspect Mister Corsi was just as frustrated as I was with the decision, and I imagine that he might've shared the Major's and the Senator's request to deliver the mail with his co-pilot. Hell, maybe even with the rest of the crew since all of the comms were working in their flight helmets, so I hope the C-I-D people speak with the surviving crew members."

A startled look flashed across the senior officer's face, but just as fast as it showed itself it was gone, replaced once again with an angry glare. Colonel Bainbridge started to respond only the Captain wasn't quite done.

"And while I was, indeed, the more experienced officer on the ground," he said, "I did, in fact, take on that role after the helicopter went down, in spite of the considerable whining done by the Major."

"He was injured."

"He had a goddamn broken arm and we had more serious injuries to deal with at the time."

"He says you usurped his authority."

Adler gave a short laugh that held little humor. "Can't have it both ways, sir, either I was the more experienced officer on the ground or he was. So, which is it?"

Lieutenant Colonel Bainbridge took in a slow, measured breath and slowly let it out.

"You may think it's your injury that ended your career, Adler, but it's your attitude. You're not a team player."

"Actually I am, for a better team," he said, bluntly.

"Excuse me?"

"Look Colonel, we both know you want my career to be over and with what the doctors are saying about my injuries, I'm sure it is. Only, if you're expecting me to fall on my sword because the helicopter went down in the storm, and the Senator died as a result, well, that's not going to happen."

"You need to accept your responsibility in this mess, Captain."

Adler's head was pounding behind his eyes. The headache had nothing to do with his injuries. He was done

"Colonel, I'd love to say that it's been a pleasure working with you and the Major, but I can't, because it wasn't. Maybe it's the drugs they're giving me or possibly delirium from the operation, but I'm tempted to tell you to go fuck yourself."

The flustered senior officer stiffened. "That's insubordination!" he cried. "I'll... I'll have you Court Martialed!"

"No, sir, that's not likely, either," said Adler, finding a surprising amount of calm. "I said I was tempted. And, by the way, you just sent the only witness away? I'm floating on some pretty strong painkillers, so it's plausible I must have mistaken you for a North Vietnamese Army soldier or Viet Cong that are trying to harm me, which might explain my agitation. Now, if you'll excuse me, Colonel, I'm in a lot of pain and your visit isn't helping to ease any of it, so it might be in your best interest for you to leave before I ask the staff to escort you out of the ward."

Tony Adler closed his eyes and waited until the pissed off Colonel got the message. Bainbridge stormed off grumbling. When he was gone the Captain opened his eyes.

He wasn't certain if Mister Corsi had told Kehr just who exactly had made the decision to deliver the mail atop the mountain. Maybe he did, and maybe the Senator's Chief of Staff might also shed some better light on how it all came about, if she wasn't already winging her way back to the *The World*.

In a better world that could happen, but Tony Adler knew that warzones were never actually in the better worlds.

Because a United States Senator had died on the VIP visit, the Colonel was looking to distance himself from the possible fallout in the official investigation on the crash. Haverly too, was scrambling to cover his ass.

Someone, officially or unofficially, would have to be held accountable for some aspect of the fatal crash, and that someone, thought Adler in resigned realization, will probably be me.

A Medical Retirement might be enough of a sacrificial offering for all involved. He'd still have his Army pension and more than likely a little disability from his previous combat wounds and this latest injury.

He didn't like the idea of going out under a cloud of suspicion, but hated the notion that others like Haverly and the Colonel playing the political role of rainmakers were trying to seed the clouds of doubt even more.

To civilians, the military was often looked upon as a fraternity, a brotherhood, and, to some extent this was true. In some units, there was a sincere and genuine feeling of brotherhood. But then civilians might've overlooked that Cain and Abel were brothers, and it didn't stop Cain from looking around for a good-sized rock.

Chapter 21

The sour mood and funk he was in from the Colonel's visit eased considerably when his next visitor came calling a short time later. Stephanie Orlov was walking down the aisle of the ward in a determined stride, towards his hospital bed. She was carrying a handful of magazines and a visitor's concerned, but friendly smile. Tony Adler found a smile of his own as she stopped at his bedside.

A little worn from her own wartime wear, Orlov sported two strips of white, white adhesive tape stretched across her nose and dark, half-circles under her eyes, courtesy of the broken, and now re-set nose. The bruise to her forehead now looked like a faded purple and green watercolor smear.

"I thought you might like something to read," she said, setting a copy of Life Magazine, Sports Illustrated, and a Stars and Stripes newspaper on his bed stand. "I couldn't find a copy of Better Guns and Gardens Magazine, so I hope these will do."

"Better Guns and Gardens, huh?"

Orlov shrugged. "Well, after all, you are a Green Beret."

She smiled and he chuckled.

"How are you doing, Major?" she asked, setting the gifts down on the nightstand next to the hospital bed. "Is there anything you need? Anything I can get you?"

"I could probably use a bird feeder," he said, pointing to his Halo Brace. "And you know I'm only a Captain, right?"

Orlov nodded.

"I know, but, if it were up to me, you'd be promoted yesterday, given all you did for us out there.

"I don't think that's going to happen, but I thank you, regardless."

"Oh?"

"Just had a visit from my boss, the Colonel, who's not very happy with me about the helicopter going down."

"None of us are happy about it! But what, does he think you control the weather?"

"He thinks I shouldn't have let the Senator deliver the mail to the GIs stationed on top of the mountain. That delay, he said, set us all up for what followed."

Orlov's face colored and she briefly looked away.

"The Senator thought it was a great idea," she said, "and to be honest, so did I. I thought it would make for great PR. We all did, except you. You were right and we were wrong, so I hope your Colonel will want to speak to me about it. I'll be happy to set him straight."

"Major Haverly has given him his side of the story, which might not necessarily play well for me, so yours would be much appreciated."

"Not to worry. I'll make sure he understands that, and that while you don't control Acts of God, either, you did perform a few miracles out there for the rest of us."

"No miracles, Ma'am. Just did what needed to be done."

"You forgot to humbly add, *Pilgrim* to the end of that last statement there, Rio Bravo. But I'll tell you what, I have a meeting with the Ambassador and a few Generals later this afternoon, so I'll be happy to let them know it was you that kept us all safe and alive after the crash. And, if my word isn't good enough, then I'll also let them know that the Senator is very appreciative everything you did."

Adler wasn't tracking that last part and gave her a confused stare.

Orlov drew closer to his bedside.

"I'd appreciate it if you'd keep what I'm about to tell you under your hat for the time being."

"Well, under my cage, certainly," said Adler. "But sure, go ahead."

She looked around the ward and after seeing that the handful of other patients a few beds down were out of hearing range, she continued.

"Senator Russell had two more years remaining on his six year term of office."

"Okay," Adler said, not really sure where she was going with this.

"Under the 7th Amendment, if a Senator dies while in office, the Governor of the State that he or she represents can pick someone to fill the vacant seat."

"Seriously? They can do that?"

Orlov nodded. "Uh-huh, they can, and they do. It's how some parties stay in power."

"I didn't know that."

"Most people don't," she said. "Anyway, when I spoke to Beverly, the Senator's wife, she told me that when the Governor called to offer his condolences, he also asked her to fill the seat until the next election."

"He can do that?"

"He can and did."

"Just like that? And she agreed."

"Yes. Just like that, and yes, she agreed."

"So, she's the new Senator?"

"She will be when it'll be announced shortly after the state funeral. The thing is, Bev's smart, savvy, and well-regarded back home, which is why the Governor was wise enough to appoint her. It's not a B-V-O-T thing."

"B-V-O-T?"

"*By Virtue of Tits*, as some might believe. There are some old school hacks out there that still believe that women don't have a place in politics, or even in key positions in the business world, for that matter, and that, if we somehow rose up through the ranks in the Old Boys' club, then he we got here..."

"B-V-O-T."

"Exactly," she said. "You'd be surprised how many key figures in Congress still don't get that it's possible we women might actually be good, or even very good, at our jobs."

"Speaking of which, so will you still have a job or are you soon to be unemployed like me?"

"I've been asked to stay on."

"Then I'd say the new Senator's lucky to have you, Ma'am."

"Stop calling me *Ma'am*. My friends call me Steph, and you've earned that right, Tony Adler. Try it."

"Steph."

"There you go! We were very lucky, blessed, and both to have you on that helicopter flight with us because when we went down the Major wasn't much in the way of help out there."

"He was out of his element."

"We all were, except you, and those Rangers."

"But, other than the Major, the rest of you stepped up when it was needed."

"Out of fear, maybe."

"Maybe, but that fear that didn't overpower you, and you did what needed to be done."

"I told Mrs. Russell all that you did for her husband and son, and she wanted me to personally pass along her sincere appreciation and thanks. She's grieving, but she's also very grateful, and, so am I...and before you give me that *'aw shucks, just doing my job, Ma'am'* stoic cowboy shtick, you and those young Rangers, those Larps, are genuine heroes..."

"Lurps- LRRP, Long Range Reconnaissance Patrol. But you're right, they were, and are."

"My God, they all looked too young to be doing what they're doing."

"I'd nod, but I can't with this damn thing hammered to my head," he said.

"The doctor said you were almost paralyzed."

"Almost doesn't count, Ma'am..."

"Steph."

"Steph, " he echoed. "The Doctors said, given time in this thing, I should be fine."

"And they're recommending a medical discharge?"

Adler gave a downcast sigh. "That's what I'm hearing, yeah."

"You don't sound or look like that's good news?"

Tony Adler was quiet for a long moment, hesitant for what he was about to ask, and his face must've given him away.

"Something more on your mind, Tony?"

"I'm afraid any influence I had with the Army is over, so I'd like to ask a personal favor, if I could?"

"I'd say you've earned a few, so ask away."

"Can I get you to use whatever influence you have with the Ambassador, Generals, or even the new Senator to see that those young Rangers and surviving helicopter crew members get put in for medals for all they did?"

"Medals? For them?"

"Uh-huh."

"And nothing for you?"

"I have all of the medals I need, and to be honest, I'm not too damn thrilled about another Purple Heart. It speaks poorly to my ability to duck in time when things are coming at me."

Adler smiled, as did Orlov.

"That's it? That's your favor?"

"It is," he said. "I seriously doubt we would've made it out of the jungle without them. I'd write them up for awards, but I don't think my boss, Colonel Bainbridge, is much interested in anything I have to say, let alone, submit."

"Because of the helicopter crash?"

"Well that, and when he thought I might roll over and take the blame for everything, I might've told him to go screw himself."

Stephanie Orlov let out a raucous howl and the laughter drew the attention of a medic at the end of the ward who was making up an empty bed four beds down the near empty ward.

The laughter also startled Lieutenant Price standing at the nurse's station. The duty nurse looked up, stared for a questioning moment, until Orlov held up an open hand and mouthed, *"I'm Sorry."* Lieutenant Price smiled, nodded, and went back to work at the desk.

Orlov said, "I take it you told him that after you were informed of a medical retirement?"

"Timing is everything, I'm told," said Adler.

"Tactical move on your part. So how about you? Are you sure there's nothing I can do for you?"

"Naw, just put in a good word for the co-pilot and door gunner, and those Rangers, and maybe set the record straight about all that happened out there. I have a feeling the Army might try to say it was pilot error instead of the weather. His family deserves better than that."

Orlov nodded. "I'll make sure those with say get the message, loud and clear, and I might even shout your praises while I'm at it."

"That's not necessary. I think the retirement will be good enough."

"So what will you do when you retire?"

"I don't know," he said. "Maybe do a little fly fishing in Montana."

"Are you from Montana?"

Adler laughed. "No, and I don't know the first damn thing about fly fishing, either. I'd just like to go someplace quiet for awhile where I can contemplate the hell out of the scenery when no one's shooting at me."

"I'd say that's not a bad plan," she said. "By the way, where're you from? Where's home?"

"Chicago."

She looked disappointed, but added, "Well, if you're ever in Washington DC, I hope you 'll drop in and say hello."

"The Doctor said they'll eventually be sending me to Walter Reed."

"Bethesda! Terrific! The least I can do is take you out for dinner."

"If I'm still wearing this contraption, just order bird seed."

Orlov chuckled as she took out a pen a paper, wrote something down, and handed it to him. "It's my private number. I'd love to buy you a drink or two, Captain."

"I'll do that, and see, you remembered my rank."

"And I won't ever forget it or all that you've done. Take care of yourself, Tony Adler. You are truly one of the rare good guys we all hear about, but seldom see."

She put out her hand to shake and when Adler shook it, she held onto his hand for a moment.

"Call me," she said.

"I will."

"I mean it, call me. Take care, Tony."

Adler smiled as he watched her walk away. This time the tingling he felt had nothing to do with his fractured vertebrae.

With the visitors gone Nurse Price made her way back to him returning with a second cold Doctor Pepper and a new straw.

"Well, you're a popular guy," she said. "However, that Colonel earlier didn't seem to be in a good mood when he left."

"Mission accomplished," said Adler.

"But that VIP that just left was," added the nurse. "Out in the hallway where her escort of Colonels were chatting with the hospital's Chief of Staff, she made a point of saying that she wanted us to take good care of you."

"Hence the second Doctor Pepper?"

"The more fluids, the better, but what say we switch you over to ice water after this?

Adler smiled. "That'd be fine. Thank you."

"More Jell-O?"

"You mean with the piece of green bean wobbling in the middle of it?

"Uh-huh."

"Oh God, no!"

Chapter 22

"Yo! Carey? Thomas?" yelled First Sergeant Poplawski, shoving the creaking, spring-loaded screen door open and roaring into the Platoon's hootch like a bull in a Celestial China shop.

"Yes, First Sergeant?" Carey said, coming to his feet out of the folding chair. The bandage that had once covered the small wound over his left eye was gone and a small purple welt with several looping stitches remained.

Dressed in flip-flops, cut-off jungle fatigue pants, and what Poplawski thought was the ugliest fucking Hawaiian shirt ever made, Ben Carey had been penning a letter home during his free time and had set the Bic ballpoint pen and PX stationary down on his bunk as he stood.

"Where's Thomas?"

"He's with Doc Moore. They're teaching the new arrivals a better way to deal with sucking chest wounds."

"Go get them and when you do, find Specialist Warren and the New Guy..."

"Bowman."

"Bowman, huh?"

"Yes, First Sergeant."

"Tell Bowman and the others to shit, shower, shave, and be in their cleanest jungle fatigues, polished boots, and beret at 12:45 hours for the CO's inspection. I say again, 12:45 hours."

"What's up, Top?"

"Some MAC-V General is flying in from Saigon to pin medals on your scrawny chests this afternoon. Apparently, they had some extra ones cluttering up their air-conditioned offices and decided to bestow them upon you and your team mates."

"Medals?"

"Yeah, they're like shrapnel only with pretty ribbons. Now shut the fuck up, nod, and say, 'Yes, First Sergeant. Will do, First Sergeant.' You copy?"

"Yes, First Sergeant."

"And?"

"Will do, First Sergeant."

"There you go. Now was that so difficult?"

"No, First Sergeant."

"See, you got the hang of it," said Poplawski turning to leave. "Oh," he said, turning back around, "and tell the New Guy..."

"Bowman?"

"Yep, him. Anyway, tell him he's now a Specialist-Four and that he needs to be wearing the appropriate rank and his brand new CIB on his uniform in the ceremony. Make sure one of you shows him how to straighten out his beret while you're at it. The last time I saw him in it he looked like the Pillsbury fucking Dough Boy turned Paris pimp. Square him away."

Carey nodded.

"By the way, Thomas is no longer your A-T-L. We're giving him his own team? You think he's ready?"

"He's ready, First Sergeant."

"Good, that'll leave Warren as your new number two. That work for you?"

"It does, First Sergeant."

Poplawski nodded.

"Who you writing to?" he said, pointing to pen and paper.

"My folks."

The First Sergeant nodded. "Tell 'em you're getting a medal, and that you done good and, oh, tell 'em that it's possible you want to re-enlist to go Special Forces so you can be a man among men."

"No offense, Top, but I want to get out and use my GI Bill for college and be a man among co-eds."

"Who you kidding, Carey?" laughed the First Sergeant. "You only want to go to college to get laid."

Carey grinned, sheepishly. "Well that, too, yeah."

"Then for that, you'll certainly need a Green beret."

Book Two Coming Soon

Chasing Romeo
Nine-Four in the Belly of the Beast

CPSIA information can be obtained
at www.ICGtesting.com
Printed in the USA
FSHW011957011120
75470FS